THE SANTA FE
SECRET

MARILYN BROWN ODEN

WESTERN REFLECTIONS PUBLISHING COMPANY®

ISBN: 978-1-937851-31-6

First Edition
Printed in the United States

Cover and text design by Steve Smith
FluiDesigns

Cover photo by Dick Smith
http://www.innerviewphoto.com/

Western Reflections Publishing Company
P.O. Box 1149
951 N. Highway 149
Lake City, Colorado 81235
www.westernreflectionspublishing.com
(970) 944-0110

DEDICATION

To my Santa Fe friends

who live in the present

honor the past

and help shape the future

The one who tells the stories rules the world.

—Hopi Proverb

*Both the man of science and the man of art
live always at the edge of mystery, surrounded by it.*

—J. Robert Oppenheimer

Other Books by Marilyn Brown Oden

FICTION
The Dead Saint
Crested Butte: A Novel

NONFICTION
Hospitality of the Heart
Abundance
Through the East Window
Wilderness Wanderings
Land of Sickles and Crosses
The Courage to Care

PART ONE

THE PLAZA POISONER
Monday, 4:00 P.M.

PART TWO

THE COUNTDOWN
Wednesday, 8:29 A.M.

PART THREE

THE DECEPTION
Thursday, 5:47 A.M.

EPILOGUE

Saturday, 6:30 A.M.

PART ONE
THE PLAZA POISONER
Monday, 4:00 P.M.

No problem can be solved by
the same consciousness that caused it.

—Albert Einstein

Action is not governed by moral reason
but by political expediency . . .
translated into the simple abstract formulas of propaganda . . .
they simply condition [us]to react in a desired way to certain stimuli.

—Thomas Merton

1

Freed from others' personas and problems, I felt like a child dancing with the wind. I cradled a cup of cinnamon chai as I gazed down at the Santa Fe Plaza from my corner table on the coffee shop balcony. I took a deep breath of fresh mountain air and listened to the cathedral bells toll four o'clock. People ambled along in a colorful choreography of motion and music. The scene around me changed moment to moment and I was part of it, like at the French Quarter back home in New Orleans.

A man on a park bench below caught my eye because of his black sweatshirt with faded gold letters:

NEW ORLEANS SAINTS
2010 SUPERBOWL CHAMPIONS

His old sweatshirt turned a stranger into a friend. He glanced up at me from his Sports Illustrated magazine. I saluted and mouthed Go Saints. He tipped an imaginary cap. We both smiled.

A fiddler played a lively tune at the Plaza gazebo. A middle-aged couple began to dance. Others joined in. A young man held his little girl in his arms as he two-stepped to the beat and whirled her around. She bobbed and laughed with glee. People of all ages strolled along with dogs of all sizes. A wee toddler took a few wobbly steps on the brick sidewalk, pleased with himself for his vertical view. A circle of teens played hacky-sack. Young adults stretched out on the grass. Older folk sat on benches, a few holding hands. Three police officers talked together in front of the Plaza Café, casually observant.

I looked down at Saints Fan again, now joined by a man in unfaded jeans, Velcro-fastened sneakers and an oversized green pullover with a hood that drooped over his forehead to his large wraparound sunglasses, a visible person—but personally invisible, hidden. They talked a bit and Saints Fan offered him the magazine.

Laughter and snippets of conversations rose from the tables around me:

I'm Tewa—our Pueblo finally reclaimed our name. . . .
We need to spin it or flip it. . . .
Older people are from a different generation. . . .
You can't trust anyone who uses words with more than three syllables. . . .

Revealing tidbits. But requiring nothing from me. I'd learned that being a bishop is a dance of opportunities to the beat of discernment and a tune of delight. Well, sometimes delight. Sometimes chaos. Always complexity. It felt good to be on renewal leave. Unknown, uncalendared and duty free. No problem to solve, conflict to resolve, or event to attend.

A woman with a chocolate ice cream cone pushed a stroller. She stopped and bent down to her baby with a little pink bow in her sprig of blond hair. I noticed that Saints Fan sat alone again. I scanned the Plaza for Hoody and spotted him crossing toward my side of San Francisco with a confident swagger. He had a navy canvas backpack slung over his shoulder, the Sports Illustrated magazine under his arm, his hands in his pockets. He disappeared beneath the balcony to enter the Arcade.

Mother and stroller stopped in front of Saints Fan's bench. She greeted him with a smile as she sat down beside him. He ignored her. She let the baby have a lick of ice cream. Her chubby little arm waved in excitement and knocked the cone against Saints Fan's sleeve. The mother offered him a tissue. Again he ignored her. She dabbed at his sleeve.

He slumped against her. She jumped up. His head cracked against the bench. The mother screamed. The baby wailed.

The police trio sprinted toward them. The first officer gently walked mother and baby away. The second felt for a pulse, shook his head. The third spoke into his radio. Saints Fan was dead!

2

I watched numbly from the balcony. People rushed to help. Some stood paralyzed. Others elbowed their way forward with cells lifted to video and Facebook it. Two officers ordered them back. Sirens shrieked above the din. Shoppers poured out of the stores to see what happened. I felt a bond with this stranger I'd never met. It all happened so fast. Saints Fan tipping his imaginary cap to me . . . a man joining him for a bit . . . then suddenly falling lifeless on the bench.

Too suddenly? What if it wasn't natural? What if . . . I stopped myself and curbed my overactive imagination that yearned to write mysteries.

But the *What if* echoed. The last person Saints Fan talked to was Hoody. I scanned the crowded Plaza. No Hoody. He hadn't streamed out of the stores like the others when the mother screamed with terror. I recalled that the Arcade went through to a Water Street exit. *What if . . .*

I stopped myself again. Another trek into fantasyland.

But . . . I glanced down at Saints Fan in his sweatshirt that made him a brother. Tossed some cash on the table. Triple-timed it through the Arcade past all the shops to the other end. Rushed through the pizzaria. Zipped out to the balcony view. Stared down at Water Street. Leaned over the guard wall. Scanned the scene below. Pasqual's Café. Hotel St. Francis. The parking lot.

No Hoody.

Two men with Starbuck's coffee cups sat on a stone bench across the street leisurely watching the people go by. One looked up at me. "You better be careful leaning over like that! You could fall off the balcony!"

"Did you see a man in a green hooded pullover?"

One shook his head. The second called, "Sorry, lady. Can't help you."

I waved my thanks and scanned the area again

A man stepped into view from under the balcony and swaggered leisurely across Water Street. I couldn't see his face. He wore a tan Polo shirt and khaki shorts. Birkenstock sandals and a brimmed hat. A gold watch on his left wrist. *Come on! Come on! Look back and show me your* face. But he didn't. He carried a large black leather computer bag over his shoulder. No green hoody, no jeans, no sneakers, no small navy backpack. The only similarities between Hoody and Polo were size, swagger and hands in pockets.

I stepped back from the guard wall. Enough fantasy. I started to turn away, but he entered the parking lot. Curious about his car, I continued the game. I noted his build from behind: thick neck, broad shoulders, straight back, tapered waist. He blended in with the tourists—yet something seemed off. He stopped at a gray Ford Explorer. Turned his head toward the cars in the next row. Paused. Stiffened an instant. And then I got it! The disconnect! Beneath his casual air was a Doberman ready to attack.

He unlocked the door. Tossed his computer bag into the passenger seat. Put both visors down—face concealed—and drove to the exit gate. I added the Explorer description and tag number to my mental album.

The game ended. Just another venture in imagination. An attempt to see something that wasn't there. *Or . . .* Did I miss something that *is* there? I replayed the scene. Could Polo's clothes have fit under Hoody's? A quick change in the restroom. Remove green hoody and jeans. Swap Velcro sneakers for slip-on sandals, backpack for oversized computer bag. Add hat. Change sunglasses. Expensive watch on view. Presto! A different persona! Cram discarded clothes and backpack into computer bag. Exit on Water Street. Car in parking lot.

Again I caught myself. Imagination run amok! I watched Polo pull out of the parking lot and turn right onto Water Street. What was in the computer bag? If I knew that, I'd know what happened!

Suddenly a bigger concern hit me. If there happened to be some facts in my fantasy, what if he looked through his rearview mirror and saw me watching him?

3

I walked at my usual rapid pace toward our *casita* off Canyon Road. Galen and I had rented it for a month, envisioning a needed peaceful reprieve. A bad start! The Plaza scene returned, circling in my mind, round and round like a carousel that wouldn't stop.

As a diversion, I made a phone call to my assistant's sister, a cancer patient between chemo treatments. Fay had asked me to check on her since Denise and her husband Dan had a second home in Santa Fe.

"Dan Dickerson here," said a mellow bass voice in a no-nonsense manner.

I introduced myself and told him how much I appreciate Fay.

"She speaks highly of you," he said warmly. "Thank you for calling."

"I was wondering if Denise might feel up to going out for dinner some evening."

"It would be good for her. We return to Bethesda the day after tomorrow."

I remembered the Catholic archbishop's dinner party.
"We aren't free tomorrow evening. This is short notice, but would tonight work?"

"Absolutely." Dan's voice sounded lighter. "How about La Fonda? It's her favorite place."

"Ours too. Is 6:30 OK?"

"Yes. That will give her time to make herself beautiful.
She likes that."

I winced empathically. Chemo baldness intensifies the anguish of cancer, perhaps especially for women who've taken beauty for granted. "See you there."

"Thank you, Bishop Peterson."

"How about *Lynn*? Unless," I added lightly, "you prefer we both use titles and surnames."

"Agent Dickerson? I don't think so. Besides, I'm retired now."

Agent Dickerson! Fay had never mentioned that.

"I assume your silence indicates a double-take, Lynn. You're probably wondering what kind of agent."

He'd nailed it exactly.

"Technically I'm an operations officer. I just retired from the CIA."

4

I unlocked the *casita* door, wishing Galen were home so I could talk with him about today. Galen Lincoln Peterson—the man I loved dearly. As I texted him about dinner, the afternoon's images intruded again. I wanted to curl up in the white leather chair and distract my mind by reading one of the books I'd stacked on the lamp table beside it. My eyes focused on the treasured eight-by-ten photograph next to them. Our precious Lyndie. Taken on her sixteenth birthday, it captured her smile that lit up like dawn. It also left a hole in my heart— the final picture of our only child. Loving. Generous. Beautiful.

Killed in a car wreck.

Each day I replayed the concert of cherished memories. Every December 10th I mentally lit another candle on an imaginary cake and tried to add another year to her image. If she had lived, she'd be nineteen now. I celebrated precious Lyndie's life with all my soul. And simultaneously agonized that her days were cut so short. A Minquass proverb came to mind: *The soul would have no rainbow if the eyes had no tears.*

I took a long shower and let the water wash away my sadness and suspicion. Finally Galen arrived—too late for me to share what happened this afternoon. He had a handsome face, intense brown eyes that pierced facades and a casually neat appearance. His sandy hair was gray at the temples, but his physique still reflected his college quarterback days. He preferred sound logic to soundbites, and precise language to the superficial hyperbole of politics, media and market.

We hurried to La Fonda. My habitual fast pace barely kept up with his long legs. "By the way," I said in a pseudo surreptitious tone as we crossed Water Street, "be on guard about your secrets tonight. Dan is retired from the CIA."

He grinned. "How did you know I have secrets?"

When we entered the old hotel, a tall man and thin woman stepped forward. "Lynn and Galen?" He asked in his mellow bass. We nodded. "This is Denise. I'm Dan." He had an outgoing smile and alert gray eyes, a retired protector never off duty.

Galen shook his hand. "How did you recognize us? Lynn isn't wearing purple and carrying a crosier." That prompted our first laugh together.

Denise put her arm around me. "My sister has a framed photo of the three of you." She was blue-eyed and fair like her sister, probably a blond before chemo stole her hair. "She talks about you so often that you seem like family."

"Family," I repeated. "I like that." I vowed to myself to be fully present this evening. *Here.* In *this* moment. To walk *with* this brave woman carrying her light through a dark tunnel. "You look lovely, Denise."

"Thank you. A friend made this for me." She brushed her hand over the cap where hair used to be. Knitted from textured yarn of pastel hues, it fit loose over her head and hung down in a short oval at the back. "Isn't it pretty?"

"Yes! Cute and clever."

We were shown to a table near the fountain. Water tumbled gently in mystical magical rhythm. Tiny white lights brightened two large ficus trees in pots. High-backed chairs painted with decorative flowers circled the table.

Dan scanned the room as he seated Denise. "We haven't gone out for dinner in a long time."

She touched her cap again and gave a little sigh. Then she smiled. "But look at us! I'm able to be in Santa Fe. At La Fonda. With nice people we just met—but already knew." Her inner strength countered her fragile appearance, an orchid grafted to an oak.

"You're doing well, sweetheart."

She smiled lovingly at Dan, then turned to Galen. "Fay told us you hold Tulane's most prestigious chair in history and are here on a study leave."

"I'm a Visiting Research Associate at SAR—the School for Advanced Research."

"Tell us about your project," said Dan while we munched on tortilla chips dipped in guacamole and salsa.

Galen took off, as goal-oriented as a turnover runner headed for a touchdown. "I've studied European and U.S. history thoroughly but know shamefully little about our native history. I'm researching the Ancestral Puebloans, formerly referred to as the Anasazi, a word foreign to their language. It's Navajo—or *Diné*—meaning *Ancient Enemies*." He grinned. "Enough said about that. I tend to become a monologist when someone pushes my history button."

The server arrived. We all decided to get a Santa Fe chile fix and ordered enchiladas. "Red or green chile?" He asked.

"Red," said Galen.

"Green for me," Dan said.

Denise smiled. "Both. I'm a Christmas girl."

I noted the waiter's nametag. "Red on the side, Ramon. I'm a sissy."

When he left, Galen asked, "What's it like to work for the CIA, Dan?"

He entertained us with unclassified stories. Denise offered comic interruptions with her own slant.

I enjoyed the easy laughter together. It ended abruptly when a megaphone voice at the next table growled: *Death on the Plaza! Sit down on a park bench and a corpse falls in your lap! That's a good way to scare off tourists!*

I winced and saw Dan stiffen.

"I heard about that on the 5:00 news," said Denise. "His name was Carlos Martinez."

Carlos Martinez. I liked knowing Saints Fan's name.

The enchiladas arrived. As we ate, Dan leaned forward and said softly, "Detective Juan de Santiago is a friend. He has that case and asked me to look into it with him."

"The *case*?" I asked.

He answered barely above a whisper. "They haven't ruled out murder."

The Plaza scenario zoom-lensed on my mental screen.

Dan observed me. "What is it, Lynn? Did you know Martinez?"

My little Sherlock Holmes game suddenly seemed inane if not insane. I felt Dan reading me.

"Tell me," he said.

"I was at the Plaza when it happened."

Galen stared at me, eyebrows raised. "I didn't know that!"

"We didn't have time to talk about it."

Dan sat forward in his chair. "Did you see anything?"

"I made some observations. Probably silly ones."

"No observation is silly. We need them all to develop a pattern and build an effective strategy." He looked expectantly at me.

The scenario I'd wanted to unload on Galen spilled over—including my foolish leap that morphed Hoody into Polo with a quick change of clothes. I concluded with Hoody/Polo driving away in a gray Ford Explorer and told Dan the tag number.

His alert eyes cut like a blade to the core of the story, which didn't sound credible even to me. Embarrassed, I explained defensively, "I play around with writing a novel. Sometimes I leap to connections that aren't there." And I haven't learned to keep those leaps to myself, I thought, scanning their faces. Galen looked skeptical as though I were indeed connecting unrelated dots—*again*. Denise was wide-eyed.

Dan's face was blank. He pulled out his cell. "Please excuse me. I must send a text." In a moment he put the cell away and eyed me. "Who trained you to do that?"

"Do what?"

"Be so observant."

"I don't know." It's part of me, as common as walking, I thought with a shrug. "My vocation is people. I try to be aware of surface details that may point to some need beneath the surface." I paused. "And sometimes I get it all wrong."

"Well I'm impressed," said Dan. "You observed details, analyzed them and linked the relevant ones."

Surprised, I didn't know how to respond.

"You'd be great in the secrets business."

Secrets! "I already keep a few secrets in my line of work," I said lightly. The big one I kept to myself—being distantly related to the President. We shared the same great-great-grandparents—which had resulted in her occasional request for a "simple favor." *Simple* favor! Right! Asking me for confidential help showed how desperate she was for people she could totally trust. The first and only sentence of my novel popped to mind: *Secrets take us on a journey*. I wondered if I would ever get around to writing the second sentence.

The dessert menu lightened our mood. Denise wanted flan. We all succumbed, telling more stories, sharing more laughs. I had expected that tonight would be my gift to Fay and Denise. Instead, I had received a gift.

Dan's phone beeped. He read the message and explained softly. "Earlier I texted the Explorer's tag number to Juan." He looked at me. "I didn't name my source, Lynn. You don't need to spend your renewal leave hounded by detective types."

"I appreciate that."

"He says it's registered to a car rental company and was leased at the Santa Fe airport yesterday to Abram Baines, who had a California driver's license. Juan checked. No record."

A dead end. Just a game of intrigue on my part.

"Baines may be a citizen whose life flies under the radar. Or he may have false credentials. I'll ask an old buddy to run the name." Dan's eyes circled our faces. "Juan said everything related to the medical examiner's report was expedited because a death on the Plaza could affect tourism. He just now received it: Martinez was poisoned. That supports Lynn's theory."

5

Ariel, as sharp and cold as a bone-handled switchblade, sat alone in his favorite Mexican restaurant in Albuquerque's Old Town, his back to the wall. The chair's red cushion matched the napkins and curtains on the windows. The crowd chattered noisily above the mariachi band. He lifted his margarita and toasted his perfect execution of the Venom Contract. *Execution*—literally. An appropriate double entendre.

He tasted the salt on the rim of his glass and basked in success. His client had not only included thorough details for the double assassination like place and time, but also the means of termination: poisoned spearpoints loaded in a miniature weapon that could be hidden in his hand. Instant death to both targets. A nice touch, adapting a weapon from 10,000 years ago for a third millennium biowarfare poisoning.

Only a precise and methodical artiste could have handled this contract's complexity. He made a mental list of people in his field worthy of the challenge. A short list: himself. Some might call me arrogant, he thought, *offensively exaggerating one's own importance*, according to Webster. But I do not exaggerate; I merely recognize my superiority. Pride is more honest than a pretense of mediocrity. He smiled to himself and took another sip of his margarita.

His mind wandered back to his time with the CIA. Trained and licensed to kill, he used a gun, knife, poison—whatever it took—to hoe weeds from the earth and clear the way for a higher human norm. His superiority threatened incompetent operatives as well as inferior higher-ups. They humiliated him by granting promotions to lesser men, even women. Then they revoked his license to kill. He downed his margarita and crunched the ice. They had robbed him of his idealism and taught him that a higher human norm was impossible. Too many inferior specimens sullied the landscape.

He raised his empty glass to get the waiter's attention. He was better off without the CIA. No boss. No boundaries. No bureaucracy—*that body of appointive government officials, marked by specialization of functions, under fixed rules and a hierarchy of authority, with an unwieldy administrative system burdened with excessive complexity and lack of flexibility.* A wordy Webster definition, but accurate. Going freelance took his clandestine career down a darker but more lucrative path. Contracts abounded. He had earned more the last two years than the previous ten combined. People would always want *one more* death. Always transfer their abstract hatred to a concrete enemy. Always want to dispose of a person or group that fostered dangerous political, social or religious views—*dangerous* meaning views in opposition to their own. His clients convinced themselves that a specific death would make their life perfect. It made them feel powerful . . . temporarily. He was an equal opportunity assassin—they were *all* enemies, clients and targets alike. Each contract fed his coffers.

Rich and free. About to become richer. Today he had not only fulfilled the Venom Contract, but he had undetectably opened and read the CIA's intercepted report before taking it to his client's drop site. A nice touch, using against the CIA the very skills it had taught him. The report revealed both the *who* and *how* of the Los Alamos National Lab toxin theft. *Blackmail* was not a word in his spoken vocabulary. He preferred to invite miscreants to purchase *freedom insurance.* Ariel finished his second margarita.

The flawless day flashed through his mind. No wavering. No weakness. No witness. Enough basking, he told himself. Time to critique, but his *chile rellenos* arrived. On the long drive home tonight he would examine each detail under his mental microscope. He muttered his mantra: *No loose ends.*

Except . . . maybe the woman on the balcony. Was she watching him after he left the Arcade and walked to the parking lot and got into the Explorer? *Unlikely. Probably* she was not a loose end. But he had no tolerance for *unlikely* or *probably.* He'd built success on methodical precision, which in this instance demanded a thorough investigation of her.

Tomorrow. For now, another margarita. Another toast.

6

At 7:02 on Tuesday morning President Helena Heffron Benedict walked quickly into the Oval Office, pinnacle of political dreams. She had short dark hair and wide-set eyes the color of a deep lagoon. She wore tailored clothes on the feminine side and limited her jewelry to wedding ring and earrings. Small in stature and long on integrity, a pundit had dubbed her *a diamond among rhinestones.*

It was a difficult time to be President. The nation was engaged in a civility war, its opposing canons blasting nuclear words. Republican against Democrat, right against left, agency against agency—the country itself was the victim. Fear snatched at its traditional courage and historic honor. The times were gray like this rainy day, and rifts roared like DC traffic. She focused on *The Shy One*, a Native American child close beside her mother. Haozous, better known as National Medal of Arts winner Alan Houser, had chiseled warm tenderness from cold hard stone. She saw the sculpture as a symbol of her purpose in this cold hard time: to serve and enfold all the people to the best of her ability each day of her presidency.

Her eyes roamed to her great-grandfather's saddlebag in the display case, a gift from her father, old Senator Heffron. He died soon after her inauguration, but she still felt his presence and heard his admonishment: *Serving boldly is more important than serving again.* She'd placed the worn saddlebag in the Oval Office as a reminder to restrain herself from expedient decisions based on reelection.

Vice-President Dwight Parker arrived exactly on time. The President genuinely welcomed him. A longtime senator, he had vast international experience—one of the reasons for his selection. His campaign-poster smile hid a will of steel, like a German Shepherd masquerading as a Labrador Retriever. She found both his smile and steel enormously helpful. This morning she and Dwight would hear briefings from the directors of National Intelligence, the Central Intelligence Agency and the Federal Bureau of Investigation. She combined the three in an effort to build more cooperation and trust between competitors—essential but historically hopeless.

The Director of National Intelligence entered a fraction before CIA. DNI was tall, rigid and linear like the Washington Monument obelisk. CIA was duly somber like Lincoln at the other end of the Mall—but she pegged him as a self-serving mutation. FBI arrived a few seconds later, the harried new kid on the block promoted from the ranks. The three held clandestine positions of power and knowledge that would require denial of reality to sleep at night. The President hoped they would begin to decrease coercion and tip the scales toward creative solutions to problems—again necessary but historically hopeless.

DNI and FBI accepted coffee. CIA declined—Director Cliff Clifford did not need a prop to feel secure. DNI reported first, then CIA. FBI came in last. The President listened attentively with no interruptions. Dwight made comments along the way. When the reports were completed, she asked questions, shared her views, and considered the meeting over. But the trio showed no signs of exit behavior. "Is there something else?"

DNI and FBI looked at each other, then FBI focused on the floor. CIA studied them both, blank face in place. DNI cleared his throat. "As you know, Los Alamos National Lab has engaged in biological weapons research." Quickly he added, "For defense, response and decontamination, of course. A current top-secret project—meaning nonexistent—is developing a toxin that causes instant paralysis and death; requires no storage care regarding environment, temperature, expiration date; and, without proper handling, could result in post-mortem contagion." He spoke robotically as though the meaning would skip past her if he used a flat tone. "They are still working on the contagion dimension." He paused. "Since the toxin is in the experimental stage, an antidote has not been developed." He paused again, focused on the floor. "Evidently some of the toxin was stolen."

"*Evidently*?" The President looked from DNI to FBI. "*Stolen*?" She looked back again at DNI. "From the LANL Biological Threat Reduction Program, I assume."

They nodded. Squirmed was more accurate.

"When?"

"About two weeks ago," said FBI.

"*About*?" More squirming. "And I'm just *now* hearing about it! Let me see if I understand." She used the calm icy tone she saved for times of total exasperation. "I'll cut the euphemisms for clarity. The biothreat *reduction* team developed a toxin that can paralyze and kill instantly, and is in the process of making that toxin contagious through contact with a deceased host. *And* they let it get stolen and created a biothreat!" More horrific to her than the biothreat itself was the reality that human beings would agree to use their brilliant intellect and biomedical knowledge to develop fatal contagious toxins, justifying it by fear of others doing the same thing.

"We recognize the potential consequences," said DNI. "When Los Alamos is vulnerable, so is the nation."

Dazzling deduction! She refrained from saying so.

CIA entered the fray. "This theft is an international threat with terrorist potential!"

"As you know," declared FBI, "federal law puts terrorism in the FBI's jurisdiction."

"*Jurisdiction* refers to where authority can be exercised," Cliff countered. "As you *should* know, the CIA is an agency without borders, responsible for national security intelligence here and around the globe."

FBI's eyes flashed. "LANL has a history of leaked secrets since research began on atomic bombs. Foreign spies walk right in and leave with our secrets. What does *that* say about the effectiveness of CIA intelligence and counterintelligence?"

President Benedict felt like a first grade teacher on playground duty. She brought them back from turf to theft. "You knew about this two weeks ago but did not notify me. Why the change of heart this morning?"

A long silence followed, the tension palpable.

Dwight lost his patience. "DID YOU HEAR THE PRESIDENT'S QUESTION?" Bye-bye, Labrador Retriever. Hello, German Shepherd.

FBI looked at the floor again. "One of the LANL employees died from the toxin."

The President glanced toward *Shy One*, the little girl leaning into her mother and trusting her protection. She sank her head and silently groaned.

"The victim . . ."

"Doesn't he have a *name*? Somebody loves him and is grieving right now."

FBI's jaw tightened as he checked his notes. "His name is Carlos Martinez. He was a custodian, basically an invisible job with broad security clearance and easy access without suspicion. He worked undercover for us. Evidently someone caught on."

Evidently again. And now he's dead because LANL and our agencies were careless, she thought but didn't say. Another reminder to serve in a way the people deserve. "Did he die at the Lab?"

DNI and FBI sat unmoving out-waiting each other to pick up the tab. DNI lost. "He was quietly murdered in the Santa Fe Plaza yesterday afternoon."

Quietly murdered, she thought, again applying self-restraint.

"When we learned Martinez was dead, we claimed the body and discovered the cause."

Dwight snarled. "I assume the cover story will be less sensational than **TOXIN CREATED BY LOS ALAMOS BIOWAR LAB KILLS MAN IN SANTA FE PLAZA.**"

This time DNI's jaw tightened. "For the record, Mr. Vice President, "the news release states that Martinez died of a heart attack."

President Benedict took charge of cooling things down. "You all have difficult positions, and I appreciate what you do," she said sincerely. Silence followed as they watched her, wondering how she would handle this. She picked up the old Mont Blanc pen her father had used, rolling it between thumb and fingers, and let them wait. Seconds dragged like minutes.

She looked from face to face, gaining eye contact with each man. "Listen carefully. I see the three national labs as potentially the most *catastrophic* threat on our home soil." Her body posture and tone accentuated the words. "I cannot—*will not*—abide ineffective security. All agencies of the U.S. Intelligence Community *must* work together. If this vulnerability is not resolved, LANL and the other national lab contracts will **not be renewed** in the private sector. They will be returned to the public sector."

Only their eyes spoke: *Would you really do that?*

She let her own eyes answer. FBI blinked first. Then DNI. Finally so did CIA. She looked at her watch and stood. They rose and offered the traditional but newly-gendered *Thank you, Madam President.*

7

I rose early to a glorious Mountain Time sunrise, soon eclipsed by memory's storm clouds. Again I saw the watchful man get into the Explorer and exit on Water Street, putting the balcony in his rearview mirror. Again I wondered if he saw me and could tell I was watching him. Abram Baines. A false identity?

I opened the front door to the small porch—portal, I corrected mentally. As expected, the Santa Fe New Mexican waited on the flagstone walk, a complimentary perk with the casita. I took it to the small table for two in the kitchenette, expecting to see a story about a man poisoned. The bold headline read: **Heart attack on the Plaza**.

Heart attack! I read it again as Dan's words echoed in my mind: *The autopsy showed that Martinez was poisoned.* "What's going on!" I said aloud.

Galen joined me. "What *is* going on?"

"Take a look at this."

He frowned. "What the . . . ." He held the article nearer as though reading it close-up would change the content. "I don't get it! Dan doesn't strike me as someone who confuses facts."

I nodded agreement.

"You don't confuse facts either." He wrapped his arms around me and, a foot taller, rested his chin on my head. "Your observations and deductions yesterday were brilliant."

"Really?" I teased. "Not a moment of skepticism?"

"I would apologize but skepticism makes me a better researcher." He smiled down at me. "All our years of marriage, and you still amaze me."

It was not so much what he said, but the love in his eyes as he said it that put me in touch with how deeply I love him. He kissed me goodbye and left for SAR. "Enjoy your research."

"Every minute of it!" He grinned. "Happy sleuthing."

I watched the man of logic double-time it down the street like a little boy on his way to get ice cream. When he was out of sight, I read the headline again. An Anishinabe Proverb came to mind: *What the people believe is true.*

I scanned my stack of books on the lamp table, curled up in the white leather chair and chose Anthony the Great. He spoke to me from the third century. Or tried to. It was difficult to concentrate. Suddenly seven words leapt out at me—once again, ancient words about thoughts. I reread them: *These thoughts do not leave me alone.* Nor me. Thoughts about Carlos Martinez. Poison or heart attack? Was the medical examiner wrong or the newspaper headline a cover-up? Thoughts about my situation rumbled loudest. Was I noticed? Was I considered a potential threat? *These thoughts do not leave me alone.*

My cell interrupted. "Hello." I expected Fay's voice and an office update from her. Instead, my name was spoken an octave lower by her brother-in-law.

"Lynn, Dan here. Did you see this morning's headline?"

"Yes. What's going on?"

"We need to talk. Can you meet me where you had coffee yesterday on the Plaza?"

I hesitated. Revisiting the balcony view of Carlos' death did not appeal.

He preempted my decline. "I can be there in ten minutes."

I sighed. "Better make it fifteen, Dan."

"Fifteen it is. Thanks."

I threw on jeans and a blue sweatshirt and fast-paced it to the Plaza. No dress code here. Not even make-up.

When I reached San Francisco Street, my eyes automatically darted to Carlos' bench. The space around it was taped off in yellow. For a heart attack? My spine tingled, and I averted my eyes to the balcony. Dan waved at me. I waved back and hurried inside the Arcade and up the stairs.

He held two cups of coffee. "Let's sit where you did yesterday."

I pointed to the corner table.

"Tell me exactly what you saw." Straight-to-the-point Dan. No prelude of pleasantries. Not even a sip of coffee.

I settled for an aromatic whiff and the warm cup in my hands. "Carlos Martinez sat there." I gestured toward the bench. "Hoody joined him, then left. A woman with a baby sat down by him. He fell over. She screamed." Story finished. I escaped into a long sip of coffee.

"What did Hoody look like?"

His use of *Hoody* felt like he was joining in my scenario. "I'm sorry, Dan. His hood reached down to the rim of large sunglasses."

"You've given a fine summary. How about details?"

I dragged myself back in time to yesterday afternoon and focused on memory's video. Dan asked questions. I answered them. It felt like an inquisition, but it helped me remember details I would have overlooked. Like Hoody's arm on the top of the bench, his hand hidden behind Carlos' neck. Like the *Sports Illustrated* magazine Hoody carried under his arm when he left. "Carlos was reading it before Hoody sat down," I explained.

Dan stared at the bench for a long moment. "Some hypotheticals: That could mean that Carlos passed him information. If Hoody is the murderer, that could mean that Carlos thought he was someone else. What information did Carlos pass on? Who did he think he was passing it to? Why was it intercepted? Why was it important enough to kill him?"

Silence followed. I waited.

"I'll find out," he said finally. "We can't go to the balcony that overlooks Water Street. The pizzaria isn't open yet. But rerun the scene. Think carefully about the details you noticed. Just like you did when you talked about the Plaza. Don't filter out even the smallest thing."

I retold last night's story at La Fonda, adding more details and answering his questions.

"I need physical features to identify Hoody/Polo."

"I only saw his back. As soon as he reached the Explorer, he looked at the parked cars in the row to his right, then flipped down the sun visors. I didn't ever see his face." The dots were too scattered to connect. "I wish I could be more helpful."

"You have been. Thank you." He smiled for the first time and shifted gears, a relaxed friend once more. "Denise and I have decided to stay in Santa Fe a while longer. Her next chemo treatment isn't for a couple of weeks and both of us enjoy being here."

"I'm glad to hear that. We want to have dinner again when she feels like it."

"We'll look forward to it." He skipped a beat and resumed the inquisition. "I have one more question. The most important. It sounds like Polo had his back to you until he got into the Explorer."

I nodded.

"Could he have seen you in his rearview mirror as he drove down Water Street?"

I exhaled. It was even more terrifying when said aloud, especially by Dan.

"Your face is answer enough. If *anyone* does *anything* that arouses your suspicion even *slightly*, I want to know. Call me *immediately*. Don't evaluate it yourself. Do *not* take chances." He eyed me, waiting. Finally he said, "Listen to me. Lynn." His eyes cut into mine. "Until we get this solved, your susceptibility to trusting people could *get you killed.*"

8

Ariel sat at his old oak desk in the gunroom of his adobe house, built over a century ago by his great-great-grandfather. The isolation of the New Mexico ranch sheltered him from inferiors on both sides of the law. "You should have seen me in action at the Albuquerque airport yesterday, General," he said to the trained-to-kill Doberman at his feet, the one living creature he trusted. "I park across from the CIA's tan Taurus. Target One approaches. I get out of my car. He glances at me and sees a man doing business on his iPhone—blazer, leather computer bag, black Chrysler. He dismisses me as unsuspicious—the final mistake in his life. A nice touch, driving my Chrysler. "Appearance shapes perception, General. Remember that when you're chasing the ladies." The Doberman's head rested on his outstretched forelegs, his eyes alert and his ears forward.

"He turns to open the trunk. I lunge. Ram the palm-size speargun against his neck. Instant death. No noise. No fight. No problem." Ariel took a sip of coffee, reveling in yesterday's success. He thought of the woman on the balcony, and his revelry dimmed. "Perhaps one glitch. Let's check it out."

He unlocked a hidden drawer in the desk and removed the three tiny video cams he'd used in the rented Explorer yesterday. Carefully he watched the people caught on rearview video as he exited the parking lot and drove down Water Street. He saw the woman on the balcony. Zoomed in. Her eyes were glued to the Explorer, the tag number visible. "The tag is not a problem, General. *She* may be a problem."

He froze the clearest video image of her, captured it as a still shot and enlarged it. Black hair with a gray streak in her widow's peak, alert blue-green eyes and an unreadable face. He wished she weren't so pretty. "We must be wary of loose ends that are pretty, General. They can hinder our judgment."

Ariel used one of his secure phones to call the man he dubbed Sclavus. *Sclavus—Medieval Latin—a slave, originally Slav because many Slavs were sold into slavery.* "Remember him, General? He is the computer genius from my CIA days who can retrieve data impossible to retrieve. I found evidence that he sent classified information to China. Unfortunate for him. Fortunate for me. It gives me permanent access to his skills. General tipped his head.

"Hello, old friend," he said to Sclavus.

A spontaneous *oh-my-god-no* sigh was interrupted as Sclavus remembered that his work conversations were recorded. "It has been a while," he said lightly.

"I have a photo from my vacation. You'll enjoy it." Nothing more was needed. "Take care of yourself." Ariel hung up and emailed the woman's photo through the secure sender's address he reserved for Sclavus. "My photo will be his top priority, General. Power has its perks."

While waiting for a response, Ariel relaxed in his swivel chair and read *The Santa Fe New Mexican.* It was billed as the **West's oldest newspaper** company, the first edition published in 1849, with four pages—two in English and two in Spanish. A nice touch, reading the old newspaper on his iPad. Today's headline stopped his musings: ***Heart attack on the Plaza.*** A cover-up! Who was it protecting? The source of the poison? The mistake of a high official? The tourism industry? "Guesses are pointless, General. But I am a beneficiary for now we know the victim's name—Carlos Martinez."

Within the hour Ariel received the report from Sclavus: *Bishop Lynn Peterson of New Orleans.* She traveled the world and had received numerous honors. He pictured her in a plush office at a large mahogany desk, backed by a vanity wall crowded with framed awards. The public display of importance would satisfy her ego and foster the pretense that she could handle a male profession. No tradition. No valor. No merit. Just another woman disappointed in her gender. He knew her kind well—so successful at pretense that they were promoted over him.

He googled her, found her website and learned what he needed to know—her office phone number and that she would be in Santa Fe for a month's renewal leave. Finding her was easy. Killing her was risky.

Three terminations so close together increased the odds of getting caught. First he needed to know whether she could identify him. That might require him to go back to the crime scene. "No one would expect that, General. Besides, maintaining the heart-attack cover-up could distract officials from looking for an assassin." He did not admit to General that killing a bishop was worrisome, especially if she were an innocent one. What if those millions of Christians for over two millennia were right about the existence of God? To be on the safe side godwise, he decided to risk seeing whether she could identify him. "If she can't, General, she and I are both better off. If she can . . ." That would call for another plan.

Step one: Call her office on his secure phone. It rang only once.

"Bishop Lynn Peterson's office. Fay speaking. How may I help you?"

"This is Andy Bush," said Ariel, oozing warmth. "I'm Lynn's second cousin. I need to get hold of her. As I recall, she's in Santa Fe."

There was a pause before replying. "Please give me your number, and I will get it to the bishop."

Her response surprised him.

Cordially she added, "I know she will want to visit with you, Andy."

Smart old bird, he thought. Kind response but no information. "We did something special together on this day at a family reunion years ago when we were kids. I just happened to think about it, Fay, and wanted to contact her and share the memory."

"She would like that. I'll be sure she gets your message. Where can she reach you?"

He made up a number with a Los Angeles area code, a city he avoided and used for bogus personal information. "Thank you, Fay." After the disconnect he added, "For nothing." But the old bird wasn't as smart as she thought. She didn't say her boss was in Santa Fe, but she didn't deny it either. "That in itself is confirmation, General. All I have to do is find out where Bishop Lynn Peterson is staying."

9

Dan's intense questioning and admonition not to trust people left me drained. I had declined his insistent offer to take me home. Tough spots in the U.S. and around the globe had taught me how to be wisely cautious and alert to my surroundings. I would do that, but I didn't intend to give anyone—even the Plaza poisoner—the power to send me scuttling home in fear. To prove it, I ambled over to the long *portal* that fronts the Palace of the Governors, constructed over 400 years ago. Certified Indian artists continued the old tradition of sitting with their backs against the adobe wall, selling their beautiful hand-crafted arts displayed on blanket-sized spaces. The only thing new was their cell phones.

I stopped in front of a blanket with beautiful silver necklaces and earrings displayed. "You may pick them up," he said with a smile.

I knew that if I touched the eye-catching pair of turquoise and silver earrings, I'd be a goner.

"Go ahead," he encouraged.

I did. And was. "I'll take them." I introduced myself as I paid. "I'm Lynn."

He gave me his card. "I'm Rudy. They go well with your eyes."

I noticed his large ring. The white gem with black mottling was set into etched sterling silver. "Your ring is extraordinary," I said. "Did you design it?"

"My father did. We call the stone white buffalo."

"Isn't the white buffalo a sacred symbol?"

"Yes." He lifted his hand to show me the ring more closely. "I don't ever intend to sell it."

I nodded. "Family heritage gifts exceed monetary value."

"Always, Lynn!" He agreed, his eyes as intense and bright as ebony in the sunlight.

"Thank you, Rudy." I walked on, feeling we were kindred spirits.

A few blanket spaces later I admired a bolo tie made of a large oval stone. "White buffalo?" I asked.

He nodded and showed me the back. "You can see that I signed it. I use only my first name."

Wolf, I read, and bought it for Galen. "Thank you, Wolf."

"That piece is one of my favorites. Your husband will like it."

Still proving that the Plaza poisoner couldn't send me scuttling home in fear, I stopped at the last blanket space and bought a silver hairclip with geometric designs from Ataloa. Her long hair was braided, her face creased with age, her perpetual smile contradicted by sad eyes. I wished I could sit on a Plaza bench with her and listen to her stories. My phone rang, ending the peaceful interlude.

"Bishop Peterson, Fay here."

"Good morning." I felt fortunate to work with her. She was courteous, cordial, completely loyal and a master at graciously protecting my time. A marshmallow with a steel core.

"Denise called me. Thank you for taking them to dinner last night. They really enjoyed it."

"Our pleasure. We felt like old friends. Are things OK there?"

"No questions about work please. A renewal *leave* means *leave* all this behind you. But to relieve your mind, all is well. Everyone knows you're not here. It's as quiet as Spanish moss on a cypress tree."

"Let's hope it stays that way."

"How about Santa Fe? Is it restful?"

I hesitated. "It's good to be here." Except for the murder of Carlos Martinez and the possibility that the killer saw me in his rearview mirror.

After an audible sigh she came to the point. "Andy Bush called. He knows you're in Santa Fe and wants your number. Since it's your private cell, I wanted to check with you first. I'm sorry if I made a mistake since he's kin."

"Who? *Andy Bush*?"

A long pause.

"Fay?"

"He said he's your second cousin and wants to get in touch with you."

I exhaled slowly. "Did he leave a number?"

"Yes." She repeated it.

"Please put me on hold and call him. But do *not* give him this number."

"I'll handle it."

I waited seconds that passed like minutes. Picked up my pace across the Plaza. Glanced toward the bench. A pointless train of thoughts about the Plaza poisoner picked up steam. I willed myself to change tracks and focus on the Plaza. Two men struggled to set up a fajita stand. Soon the smell of fried onions would drift across the Plaza. I noticed walkers and bikers, taxis and cars. I looked up at the blue sky, cloudless except for wispy airplane trails in crisscrossed arcs. All of it tainted by prevalent images of two men on a bench and only one walking away.

"Bishop Peterson, that number is not in service."

"You are *always* wise to check with me. Thank you."

"Imagine!" She said indignantly. "Posing as kin!" Mr. Andy Bush had just broken Fay Foster's eleventh commandment: *Thou shalt not desecrate family.* "Not to worry. *No one* is getting your new cell number from me without your permission."

"Did you confirm that I'm in Santa Fe?"

"I neither confirmed nor denied it."

"Thank you, Fay." A Hopi proverb ran through my mind: *No answer is also an answer.* That pseudo-second-cousin knows *where* I am and *who* I am! That call sent me scuttling home in fear.

10

Dan entered Juan de Santiago's door exactly on time.

"Thank you for coming, *amigo*." The detective had dark hair, alert eyes, and the build and tenacity of a matador. He shook Dan's hand and nodded toward a pine armchair with a green cushion.

"I hope I can help." He scanned the neat functional office that said Juan knew exactly where everything was and didn't have time for inefficiency.

Juan sidestepped before getting to the point. "How do you like living part-time in *the city different*?"

He was one of the few native Santa Feans Dan knew. "It suits me. We don't do things like other cities."

"And we're proud of it."

"Rightly so."

"We've had centuries to get it right. Founded before the Pilgrims hit the shores. The oldest ongoing seat of government in the country."

"A city of many flags," Dan added, doing his part in the litany of local pride.

On a roll, Juan bragged, "Our summer opera ranks right up there with the New York Met. Lots of people don't know that. Some don't even know *New* Mexico is part of the U.S.!"

Dan grinned. "We have to cut outsiders some slack."

Banter over, Juan stood and turned toward the window. "The Suits are infesting us like grasshoppers in a cornfield."

"Maybe they'll learn a thing or two about Santa Fe."

"The Suits? It's difficult to learn anything when you're sure you already know everything." He turned back to Dan. "No offense intended."

"None taken. I'm retired."

"Those little boys and girls can play their games on our turf. That's OK. They can even pretend death by poison is a heart attack. But *nobody* commits murder on the Santa Fe Plaza and gets by with it!" The matador waved his cape. "Not on *my* watch!"

"The Suits will protest your investigation," Dan cautioned

"*Oh-h-h*," shrilled Juan's baritone voice. "*I'm so scared!*"

Dan chuckled. "You're better at scaring than being scared."

"I can't sit back and pretend I buy their lack of logic. You know that, Dan. We've had murders here before and the Suits didn't storm the place. So why are they here now? Why the poison cover-up? What are they afraid of? Carlos Martinez worked for Los Alamos, but he was a custodial engineer not J. Robert Oppenheimer." He paused, his dark eyes searching Dan's. "You're a CIA hotshot. I need your help."

"I'm retired."

"So, you have time for this, *amigo*." Juan put his palms flat on the desk and leaned in toward him. "The M.E. told me he'd barely completed the autopsy before the Feds snatched the body."

If Juan has confidence in the medical examiner, thought Dan, so do I. "Did he offer any useful information?"

"There was a miniscule jagged scratch on the back of the victim's neck where the poison was administered. A less thorough medical examiner would have missed it."

Dan remembered one of Lynn's details. "The suspect's arm was resting along the top of the bench. His hand was behind Martinez's neck."

"Did you get that information from your witness who saw the license plate number?"

"Dot-connector," Dan corrected.

"You think he's highly credible, don't you?"

Wrong gender. Helpful to Lynn. "I'd bank on the credibility. Unfortunately, the dot-connector didn't see the suspect well enough for an ID."

"I'd like to question him."

"Sorry, Juan. Not going to happen."

"I'll bet you lunch at Maria's that the FBI or CIA insists on getting his identity."

"I'm a free man now."

"What if the CIA presses you back into temporary service?"

"No reason for them to ask. No reason for me to agree." Cliff Clifford's image popped into his mind, a friend since working together in their early CIA days. After Cliff's appointment as director, they rarely saw each other, but their calls continued on New Year's Day.

Juan's troubled face eased into a smile. "Most men have a hard time in retirement when they're as good at their job as you, *amigo*. I admire your comfort with it."

"It has to be this way. Denise put up with my secrecy and absence all those years. I'm here for her now." However long we have left together, he thought. His heart caught.

"She's lovely." Juan's eyes filled with concern. He stepped from behind the desk and put his hand on Dan's shoulder. "I'm sorry about her health."

Silence followed. Dan broke it. "I want to assist you any way I can, Juan. I conducted a thorough onsite interview with the witness this morning. Let's discuss it."

The office door jerked open. A Suit burst in.

"You forgot to knock," said Juan.

The Suit ignored him and brandished his ID at Dan. "Agent Ned Gaines, FBI."

Dan yawned.

"Excuse us, Santiago." Gaines scooted behind the desk and made himself at home in Juan's chair. He thumbed toward the door. "Close it when you leave."

Juan didn't enter the macho contest. Matadors don't bother with little steers. He winked at Dan and mouthed, *I win the Maria's bet.*

Dan rose and followed him to the door.

"Where are *you* going, Dickerson?" Gaines asked with practiced intimidation.

Too bad you're up against the master, thought Dan, walking on.

"SIT BACK DOWN!"

Dan stopped. Turned slowly around. For a long moment his steel-blade eyes stared down at Gaines with General-to-Private dismissal, a look that riveted Gaines to the chair and deflated him like a little rubber ducky. Point made. Dan turned back toward the door with a shrug. "I'm retired."

11

After Fay's call I was anxious to get to the *casita* and hurried through the Arcade to Water Street. No Explorer in the parking lot today. I saw a woman struggling with her large mixed-breed dog. He took charge and dragged her toward the tan Taurus that I'd noticed yesterday when Polo glanced that direction before getting in the Explorer. The dog barked wildly, incessantly, acting crazy.

I rushed to the woman and pulled out my cell. No need. A police officer in the area hurried to assist. His young partner joined him. Their uniforms meant nothing to the dog. I introduced myself and told them about seeing the Taurus in the same place yesterday.

Skittish after the Plaza death, the older officer called to his partner. "Ian, we need to identify this car. Get a call in for the license plate number and wait for it."

He did. After a long hold he wrote it down and grinned. "Get this, Vernon! It's registered to the CIA, and it's missing!"

Vernon got the car unlocked and checked the interior. He pushed the trunk button and the lid popped up. The woman went hysterical. The dog barked wildly. Young Ian threw up. I called Dan.

"Hi, Lynn." His voice sobered. "I hear a crazy dog in the background. What's going on? Where are you?"

"The Water Street parking lot. A missing CIA car has a body in the trunk. *Horrible!*"

"We're on our way. Don't let anyone touch anything!" I heard a muffled *Let's go, Juan!* A few minutes later they came running into the lot. Juan headed to the police officers. Dan rushed to me. "Tell me."

"The Taurus was parked there yesterday afternoon. I saw Polo look toward it."

He looked in the trunk. Even seasoned Dan winced as he took in the fast decaying body. He locked on the face. Emitted a wretched sigh. Fury in his eyes he jerked out his cell and pressed some numbers. He paced while waiting. Then stopped abruptly. "Cliff, I've got a body with gross flesh damage in a stolen CIA car in Santa Fe. It's Gary Greene, my partner after you." He listened a few seconds. "Cut the prattle, Cliff! Gary was my friend and this operation just became personal! What the hell is going on?"

As he listened, worry lines chiseled his face. Finally he spoke, "I'll control the situation until then."

Silence.

Dan huddled Juan and me and spoke softly. "The LANL biohazard team is on the way, with hazmat suits."

I put my hand on his. "I heard you say he was your friend. I'm sorry, Dan. Tell me what to do to help."

"The drive from Los Alamos will take some time. Keep these people back. Don't let anyone near that car!"

"You can count on it!"

Dan grabbed young Ian and pulled him away from the trunk.

Ian elbowed him. "Who do you think you are!"

"Right now, maybe your savior. We don't know whether this could be a post-mortem contagion." Dan gestured toward his dead friend. "Have you touched him or anything in that trunk?"

"Of course not! I'm no rooky!"

Dan glanced toward Vernon, who shook his head. He shut the trunk. "Don't let anyone near this car. If the media come, *ignore* them. *Totally.*"

Juan called for crime scene tape. Vernon called for backup. Ian helped me move the people farther back. He grinned. "You have a knack for this. Do you need a job?"

"Sorry, Ian. The one I have is 24/7."

"I don't know what you do, Ma'am, but you carry yourself like Secretariat's jockey—no need for brawn or badge!" His sincere blue eyes said he intended it as a compliment.

Dan turned me away from the crowd. "Thanks for calling me about this."

I nodded and debated mentioning Fay's episode with "Andy Bush." Bad timing.

"What is it, Lynn?"

"It's nothing."

"Tell me."

I used a quick monotone. "A man phoned my office, identified himself as my second cousin Andy Bush, told Fay he knows I'm in Santa Fe and wondered how to contact me. I don't have a relative named Andy Bush. At first I went paranoid, but then decided he was probably just a reporter wanting to blindside me and get a careless spontaneous quote on something controversial."

"Has that ever happened?"

"Blindsiding me for a quote? Yes. Calling Fay to see where I'm staying or to get my private cell number? No."

"Did she give him the information?"

"No."

"Did she refute that you are here?"

"No. Nor confirm it."

"Did he leave a callback number?"

"She tried it. Not in service."

"Forget your reporter theory!"

"He can't identify me. Even if he did see me in his rearview mirror, that wouldn't be enough to get my name, occupation and office number."

"Unfortunately there are ways."

When the biohazard team finally arrived, they put on hazmat suits and gloves and manhandled Dan's friend like an untouchable. I cringed. Many uniforms were on the scene now. No longer needed, I told Ian I was heading home. I texted an update to Galen—*2 deaths, not 1.*

12

The small office at SAR suited Galen. He had turned off his phone and buried himself in his research project, the intellectual realm as stimulating to him as the clandestine realm to heroes in spy novels. He sifted through data and writings about the Paleoindian site on an isolated butte west of the Plaza. He looked out the window and, like a time warp, saw the same mountainous horizon the ancient peoples saw, an unchanged connection through the millennia.

He opened one of his research books to the page that pictured a variety of spearpoints. He gazed at them, and feeling left-brain weary he shifted to his right, aware that facts sometimes stop short and we have to add the brushstrokes. He let his mind roam free. A little Paleoindian girl flashed on his mental screen. She seemed so real he gave her a name: **D**aughter-**O**f-**S**un-**A**nd-**E**arth—DOSAE.

A little girl ran naked through the lush meadow in the foothills of the mountains. She liked to watch them turn blood red as the sun went to bed. She raced as fast as her short legs would carry her, a breeze catching her black hair, her feet pounding the warm earth. But she couldn't keep up with the birds soaring fast in the clear blue sky. Disappointed, she watched them fly away.

Running with the birds made her thirsty. She sat down beside a fresh spring and scooped cold water into her small hands. The river sang nearby. She skipped to its bank to watch the fish dance. Dosae liked fish.

Her mama gathered fruit and nuts and seeds in the rolling hills surrounding them. Her daddy hunted for big animals with the other men. They might bring home meat tonight. Dosae liked meat. She saw a doe and fawn in the distance and wondered if her daddy could see them too. A few sunrises ago they had killed a huge deer. It had things growing out of its head that looked like leafless branches from a tree. Her daddy had given her the flint spearpoint he'd used. He had made it himself. She was proud of it, the only thing in the world that belonged to her. It reminded her of a flat finger that grew to a point, but it was hard and sharp.

Dosae liked this camp better than any place she'd ever been. But they wouldn't stay here long. They had to follow the game for food and for hides that kept them warm when the sun got lazy and darkness chased the light away longer and it was cold and the soft white flakes came down from the sky and covered the earth. She and her mama and daddy and the others wouldn't get to see decades and decades of white flakes on the mountains. Life was short. Each day was precious.

Later that afternoon the little girl lost her spearpoint and couldn't find it. That night as the fire gave them a circle of light, tears filled her eyes. Though Dosae didn't know it, she was there when Santa Fe's cultural history began ten thousand years ago. And one day in the far distant future someone would find her spearpoint.

The fantasy brought the man of logic a sense of reverence that he did not understand, but savored.

"Knock-knock." He heard the voice in sync with the taps.

"Come in."

"I'm Cheveyo Tupatu." His black hair appeared short from the front but hung in a long braid down his back, a contemporary man proud of his heritage. The confident smile and creases at the corners of his dark eyes added to his charm.

Galen rose to shake hands. "I'm . . ."

"Dr. Galen Peterson," Chev finished. "You hold the Jefferson Chair in History at Tulane. I teach at the University of New Mexico. We both went to Harvard. You received your Ph.D. in history two years after I received mine in cultural anthropology." He chuckled. "I googled you when I heard you were accepted as a Visiting Research Associate."

Galen liked his straightforward style. "I wonder if our paths ever crossed in Cambridge."

"They've crossed now. I'm glad you're here. I read your proposal to do research here on the Ancestral Puebloans."

"I want to know more about the Pueblos and Native American heritage, Cheveyo."

"My friends call me Chev."

"Mine call me Galen." He grinned. "My adversaries use epithets."

Chev smiled and studied him. "Your research project isn't just a way to get to be in Santa Fe. You're genuinely interested, aren't you?"

"Absolutely. I have a significant hole in my historical knowledge and cultural experience. This is an opportunity to begin to fill it."

"OK. I can help with that." He checked his phone. "I'm free tomorrow. If you are—and would like to—we could go to San Ildefonso, my pueblo. It's out toward Los Alamos. Then we could go to the Tsankawi ruins if you're interested."

"Definitely!"

"At 9:30 in the morning? Meet at SAR?"

"I look forward to it, Chev," he said, eager for a new experience in a historical perspective. He looked out at the mountains and thought again of Dosae. Freed from factual constraints, he decided that the people in the nearby pueblo of San Ildefonso were descendants of her tribe and that she was a direct ancestor of Chev. Galen found that satisfying.

13

The empty *casita* did not welcome me. I checked my phone. Galen hadn't responded to my text. He'd probably turned off his phone, totally engrossed in his research. I looked at Lyndie's photo on the lamp table. Some parents grow apart after the tragedy of losing their child. But we had grown closer, stronger, our love deeper, grateful we still had each other. I stared out the window longing for him to appear on the flagstone walk, tall and lean and taking long strides, a prince without a realm. In my heart world he would leave SAR early today. In the real world he was far more likely to be so engrossed in his project that he'd forget about dinner with Archbishop Hannahan. "*Come home, love*," I said aloud, hoping for the hopeless.

Enough! Determined to derail my mind from rerunning the Taurus trunk scene, I focused intently on our *casita*. It was very small, but suited me. The living area, kitchenette, bedroom and bathroom fit into 270 cozy square feet. Three vertical piñon logs stood in the small corner kiva. A painting on the mantel in pastels matched a morning sky. I studied the Navajo rug and took in the high-desert paintings and clay pots of all sizes. Galen and I shared the floor-to-ceiling shelves on the side wall. I'd placed a small desk beside them for my work, and Galen had a larger worktable beneath the front window. Cozy indeed. Focusing on our surroundings did not dispel my IMAX mental images of Gary Greene in the trunk.

I listened to Andrea Bocelli who saw through blind eyes and sang through a heart that touched mine. I concentrated on making a sandwich. Slice ripe tomato. Spread pimento cheese on whole grain bread. Ice diet Dr. Pepper. Watch foam rise up glass. Add stemmed maraschino cherry. Put on polka dot tray. Carry to white leather chair. My mental images walked with me.

I armed myself with the top book on the stack beside precious Lyndie's picture, an anthology of sayings from the desert fathers—and a few mothers. I marveled that their ancient wisdom is still relevant in our world of science fiction realities like spaceships, global instant communication, and potential nuclear and biowarfare destruction. The Taurus trunk image was triggered.

I refocused, thumbed through the book, and selected Amma Syncletica. She cautioned to *repel the interior onslaughts of our thoughts.*" I'm trying," I said aloud. I flipped to Abba Arsenius who moved from thoughts to speech: *I have often repented of having spoken, but never of having been silent.* Ouch! Abba Poeman moved from words to heart: *Teach your heart to keep what your tongue teaches others.* But my streaming mental images defeated even these words. If the Plaza poisoner had access to more toxin, he could do it again. My hand began to shake so badly the ice rattled against my glass.

Galen rushed in. "*Two* deaths?" He enfolded me in his arms. "My phone was off. I'm sorry."

My words overflowed. Dan's questions at the Plaza, Fay's call about Andy Bush, the Taurus trauma, LANL's biohazard team with hazmat suits. Saying the words aloud brought the horror close-up again. Pent-up tears rolled down my cheeks. The person I love and trust most in the world held me close and listened with eyes full of love and compassion. Gradually horror's power ebbed.

"My darling Lynn," he said gently, like a plea, like a prayer. "I am here. You are safe." His strong arms shielded me from the shadows. He began to sway slowly, gently rocking me. His strength comforted me. His comfort strengthened me.

14

When the biohazard team finished, Dan realized Lynn was gone. He asked Juan where she went.

Ian answered instead. "You mean after she got the whole crowd under control?" He grinned, not one to let a biothreat throw him.

What rookies lack in experience, thought Dan they make up for in resiliency.

"That lady gets people to do exactly what she wants without even raising her voice," Ian continued.

"Do you know where she went?"

"She said she was going home."

Dan called her immediately. "Lynn, it's Dan. Are you OK?" He smiled. She'd made it home, and Galen was there.

He went back with Juan to his office to recap the scenario. They reviewed every detail about both deaths, evaluated all their information and developed various possibilities. Juan shook his head. "Too many options."

Dan nodded. "But we'll get there." He looked at his watch and stood. "I need to go check on Denise." As soon as he drove into his driveway, his cell vibrated. He saw the name and skipped the greeting. "It's done, Cliff. LANL has body and car."

"Your fabled name made an FBI report from Santa Fe this morning. The report says you refused to talk to their agent." Cliff chuckled. "My old partner hadn't changed!"

Dan recalled Ned Gaines barging into Juan's office and giving orders they ignored. "Gaines needs to change his bedside manner," he said lightly. But his guard went up. The report would include the interview's failed purpose—the name of the Plaza witness. Cliff would do everything possible to get him to reveal it.

"I want to give you some information. Friend to friend."

Cliff didn't give; he traded or bought. Dan pictured him on Blue Tooth, sitting at his desk, fingers steepled righteously, green eyes guarded even on the phone, strategically leading up to getting the name he wanted. *Let the game begin!*

"Both Greene and Martinez were killed with the top secret toxin stolen from LANL."

Top secret and *stolen*—an interesting contradiction.

"But Martinez had the advantage of a quick autopsy and cold storage to halt damage. Greene didn't. His plane arrived in Albuquerque around two yesterday afternoon. He was killed soon after and his body remained in the trunk until discovered this morning." Cliff was factual, distant, his Chess board filled with replaceable pawns.

Gary Greene was not replaceable. How did the killer get close enough to kill him? Gary was always alert, but he was unsuspicious during those few seconds. Lynn's details indicated that the assassin was skilled at changing his appearance. How did he dress at the airport? What did he do to radiate *no harm here*? "Was Martinez undercover for the CIA?"

"Also for the FBI."

For someone else too? Undercover for one, thought Dan. Then two. Why not three? "Any ideas about who leaked the flight and Plaza details?"

No response.

"It had to come from inside, Cliff. You know that."

"*We're on it, Dan.*"

He pictured Cliff's fuming face. Get over it, he thought, and probed on. "The assassin transferred the CIA's tracking device from the Taurus to another vehicle." He skipped a beat. "Since he knew to look for it, could he be a former operative?"

"We're considering that."

"Have you found the Ford Explorer?"

"This morning. At the Albuquerque airport. No prints of course. That's everything we have." Cliff's turn to skip a beat. "Now a question for you."

Here comes the first move, thought Dan.

"Who gave you the Explorer's license plate number?"

"Sorry." A predictable silence followed. The Director of the CIA wasn't used to resistance. Dan outwaited him.

"You have no choice!"

"*Choice* is one advantage of being retired."

"Getting that name is essential—*one way or another!*" Cliff came through on the cell as he did in person: confident, expecting to get his way, and the power of the CIA at his disposal.

"Waterboarding won't work," Dan joked to ease tension.

"*You know* we have to interrogate him," Cliff said icily.

Like Juan, he jumped to the wrong gender. "I already did, and *you know* I'm one of the best you have—rather had—at getting accurate information." A longer silence. I won't blink first, old friend.

Finally Cliff spoke in a soothing voice, changing tactics. "If the killer is aware that your witness can ID him, he will find him. We want to be there when he does."

"So my source would be bait."

"He already is, Dan. The *Central Intelligence Agency* can provide protection. Or you can hang him out there alone to fend for himself."

Protection for Lynn. Game over. I win. The call from fake cousin Andy Bush had annulled confidentiality: Lynn's *life* could be at stake.

Cliff broke the silence. "I want to help here. We can't protect him if we don't know who he is."

Their years of working together had taught him that Cliff could be a good friend, but he would use any tactic including deceit to get what he wanted.

"Dan, are you there?"

"I have conditions, and I need guarantees."

"Go on."

"First, *complete* confidentiality. You do not link my source to this case, and you provide a false reason for protection. No *accidental* self-serving publicity leaks to the press." Dan paused.

Silence.

"Second, no interrogation—my interview suffices. No bugging. And no *overt* protection. My source is here for privacy."

More silence.

"Third, I'm to be a consultant, fully in the loop regarding all decisions related to protection, and immediately notified of any hint of danger."

Cliff shot his favorite expletive. "Dealing with retirees is worse than dealing with terrorists!"

"I must have your word. *Friend to friend*, as you said earlier. Otherwise, no deal."

"Agreed."

That was too fast. "Guarantees of *all three* conditions?"

"I'll honor the first one with everyone my level and below."

Meaning he would use the information to beat the FBI to the President. First in line with the info—always good for Cliff's ego. Dan understood that.

"You get your terms, and you have my word. Would you like a massage also?"

Dan didn't respond. Once he said Lynn's name, he couldn't undo it.

"*Who is he?*"

"First, who do I meet with to plan the covert protection?"

Caught off guard, Cliff was silent for a moment. "*First* they need his name. Then they'll organize it."

"Come on, Cliff. I know they've already been contacted and there's a plan in process."

"*Who is he?*"

"Your game turf. My rules. You get the name *after* you officially appoint me as their consultant and also affirm the restrictions to invisible protection and no additional interrogation—and I receive an official copy."

Cliff's turn to be silent. I could almost hear him steam. "You forget that I'm the *Director of the CIA*!

Time to polish his ego. "Not at all, Director," Dan said in a conciliatory tone. "I respect you and your position—which gives you the power to send an email to Santa Fe and a copy to me. You get the credit with the President for discovering the source, and the source gets protection without sacrificing normalcy. You both win."

When Cliff spoke again, I heard my old partner's voice. "I can do that, Dan. You should have your copy within 30 minutes." He paused. "I suppose it would be pointless to ask you to trust me enough to go ahead and give me the name now so we can move immediately on this."

Dan put a smile in his voice. "Sorry, Cliff. That would be in opposition to what I learned from my old partner long ago: First the deed; then the reward."

Cliff cut off the call without a word.

Dan got out of the car and went inside to check on Denise. She was asleep, so he tiptoed out and stood by a window watching the chipmunks scurry across the patio. He dreaded telling Lynn about this, expecting her to feel betrayed. Galen, however, would be relieved. Dan was mentally plotting against "Andy Bush" when he received the email Cliff—the official letter copied to him. Cliff had played it straight—invisible protection, no interrogation, and Dan as consultant. His phone rang. "Thanks, Cliff."

"*Who is he?*"

Dan paused, then traded her betrayal for her protection. "She's Bishop Lynn Peterson. From New Orleans. Here on renewal leave."

"Thank you, old buddy." Cliff hung up.

Dan stared at the dead phone. The ring of triumph in Cliff's voice rippled in the silence. He was probably calling for an appointment with President Benedict right now. Dan too made a phone call and thought of Benedict Arnold, not in regard to Cliff, but himself.

15

My cell disturbed the comforting strength of Galen's presence. It was time to move on. I thought of a Cherokee proverb I'd read while flying here: *Don't let yesterday use up too much of today.* I needed to practice that. "Hello."

"Dan here. I appreciated your help this morning."

"I like to be useful."

"It was rough. Are you doing OK?"

"Fine," I euphemized.

"Sure, Lynn. Everything is just *fine.*" He paused. "We will solve this."

I caught the *we.* A shift from his retired *they.* I had watched him handle things this morning—in his element despite grieving for his poisoned friend. You can take the person out of the profession, but you can't take the profession out of the person. "I'm glad you're on the job."

"I'm retired. Just helping out." He skipped a beat. "I need to tell you something."

There's *more?*

"I just had a *tête-à-tête* with an old friend who requested the name of the witness who saw the Explorer tag number."

I feared I knew where this was going and punched the speaker icon so Galen could hear.

"You put your phone on speaker. Who's there?"

"Trustworthy Galen."

"I'm glad you're listening, Galen." Dan hurried on. "He will provide the kind of protection you need, Lynn. He gave me his word that it will be unnoticed in the background, and you won't be questioned again. Our conversation this morning suffices. Also you can count on confidentiality. "

Sure, I thought, just like *you* kept confidentiality. I felt betrayed.

Dan broke the silence. "Are you there?"

"You gave him *my* name without *my* permission."

"Lynn," he said firmly, it isn't my style to pause for permission before accepting protection for a friend who needs it."

Galen eyed me, shook his head and spoke for the first time. "It was the correct decision, Dan. Lynn's permission is secondary to her protection. Thank you."

The phone silence rose like steam on a river. I couldn't counter Galen's logic. I didn't like the odds of a *tête-à-tête* with Dan. And I had assumed confidentiality but hadn't directly asked for it. *Don't let yesterday use up too much of today.* "What's done is done, Dan. I have one request."

"OK."

"Since this *old friend* of yours knows my name, I want to know his."

"Fair enough." He skipped a beat. "Clayton Clifford."

"*Clayton Clifford*," repeated Galen. "The *Director* of the CIA?"

"We used to work together."

The person he'd called this morning was named *Cliff*, and had arranged for the biohazard team from LANL. "Was he the *cut-the-prattle-Cliff* you were talking to this morning?"

"Right."

I recalled Dan's tone during that conversation—intimidating rather than intimidated. I thought of Denise and his gentleness toward her. I thought of his strength to fight off living in a trance of sorrow. I thought of his shock and anger and sadness this morning when he recognized that the ravaged dead man was his friend. Empathy didn't erase my anger, but it eased it. "I know you have my best interest at heart, Dan." I couldn't muster a *thank you*.

"I'm sorry I upset you. Frankly, not for getting you protection, but for not discussing it with you first."

"The Director of the CIA's interest scares me as much as the interest of the poser who called Fay. I'm here to get *away* from people watching me."

"They won't bug you."

"Literally?" I put a smile in my voice to help break the tension.

"You won't even see them. That way, if the Plaza poisoner shows up, he won't see them either, and they'll get him."

"Am I bait?"

"If he's coming, he's coming. But now they'll be there. And, as I said, he will keep your name confidential."

Galen spoke up in his professorial lecture tone. "You may want to rethink that part, Dan. The CIA director won't keep a useful name confidential. He owns it now."

"Cliff's word used to be good. I hope it still is. You can totally trust the people assigned to the details. Lynn, I encourage you to be suspicious of any stranger who remotely reminds you of the man you saw Monday afternoon."

Living suspiciously isn't *Life*, I thought. The bad guys win. But instead of arguing, I repeated a phrase Fay often used. "Not to worry."

"*Hear me*! A killer is trying to *find you*! He probably already has. Your lack of suspicion is *suicidal*." He ended the call. His tone, more than his words, turned my blood to ice.

16

Cliff hurried into the Oval Office. "Thank you for seeing me, Madam President. My FYI moment really will be a moment."

She smiled. "I value CIA information. We have ten minutes." She sat expectantly, her Katie Couric voice wed to flawless diction, her small fingers intertwined and resting on the large historic desk.

He admired the way she presented herself, always camera ready: striking dark hair, tailored clothes complimenting her gender, simple jewelry, and as manicured as the garden outside her window. Her alert blue-green eyes missed nothing and gave nothing away, like watching the world through one-way windows. He steepled his fingers, posturing to fit his position—responsible, reliable, resolute. "I chose not to prolong the fray this morning by adding that Martinez also worked for us." He paused.

No verbal or nonverbal response from her. He'd hoped for clues so he would know how to slant this. "To do my job well I need full information—not the scraps other agencies toss our way."

"So does the FBI." Her eyes added *and so do I.*

He ignored her subtle criticism and lobbed a spear at the Bureau. "The FBI may not have covered up Martinez's cause of death as well as portrayed this morning."

"Say more, Cliff."

"The Santa Fe medical examiner determined poison to be the cause of death, and that word surfaced among local officials." He paused. Her silence and face revealed nothing. This was not going as well as expected. He took a different tack. "But that is not my purpose for coming. I have significant information."

She waited.

"To summarize the situation: "Evi . . ." He remembered her *Evidently?* From this morning's meeting and decided to be direct. "Martinez was the second toxin victim. The first was the CIA operative tasked to meet him and receive his report on who stole the toxin and how." Another snippet from this morning echoed back to him. *Doesn't he have a name?* "The operative was Gary Greene, who served us long and well."

"Does he have a family?"

Cliff hesitated. He hadn't predicted that question.

"Please find out."

"Yes, Madam President. I have learned three significant new facts: First, both the toxin theft and the killings required inside information. Second, Martinez and Greene were killed by the same man, likely a contract assassin. Third, the assassin is highly skilled, leading to the possibility that he was trained by an intelligence agency and could have undetectably viewed the CIA report before delivering it." He paused. "Most important, the amount of toxin required for the two deaths likely equals the total missing from the lab." He noted a quick shudder of the President's shoulders.

"*Likely?*"

"It was a very small amount."

"Our poisoner has been busy."

"An astute observer was having coffee on the Plaza when the murder occurred. She connected the dots, but she didn't see him clearly enough to provide a good description."

"Is that information reliable?"

"Yes. She shared it with a newly retired operations officer who has a condo in Santa Fe."

"Who?"

The question threatened him. "He doesn't run in your circles, Madam President."

"Who?" She repeated.

"Dan Dickerson."

"I've heard of him."

Cliff tried to hide his surprise.

She answered his unasked question. "After my election I asked Vice President Parker to share his insights about all the intelligence agencies and their major players. He spoke highly of Dickerson's skill and judgment."

Cliff's old competition with Dan jumped to the surface. He checked it. "He's the best. I heard that an FBI agent tried intimidation on him this morning." He grinned. "I wish I'd been there to see it."

"Is Dickerson's *astute observer* credible or perhaps a setup?"

"She's credible all right. A bishop, no less." He perceived a nanosecond flash in the President's eyes.

"Who?" She asked.

This time he answered immediately. "Bishop Lynn Peterson from New Orleans. She's in Santa Fe on renewal leave." He curbed the impulse to ask, *Have you heard of Peterson too?* Instead, he steepled his fingers again.

"Thank you for the update, Cliff. Let's see if I understand. A man with access to lethal LANL experimental toxin poisoned two operatives, intercepted a secret CIA espionage report, and the only clues to his identity come from an astute observer having a cup of coffee." Her eyes were as piercing as her words.

He felt his jaw tighten as DNI's and FBI's had this morning.

"This time we're going to try cooperation, Director. Inform the FBI of three things. First, that Martinez was on your payroll as well as theirs. Secondly, that he had prepared an espionage report for the CIA. Thirdly, that the double-murderer intercepted it and may have read it. Do it *today*," she added.

He rose and forced a "Yes, Madam President." He'd come for points. Zip.

"Cliff," she said, her tone warmer, "I appreciate your transparency with me and highly value it. Please understand that I consider cooperation between the intelligence agencies—including the CIA and FBI—to be vital to our national security."

He nodded and started for the door, then turned back to her. "You are not wrong about the need for agency cooperation, Madam President, but you are naïve about its achievement." He closed the door behind him. How's that for risking transparency!

Alone in the Oval Office, the President opened the display case and removed the old saddlebag. Its worn brown leather smelled of family history. She hugged it to her and wished her father were alive and here with her today. Old Senator Heffron understood that coercion is the native language of governments and that creativity is a second language few political leaders bother to learn. When to speak which language, that is the dilemma. His voice echoed: *Instead of shaping the horseshoe to fit the hoof, political leaders try to force the hoof to fit the horseshoe.* She thought of Cliff's parting shot in his climate-controlled voice. She refused to give up on inter-agency cooperation. But this issue was urgent. She couldn't wait until they outgrew their dysfunctional patterns. She needed her own creative solution, her own trustworthy source.

17

Dan's words rang in my ears: "*Hear me! A killer is trying to find you!*"

In a counter effort, Galen fixed soothing hot chocolate, and we sat at the small kitchenette table. "Dan means well. I'm relieved that you'll have protection."

Usually quiet about his work, Galen led our conversation in his soothing baritone voice. He talked about his research and Cheveyo Tupatu, sharing his day lightly and trying to spray paint over my images of horror. He partially succeeded, primarily because I felt enwrapped in his love.

I heard the cathedral bells toll one-two-three-four. *Déjà vu* yesterday afternoon. Twenty-four hours ago Carlos Martinez was killed. *May the next twenty-four be better.* With an inner sigh, I stood and kissed Galen on the forehead. "Thank you, love. I'm going to take a shower and get ready for the archbishop's dinner."

"I forgot! What time?"

"Six-thirty." The bolo tie! "I forgot something also." I took it from my purse and gave it to him. "Just pretend you're unwrapping it," I said as he removed it from the sealed plastic bag. "The stone is called white buffalo."

Galen examined it. "I know the white buffalo is a sacred symbol, but I didn't know there was also a gemstone."

Wolf was right. He likes it. "The artist signed it on the back. He doesn't use a last name."

"*Thank you.* I think I'll wear it tonight."

I knew he intended to, but wouldn't. He was strictly a striped tie and blazer man at a dinner party. I headed to the bathroom, eager to bathe away the day that stained me with red ink. I went through the motions of dressing—a teal blouse that matched my eyes and a skirt in swirling shades from blues to greens that swished when I walked. I like to swish—sometimes. But tonight it felt superficial. I put on makeup and peered at my image in the mirror. Ataloa's silver clip held my hair back at the nape of my neck, and Rudy's earrings dangled slightly. Bought this morning. *This* morning? Unbelievable.

I walked back into the living area. "Your turn."

He looked up from his computer, stood, and gave me an exaggerated head-to-foot once over. Twice over. "Bishop Peterson, you look lovely."

"I'm escaping *bishop*. Remember? I didn't even bring my black dinner dress."

"It isn't the dress. It's who's in it that counts. And for me," he said with a bow, "that will always be you, Mrs. Peterson."

I laughed. "Go get your shower!"

I looked out the window and took in the view. Another cloudless blue sky. I admired the colorful flower garden next door and the way sunlight danced with the blossoms. Despite the chaos, I was glad we were here.

The phone interrupted my musings. What did you do to us, Alexander Graham Bell? I realized it wasn't my cell but the condo phone on Galen's desk. I didn't even know the number. "Hello."

"We attended the same funeral," said a well-modulated voice with perfect diction.

I nearly dropped the receiver. I'd learned from doing "simple favors" for the President that she is so full of surprises that surprise is not surprising. I focused. Steadied my voice. "I remember." I reined in the impulse to add *Madam President*. The nameless greeting meant this was to be a nameless call.

"I understand that you are on renewal leave."

How does she know where I am? Why I'm here? This phone number? *She's the President.*

"You witnessed yesterday's incident." A statement, not a question.

"Yes." Dan's friend Cliff must have gone straight to the top.

"I have a simple favor to ask."

Those words again. A *simple favor* for her was like a chamisa bush—it starts out small but begins to invade all the space around it.

"People in the field filter reports to fit what their supervisors want. Their supervisors do the same thing on up the chain of command. By the time a report reaches me, there may be little resemblance to initial reality."

"I understand." People want to please and be praised by their supervisors.

"I need boots on the ground—please pardon the over-used phrase. A contact outside the system, without a personal agenda. Someone I totally trust who has been tested—and excelled."

"Thank you." I realized I too liked praise from the top.

"There's no risk involved. As I said, a simple favor."

Until it gets complex and complicated. But I couldn't refuse. "Of course I'll help any way I can."

"Thank you. It means a great deal to me to be able to count on you again." She paused, and Lynn knew she was about to give instructions. "You are acquainted with a newly retired operations officer there." Another statement. "He is highly respected and is now free from his former chain of command."

I assumed she meant Dan. "Yes."

"Tomorrow you will receive a package that contains a secure means of communication with me."

There goes my renewal leave.

"Turn it on. Push the star key once to activate it. Listen for a beep. Push the star again for instructions. They will repeat once and delete."

"I understand."

"Thank you also for your helpful observations yesterday." When she spoke again her voice was wrapped in a smile. "From what I've learned about the Suits, you were the only one on top of it."

The call ended.

18

I stared at the receiver. My sense of inadequacy overshadowed the President's trust. *If you want to make another call* the robo voice reminded. I hung up and looked out the window.

A man was tending the neighboring flower garden, gray sunhat and gloves, sunglasses aimed at the *casita*. I waved through the window.

He ignored me, bent low, head down. His black plastic trash bag bulged, something concrete to show for his efforts. Generally my efforts as a bishop left few visible results. Why couldn't I bag up the "weeds" in my episcopal area so they wouldn't overtake the "blossoms" and transport them to another denomination? Actually, there were only a few weeds—just enough to make me grateful for all the colorful blossoms instead of taking them for granted.

I heard Galen and turned away from the window. As predicted, he wore his usual uniform—khaki pants, blue oxford shirt, navy blazer, striped tie. No bolo. Classic colors. Classic attire. Classic Galen. Casually I said, "The President called."

"The *President!*" His eyes widened, pupils dancing back and forth. Thinking. Predicting. "And?"

Honoring confidentiality was a silent vow that came with our *I do* at the altar. I trusted him completely and wanted his insight. "She wants a simple favor . . . "

"Not again! Not here!"

"Just information from someone without turf and ego battles to skew the view," I paraphrased.

"And you're the lucky one whose eyes and ears she can trust." He sighed. "I understand that need, but *simple* favors tend to get out of hand."

"Last time we were out of the country. That made things more difficult."

"A weak defense. What does she have in mind?"

"She wants 'boots on the ground' here, to use her phrase. A secure phone will arrive tomorrow." I didn't mention her interest in Dan—his to tell, not mine.

"She's wise to seek outside channels. I recall something Einstein said: *No problem can be solved by the same consciousness that caused it.*" He looked thoughtful. "Her personal interest in this situation tells us she sees national—perhaps international—ramifications. Her confidence in you is a high compliment, but we already have enough going on here."

"*Galen,*" I said, using the tone I saved for nonnegotiable disagreements, President Benedict can count on me."

He eyed me. Conceded. "OK. Patriotism wins. Again. However we must be prudent. *Both* of us."

"Prudence is good."

He shifted to the Archbishop's dinner. "What time to do you want to leave? I'll call a cab."

"It's a pleasant evening. If it weren't for all this mess, we would walk."

"*Mess.* A handy euphemism."

"Let's walk anyway."

"What happened to *prudence is good*?"

"There's being prudent. And there's quaking in cowardice."

"Your justification lacks logical cohesiveness—but it is a pleasant evening."

His agreement was too easy. Perhaps he was confident in the invisible protection Dan had mentioned. I knew he was confident in a close-up encounter—that man-to-man thing. Sometimes, like now, it felt good.

As we stepped outside, Galen flipped on the *portal* light. "We'll need it when we return." He grinned. "Unless you see turning on a porch light as quaking in cowardice."

I ignored him and noted the gardener still busy with weeds and flowers. He had only reached the border of our *casita* lot. How could his work take so long?

He glanced up and quickly looked down again.

Dan's words about suspicion echoed. My yellow flag rose. A danger to us? Protection of us? An honest laborer toiling for his wages? I started to lower the flag. Fear and suspicion aren't helpful. *But they sometimes motivate wise awareness.* My yellow flag had served me well in the past. I trusted it. With an inconspicuous movement I scooted a corner of the mat out from the doorstep slightly, the width of the tip of my high heel. Immediately I felt foolish. I'm getting paranoid.

Or prudent?

19

Ariel commended himself for the string of vehicles he had used for the Venom Contract. Yesterday his Chrysler and the CIA Taurus at the airport, then the Explorer at the Plaza. Today his Ram. His many personas served him well. He parallel parked his Ram on a road that intersected the Petersons' street. It was a secluded area far enough away not to be notable, yet close enough to see their *casita*—kiva chimney, small *portal*, teal door, flagstone path.

A gardener worked busily on the yard that bordered the casita. Habitual suspicion kicked in. Was he a hard-working man or was gardening his momentary cover? The *casita* door opened, and the Petersons came out. He watched them walk down the flagstone path. Her husband's size surprised him, a foot taller than his wife and the physique to match it. From the Google-search bio, he assumed the scholar would be a wan brainy wimp. Assumptions are dangerous, he reminded himself.

They turned left from their path and walked on across the intersection. Confident in his skill to blend in unnoticed, he gave them a long lead then got out of the Ram and followed. He thrived on daring to take risks. They demonstrated his courage. Few men besides himself—perhaps none—would have the benevolence to test whether a potential witness was a real threat before disposing of her. He ambled along, just a man enjoying a walk, his iPod in his ear. Gradually his long gait would narrow the gap between them. He planned to pass them with a friendly nod and read her eyes for recognition. She would pass his test and live or fail it and die at a strategic time.

Unexpectedly her husband opened a fancy gate. Ariel could barely make out the framed sign on it: ***Archbishop's Residence***. He thought again about the god factor. The God factor? Trying to shuck off his foolish apprehension, he watched them disappear inside the courtyard.

Test delayed. Frustrated, he ambled on around the block and retraced his steps to his observation point near their casita. He climbed into the Ram, binoculars and night goggles within reach on the seat. The gardener was gone, his hard day's work completed. Nothing to do now but watch the sun set and resign himself to boredom. Precise and methodical implementation included the patience to wait.

20

Before Galen could ring the doorbell, Archbishop Joseph Hannahan opened the door. "Welcome!" He had a snowy mane, contagious smile and kind blue eyes.

I liked him immediately. "We've been looking forward to dinner with you, Archbishop Hannahan."

"Please call me Joe. Titles for you?"

"We're in Santa Fe to escape them. I'm to bring you greetings from Archbishop Braud. He speaks highly of you."

"And also of you, Lynn."

"He just likes my bread pudding."

Joe laughed. "Dominic admonished me to take good care of you both." He led us from the hall toward an archway. "Galen, as a historian, you may know that Santa Fe is a year older than the King James Bible. An appropriate place for your renewal leave, Lynn."

I nodded. "Appropriate indeed." We entered a sparsely furnished room dominated by a heavy square coffee table with carved legs. Vanilla votive candles scented the room. A cello suite by Bach played in the background. Four pairs of chairs upholstered in chromatic shades of white to ecru stood around the coffee table which held crystal goblets and a pitcher of white sangria garnished with green grapes and thin slices of oranges, limes, lemons and green apples. A large fireplace stood on one wall. Above its marble mantle hung a somber portrait of Jean-Baptiste Lamy, the first Archbishop of Santa Fe—his fame perhaps due more to Willa Cather's *Death Comes for the Archbishop* than to historical fact. The shiny wood floor was bare of rugs. This old Spanish style residence felt like a safe haven. I was ready for one.

A man stepped into the room. He had thick dark hair and brown eyes, a man as polished and uncomplicated as a piece of Shaker furniture. His arms were outstretched in greeting.

"Matt!" I hugged him.

Galen shook his hand. "I hear you are *Bishop* Matthew Langham now. Congratulations!"

He smiled broadly. "Getting to see you both is a wonderful surprise!"

Joe's blue eyes twinkled. "I love surprises! I asked you to come early so we could have some time together." He filled our goblets and offered background snippets about our links to the guests arriving later. "Hiroshi and Amaya Takahashi live both here and in New Orleans."

"I've heard of him," said Galen.

"Hiroshi serves on the Board of Directors for GANNS—Global And National Nuclear Security. It runs Los Alamos National Lab, known locally as LANL—*lăn-əl*. Kwang-Sun Rhee is a scientist there. His wife is Sue Min Park, an archeologist. Like you, Galen, she is also is working on a project at SAR." He looked at Matt and explained, "The School for Advanced Research."

I smiled at Joe. "You are a master of connections."

He gave an affable shrug. "Matt tells me he hosted you as guests of the Vatican when he served on the Holy Father's ecumenical staff."

I nodded. "An excellent host. Matt's genuine interest in people brings out the best in us."

"He'll be an excellent bishop."

Matt winked. "The good archbishop is my mentor. He's biased."

"If his thirty-day crash course goes well, I'll write a book: *The Episcopacy for Dummies*. We can co-author it, Lynn."

As the four of us shared stories and laughter, a sense of well-being embraced me. Joe was indeed taking good care of us. The doorbell rang, and he excused himself.

Matt turned to me. "I have a favor to ask."

"Sure. Name it."

"Joe asked me to make a pastoral call in the morning on a woman who just lost her husband. He can't go because he has a long-standing speaking engagement in Albuquerque. She lives in Los Alamos now, but she grew up here and he's close to her family. The bottom line: I didn't make pastoral visits in my position at the Vatican, so it has been a long time. Would you be willing to go with me?"

"I'll be happy to."

Matt's relief was obvious. "Thank you. I think she'll draw comfort from a woman who has also experienced . . . painful loss." The last two words were wrapped in compassion.

Painful loss. Lyndie. A common denominator for so many people.

"I'll pick you up about 9:15. Her name is Marta Martinez. Her husband died of a heart attack on the Plaza yesterday."

21

Surprised, Ariel saw the *casita* door open again. He grabbed his binoculars in time to see the gardener pause, then lock the door behind him. Interesting that he had a key. Also interesting that he was empty-handed. The gardener was no gardener! A Suit seemed logical. Guarding Bishop Lynn Peterson? If so, he thought, I have my answer about her. But why would he enter the *casita* in their absence? Were they being spied on? Protected? A crucial question.

He was reflecting on a new plan when he noticed another man walking down the street. Ariel watched him through the binoculars. With the exception of his khaki vest, he was dressed all in black for night mischief—shirt, pants and shoes. When he reached the flagstone path, he turned in instead of walking on. A busy night for the *casita*.

Ariel examined him carefully. The only thing notable about him was the lack of anything notable. Intentional? The mystery man opened the door easily. No lights came on, but the windows revealed the dim glow from a pinpoint flashlight. It moved slowly and methodically, room to room, sometimes stopping for a few minutes. The door opened again. Ariel had timed him—seven minutes. Like the gardener, this intruder also exited empty handed and returned casually down the flagstone path. Was he genuinely nonchalant or skilled at appearing so? Simply nondescript by nature or carefully indistinct? Ariel observed the mystery man until he reached the corner and turned north toward Canyon Road. Who is he? Why is he here?

Two men here tonight. Likely no connection to each other. Plus me. Why all this interest in the Petersons' *casita*? He didn't know whether it should increase or decrease his suspicion of her. It heightened his curiosity. He decided to observe through the night and see if there were any more surprises.

The street was quiet. No more action. No bishop. No way to fast forward through limbo. Bored and sleepy, he selected a run of lively tunes on his iPod with the earbud in his right ear, his left one listening to the night sounds through the open truck window. He settled in to wait for their return. Tomorrow would be decision day.

><∻>< ><∻>< ><∻><

The man dressed in black except for his khaki vest ambled back to Canyon Road. He had flown to Santa Fe for one purpose: Pretty *Frau* Peterson was in trouble. He thought about his informative and effective visit to her little house tonight. He had checked it thoroughly and done what needed to be done. Most important, he had seen the spy sitting in the green Ram on the side street, likely waiting for his prey to return home. Not smart of Herr Ram to provide a quick glint of binoculars. No.

So, this little charade of leaving and not returning. Beneath his practiced casual façade he was focused, alert to each person and car. He strolled along on Canyon Road, moving faster than the long line of cars. One honked, the driver's impatience pointless. He glanced at his rented white Volks Eurovan parked in the lot across the road. In the shadow of nightfall he reversed his khaki vest to black and dubbed himself the Black Knight, here to save a damsel. He turned at the next corner and circled on around the blocks until he reached a clump of *piñon* trees that would hide him, only half a block behind Herr Ram's truck. So easy.

He removed his night goggles from his vest and peeked through a piñon pine to get the truck's tag number, predictably mud-spattered and unreadable. Herr Ram sat behind his steering wheel, still waiting and watching. Or perhaps, bored by now, had fallen asleep.

He scanned the nearby condos. Three were wrapped in darkness. He made out a rocking chair on the front porch of the nearest one. A bushy cedar tree concealed it from Herr Ram. He walked silently through the darkness toward the condo and sensed its vacant ambiance. He eased himself creaklessly into the rocker to spy on the spy.

Bored, he reflected on his move from Vienna to Calgary, Canada, which put him just a few hours flight away, but safely outside the U.S.

where he was a wanted assassin. Pretty Frau Peterson was unaware of his presence or protection. She did not know that her cell phone was monitored by spyware. It gave him the power to listen to her conversations, access her texts and emails, and he could even activate it to serve as a bug-like device that picked up surrounding noises and conversations. In Canada he used none of these capabilities. He would not dishonor her privacy. No. He had programmed the spyware to log words that could point to a threat. If needed, he could get the full message. He also had the help of his computer, fondly called Mutter. She was protected by impregnable virtual walls and loaded with the latest software stolen from China. Mutter could hack into "secure" files and catch potential searches for Bishop Lynn Peterson. So easy.

Red flags had waved this morning: Her assistant's call about Andy Bush posing as *Frau* Peterson's cousin. A text to her husband: *2 deaths, not 1*. Two CIA computer searches from different departments scanning for her name. Despite the risk of entering the U.S., it was time to get on a plane. So here I am, he thought, sitting in a rocker on the porch of an empty Santa Fe condo. Once again protecting pretty *Frau* Peterson, and cherishing memories of her, a beautiful woman, innocent and vulnerable.

It began to rain. He breathed in the smell and smiled. It would help wash mud off the Ram's tag number. He took his black handkerchief from his vest. White handkerchiefs were dangerous at night. Also pointless. He would never wave a truce flag. No. He extended the handkerchief beyond the covered porch to catch raindrops, then checked on Herr Ram through the night goggles: neck bowed, head slumped. Dream away!

Soundlessly he wove his way to a cluster of chamisa bushes near the truck and peeked through them. Herr Ram still slept. The Black Knight put his wet handkerchief in one hand and tracking device in the other. Crouching, he moved noiselessly to the truck bed. Knelt beside the bumper. Wiped the license plate clean with his handkerchief. Lodged the number in his mind. Noiselessly attached the tracking device beneath the truck. A squirrel skittered over his shoe. He had trained himself not to react when startled. He listened. Its claws and the raindrops were the only sounds in the moonless night. He made his way undetected back to the rocker. So easy.

Do not worry, pretty *Frau* Peterson. Zechariah Zeller is here.

22

Joe poured drinks for the other guests and began introductions. "Bishop Lynn Peterson and Galen, may I present Soo Min Park, archeologist, and Kwang-Sun Rhee, scientist." The thin man wore his smile like an accessory donned for the night. His wary eyes circled the room, missing nothing.

Following Korean custom, I bowed my head as I greeted them with the formal version of hello, "*Annyông hashimnika.*"

"So, you speak Korean," he said.

"Just a few words," I confessed, merely learning words of courtesy and common customs in preparation for official international visits. "Last fall I had the pleasure of being in Seoul, Kwang-Sun."

"Please call me Kwang."

Soo Min smiled at me. "Your pronunciation and inflections were flawless."

"*Kamsahamnida.*" I bowed again with my thank you.

Joe gestured to the second couple. "Hiroshi and Amaya Takahashi." Hiroshi seemed to fill the room despite his small frame. His tailored attire made a public financial statement. Amaya wore a beautiful black dress with simple lines and a multi-carat diamond solitaire at her throat, her dark hair in a French roll. She stood by him, yet a small step back, as though the space he filled left no room for her and she was content to be invisible.

"And finally," said Joe, "Bishop Matt Langham."

"The first shall be last," Matt quipped jovially.

Joe whispered an aside: "New bishops tend to quote scripture to prove their worthiness." We laughed congenially.

"I've heard of your international reputation as a shipbuilder, Hiroshi," said Galen as they shook hands.

I placed him then, envying Galen's ability to recall names and link details. "And I've heard of your generosity to good causes." I smiled. "It is an honor to meet both of you, Amaya and Hiroshi."

"Perhaps your episcopal area has a *good cause* we should consider," he said affably.

"You can trust Archbishop Braud with your funds in New Orleans and Archbishop Hannahan here in Santa Fe."
Hiroshi raised his dark eyebrows in mock disbelief. "She turns down money! It is good that women aren't bishops in the Catholic Church, Joe. They might give away the Vatican treasury." Everyone laughed.

Charming Hiroshi, I thought.

"I'll tell you a story about the Pope and Lynn." Joe's eyes twinkled. "As all of us know, he can't approve women priests, let alone women bishops. But Cardinal Bolten at the Vatican told Archbishop Braud in New Orleans that Lynn's private audience with the Pope gave him a moment's pause." Joe lifted his goblet to me. "It seems he highly approves of you, Lynn."

"And you didn't even take him bread pudding," Galen said with a chuckle.

Myths begin with stories, I thought, glad that this one about a *woman bishop* didn't end with disapproval of me.

Joe ushered us through ornately carved half-doors into the dining room. A delicate blend of aromas wafted from the kitchen. The center of the table held a vase of colorful flowers surrounded by candles. The elegant dinner blended Asian and American cuisine with lively conversation. Kwang stated opinions. Soo Min talked about favorite archeological sites. Matt was attentive to everyone. Galen brought in interesting bits of historical trivia. Hiroshi continued to be charming. I felt he could tell us *The sun rose this morning*, and we would all want to please him by acting surprised by the good news. Amaya remained silent, her alert eyes attentive. I sensed tension behind her passivity. I wanted to know her better and decided to invite her to lunch. Maybe one-to-one she would risk visibility. I felt happy to be at this delightful dinner party. A needed reprieve. Until Soo Min clouded the atmosphere. "The death on the Plaza was a terrible thing."

Not that topic, I pleaded silently. Raindrops began to fall outside, sound effects for the shift to gray inside.

"I knew Carlos Martinez through my work at LANL," said Kwang. "Not well, of course. He was just a custodian."

I caught the word *just*—a window to Kwang's worldview.

"The conspiracy-minded try to sensationalize everything," he continued. "I heard someone is even trying to turn a heart attack into a murder!" He frowned and shook his head. "Let him rest in peace!"

The Medical Examiner knew it was poison. And Juan, Dan, Denise, Galen and I. Who are the *conspiracy-minded* others? Or was this merely the kind of dramatic overstatement not uncommon from people posing as confident?

"I think that we can trust that Carlos is resting in peace," said Joe. "He was a good man, well loved by his family."

Kwang looked at me. "As a tourist, Lynn, what if you had witnessed that death?" His wary eyes searched mine.

Dan's warning to be suspicious amped up.

"What would you think about a rumor of murder on the Plaza?" He pressed.

I'd only told Galen and the Dickersons about being there. From Dan to his CIA buddy—and from there to where? Am I overreacting? I reran Kwang's tone and tried to read his face, but my suspicion blocked objectivity. "I think his death is heartbreaking."

Before Kwang could speak again, Galen intervened. "While I'm in Santa Fe, Kwang, I'd like to do some research on LANL's history. I'm considering writing an article."

That was news to me. Then I got it. If he could get on site, Kwang's colleagues might be less guarded with another scholar than with an investigator.

"If Galen Peterson, Ph.D. writes an article," said Soo Min to the group, "it will be excellent. When I learned he was selected as a Visiting Research Associate at SAR, I read some of his work." She looked at him. "You mix thorough research with an inviting writing style. A rare combination."

"Thank you. I look forward to reading some of your archeological treatises." He turned back to Kwang. "Perhaps I could visit with you at the Lab."

"I suppose I could find time to show you around."

"Good. I know you have valuable knowledge."

"I could try to arrange for you to meet some of my colleagues also."

"I'd be honored. When would be convenient?" Galen pressed.

Kwang took out his phone and puzzled over his calendar. "I could rearrange my schedule and meet on Thursday morning at eight o'clock.

I know that's early since you would drive from Santa Fe, but that's the best I can do."

"I'll be there. Thank you."

"I am very proud to work there. Our early Los Alamos scientists changed the planet," Kwang said with admiration. "In Hiroshima alone one bomb killed an estimated 70,000 to 80,000 people! And an equal number were injured! I call that success."

I glanced at Hiroshi and Amaya. Silent voices, blank faces, but their eyes spoke. He placed his hand tenderly over hers.

The Archbishop's gentle authority reclaimed the table. "Sometimes the world moves forward in mysterious and healing ways. Today Hiroshi, a fine American of Japanese descent, is on the GANNS Board."

Hiroshi nodded thoughtfully.

Soo Min smiled at Hiroshi. "A fine board member." Covering for her husband, she added, "Kwang has spoken of you with admiration, Hiroshi."

Kwang nodded and lowered his eyes. "Sometimes we scientists get overly zealous about powerful new discoveries."

The rainstorm continued outside, but the storm inside had past. Throughout the rest of the evening, Joe conducted us in harmonious conversation.

"Is your car here?" Hiroshi asked Galen as dessert arrived—*natillas*, a Spanish custard that awoke our palettes with an aroma of vanilla and cinnamon. "I didn't see one by the gate."

"No." Galen glanced at me. "We walked."

Touché, I thought. "We'll rent one when needed. Otherwise we want to walk and live simply while we're here."

"Simple is one thing. Wet is quite another," said Hiroshi. "I would drop you off, but my Aston Martin convertible only holds two." It was a complaint, not a boast.

"We'll take you," said Kwang.

My suspicion resurfaced. More pressure on me regarding the Plaza? A furtive grasp for our address? I feared my wary eyes matched his, giving away my unkind response to a friendly gesture.

Hiroshi stood. "No need, Kwang." I thought I saw something in his face, a reflexive response masked so quickly I wondered if I'd imagined it. "The least I can do for a bishop who doesn't have a hand out for my money is to keep her dry when it rains. My driver will take you home."

23

Zechariah Zeller remained in the rocker on the stranger's porch. He watched the spy, waited, practiced patience and vigilance. He used his travel vest to conceal his computer screen light. He must not be seen. No. Tonight *Mutter* searched for the Ram's tag number and discovered the owner's address, driver's license number and name— Abe Buchanan. Is this another false identity for you, Herr Ram? Probably. Yet perhaps informative. Good job, *Mutter*. He gave her a pat and put her back in his large Velcro pocket that ran across the back of his vest.

As he waited for pretty *Frau* Peterson to come home, images of her filled his mind. He was eager to see her again. Her episcopal area's website did not require spyware. He continually kept up with her through it: *Bishop Peterson is currently in Santa Fe on spiritual renewal leave for a month.* So easy! And easy also for those who would prey on her.

He reflected back on his profession. It had begun when his mother was tortured to death before his six-year-old eyes. They had strapped him in a chair, forced him to watch, helpless to help her. He had never learned who they were or why they tortured her or why they made him watch—unless to further torture her. He only knew that they left her dead and drove him away and dumped him on a strange street in a strange city. From that moment, he had been on his own. Shooting those men over and over again since his first contract on his sixteenth birthday.

His profession required him to terminate lives for pay. Many lives. Much money. That is what a world-class sniper does, he thought unapologetically. But his last two shootings were not the same. No. He had used those bullets to save the lives of two people instead, and something within him had been triggered. Something foreign to his cold isolation. Something that he had not experienced since the horror of his mother's death had transformed a little boy into a man—an iceman. Was this strange new feeling what people meant when they spoke of the heart?

He felt linked to the two women he had saved—President Benedict and *Frau* Peterson. Connection brought a sense of responsibility that complicated his lone wolf lifestyle. Yet, he could not shake it—no. The President had the Secret Service to protect her, but pretty *Frau* Peterson had no guard to watch her back. It would be easier now if he had come forward and received national credit for saving the President's life. But he had run away. The brutal men who tortured and killed his mother had permanently instilled in him that people cannot be trusted.

He had new IDs and a new purpose: keeping one person alive instead of continuing to kill those men who had killed his mother. He still ruthlessly calculated strategy, but something had shifted deep within him, as though his mission to protect pretty *Frau* Peterson was beginning to melt the iceberg around his heart. It left him unsettled.

Car lights came down the street. He saw Herr Ram stir. The car stopped in front of the little house. The driver got out and advanced alone up the flagstone walk to the portal. Evidently satisfied, he returned and opened the car door for the Petersons.

Ready for action, Zeller carefully observed Herr Ram. He remained in his truck. Sat still. Binoculars, not a gun, in his hands.

As he watched pretty Frau Peterson walk toward the portal, he wondered what she thought of him—a man seen as Satan by some, as a savior by two, feared by all. He settled back in his rocker, watching Herr Ram watch them. You can rest well, pretty *Frau* Peterson. He will not cause mischief tonight.

24

We thanked Hiroshi's driver and walked toward the door in the dim *portal* light. Eerie shadows played tricks in the mist. The *piñons*, cedars and rose bushes offered a haven for night hiders. I thought of the man weeding all afternoon. Weeding and watching outside? Watching and waiting inside? I peered down at the mat I had angled out with the tip of my heel before we left. Startled, I looked again. It stood flush against the doorstep. Automatically my peripheral vision scanned left then right. I stepped beside Galen as he put the key in the lock. Touched his hand. Signaled *shhh*, forefinger to lips. Patted the back of my hand three times quickly, sign language for *caution*. Pointed to the mat. Then to the doorsill. Then to myself and mimed moving the mat back from the doorsill before we left.

Strong enough to be gentle and astute enough to be forceful if necessary, he nodded and mouthed, *Wait here*, edging me beyond the doorway.

I pulled out my cell and punched Dan's number, ready to tap *CALL* if needed.

Galen silently turned the key and knob. Backed up. Entered with a spin kick. Arms bent. Elbow points extended. Powerful weapons magnified by motion. An eerie silence greeted us.

He waited for me to enter. My phone to my ear, I started a conversation with no one so a hidden welcoming committee would think my listener could hear threats against us and call for help.

I sensed something different and stopped. Someone had been here! Was still here? I moved close behind Galen, chattering into the phone while we scanned the small living-kitchenette area.

Nothing disturbed.

He moved warily into the bedroom. I followed.

Nothing.

Checked the bathroom.

Nothing.

He moved toward the closet door. My mind streamed movie scenes of scary closets where bad guys hid or bodies fell out. He pulled the knob. The door creaked open. I curbed the impulse to close my eyes.

Nothing.

I stared into the closet. Sensed the residue of a stranger's presence. Someone had stood here! And not only here. I sensed, intuited, *felt* that someone had walked on our floors, gone through our drawers, perhaps looked at the files on our computers. Maybe even sat on our bed. Someone skillful enough to leave no trace. Yet I *knew*.

Why come here? To steal? Nothing missing. To be destructive? Nothing damaged. To bug us?

Fury detonated. I shoved hangars aside. Jerked the fuse box open. Flipped off the master switch.

"What the . . ." Galen's arm swept protectively around me in the dark.

I turned on my cell flashlight.

He stared at me, then shook his head. "Let me guess. You had a sudden urge to go green."

"Can't you feel it, Galen? Someone desecrated our space!"

"It's OK. No one is here now. You're safe."

"Maybe someone bugged us!"

He paused. "Who?" He whispered.

"*Him*?"

"He wouldn't bug us. He'd attack us."

I shivered. "Maybe the CIA?"

"Surely they wouldn't enter without our permission, and Dan said they wouldn't bug us." He wrapped me in his arms.

Gradually my tunnel of fear and anger shifted to an echo chamber of his many comments about my overactive imagination. I felt a presence. But had I conjured it? Maybe a squirrel moved the mat. Had I let a little animal motivate all this drama? I almost tittered. It would be a hoot if it weren't so paranoid. I freed myself from his arms and reached into the closet to flip the master switch back on.

He touched my hand gently. "Leave it," he whispered.

Surprised, I looked up at him.

He pulled me close again, his breath against my ear. "I've come to trust your *little yellow flag*. Let's keep in mind that bugs can operate on batteries also."

His words turned my yellow flag to red. My cell rang. I jumped. "Hello."

"You will find a gift on your pillow. You were bugged. Your home is being watched. I am watching the watcher. He will not harm you tonight—no."

I dropped the phone.

Galen caught it. Listened to the silence. Punched *END*. Checked *Received calls*: *Caller unknown*. Number blocked. "Who was it?"

I grabbed my phone again. Turned its flashlight back on. Hurried to the bed. Flipped back the bedcovers. Three bugs formed a triangle on my pillow.

"Lynn! Who was it? You're ashen."

I would never forget that voice from the past. "Zechariah Zeller."

25

I awoke at sunrise Wednesday morning, my heart heavy. Violated *casita*. Bugs. Being watched. Zeller's call. Was he still out there *watching the watcher*? I wanted to get *away* from here! "Let's go out for breakfast, Galen."

"I was thinking the same thing." He brushed his hand tenderly across my cheek. "This is not what we expected."

Tenderness evoked my tears. I blinked them back.

"How about the Plaza Café?"

"Good idea." I felt watched as we walked down the flagstone path and curbed an absurd urge to shout out, *We're leaving now. Come on in!* Instead, I focused on the crisp sunny morning and turned my thoughts to last night's dinner party. "I think Joe will be a lifelong friend."

Galen nodded agreement.

"It was good to see Matt again too. Don't forget that I'm going to Los Alamos with him this morning. I'm not sure when I'll be back."

"That's the way Chev and I are heading too. We're going to San Ildefonzo, his pueblo. Then to the Tsankawi ruins."

"You sound like you're looking forward to it."

He nodded. "Chev graduated from Harvard two years ahead of me. He's a cultural anthropologist and a holistic blend of past/present/future."

"I'd enjoy meeting him." I thought of Kwang. "You'll be going back that way again tomorrow to see the lab."

"And get an inside view from Kwang and his co-workers."

"*Los Alamos National Lab.* There's a mystique about all that, isn't there?" I corrected myself. "No. There's an attitude of mystery, but not reverence."

"Perhaps the word is *mystifying*. It perplexes the mind." He looked down at me. "Like Zeller."

There it was, the elephant in our midst. "We've avoided talking about him this morning."

"He might be following us right now, Lynn."

"I'm more concerned about the watcher he was watching."

"That too."

"We have no way of knowing whether Zeller is protecting us from protection or from Polo."

"What are we going to do about him, Lynn? His many assassinations put him on the wrong side of the law." Galen put his arm around my waist. "But he also saved a life I cherish."

"And a President the country needs." I sighed. "He scares me, yet his presence is a comfort. He shows me the dotted line that exists between villain and hero." I inhaled deeply and slowly exhaled. "I've made an ethically paradoxical decision." I looked up at him. "You follow your own conscience. I'm not going to do anything. I will not help take his life."

Galen leaned down and kissed my cheek. "No, we can't do that. I'm forever grateful to him for saving yours." We walked along silently hand-in-hand. When he spoke again, he changed the subject. "We should probably tell Dan that bugs were planted."

"Show and tell." I pulled them from my pocket. "Do you want to call him or shall I?"

"Go ahead."

Dan answered immediately. "Hello, Lynn."

"How is Denise?" I hoped for a good report.

"She had trouble yesterday. Last night she rested well. I hired a home care nurse. Denise thinks it's silly, but I feel better."

I found it difficult to move from Denise's battle with cancer to something trivial like bugs.

To-the-point Dan shifted routinely. "We—and it's a broad *we*—can't identify the phone used by your fake cousin Andy Bush. For me, that plus the timing plus obtaining your personal information confirm him as the poisoner. At the least, he's our best lead. I hope you're practicing suspicion."

"Apparently good advice, Dan. I set a doormat ruse as we left last night. When we came home, the mat had been moved. Also someone bugged the *casita*."

He skipped a beat. "I'll get rid of the bugs for you. I may be able to identify their source."

"They've been removed. I have them with me."

"Where are you?"

"On our way to the Plaza Café for breakfast."

"I'll join you. The nurse is here, and Denise will sleep for another couple of hours."

"See you there." I punched *END*. "He's having breakfast with us."

"Good. I admire the way they are handling Denise's situation." He squeezed my hand tenderly. "We know he would do anything to reverse it."

"Yes we do, love." Old memories of Lyndie billowed in, and neither of us spoke again until we entered the Plaza Café. We were greeted by murmuring voices and the aroma of coffee, bacon and cinnamon rolls. Galen asked for the sunny corner table by the large front window.

A woman with *Antonita* on her name badge appeared with menus and coffee, followed a bit later by the entry of a man in a plaid shirt and denim shorts. His intense demeanor contradicted his attempt to act like a tourist. He looked somewhat familiar but I couldn't place him. He eyed the café and claimed the table across the room in my line of vision. Which put me in his line of vision.

I felt his gaze as I focused on my menu. An old watcher? Or a new one?

26

As Herr Ram followed the Petersons at a distance, Zeller's rented white Volks Eurovan covertly followed the green truck. So easy.

He had listened in on pretty *Frau* Peterson's call to the man named Dan regarding the bugs that had been removed. As he drove toward the Plaza, he pondered the call's new information. She had felt unsecure last night when she left the little house and had set a trap that fooled the bugger. He had either made an unmindful entry and accidentally moved the mat inward, or had noticed the moved mat as he left and thought he'd done it, so aligned it with the door. Either way the bugger was an amateur. Herr Ram was not. He had dared pose as pretty *Frau* Peterson's fake cousin to get information from her secretary. I do not like that. No.

Herr Ram seemed to have a flair for fake names. Fake truck owner Abe Buchanan and fake kin Andy Bush. Zeller caught the *AB* initials of both names. Is that on purpose? Perhaps. Using the same initials in aliases simplies fraud. Monogrammed items support authenticity, and the same monogram always fits. But two names are not enough to validate a pattern. No. Play on, Herr Ram. I will get you!

He saw the green truck turn into the bank parking lot, the license tag muddy again. Zeller drove around the block and parked near the corner of Palace and Lincoln. His Eurovan would not win in a chase, but he could sleep in it and avoid hotel check-ins and security cameras. His parking place was close enough to observe the Plaza Café but distant enough not be noticed. He reflected again on pretty *Frau* Peterson's conversation with the man named Dan. He was pleased she had omitted his call and how the bugs were found. She will not lie, he thought. But she is content to wiggle around my part in the story.

He had taken a risk in calling her. But he wanted her to know she had been bugged and was being watched.

And I wanted to be her hero, he admitted.

And I wanted to hear her voice again.

27

"Good coffee," commented Galen, typically his first evaluation of the day. He closed his menu. "Blue corn *piñon* pancakes. I can't get that in New Orleans."

I felt him looking at me as I read through the entire menu before deciding. "I think I'll get the . . ." I began and looked up at him as he grinned and mouthed *yogurt parfait* in unison with my spoken words. I laughed. "I like to see all the options before I decide."

"And then you generally order the same thing anyway." He reached over and entwined his fingers with mine, his eyes smiling. "I love you, Lynn. Quirks and all."

My heart filled with the deep joy of awareness that I was loved, even cherished, by the one I also cherished. I placed my other hand on top of his. Feeling watched, I glanced at Plaid Shirt taking it all in. "Not now, Galen, but later check out the man in the plaid shirt. Does he look familiar to you?"

Galen's eyes met mine. "The one posing as a tourist and lacking the covert skill to watch our table unnoted? He's not wearing a cap or sunglasses, but he's the gardener from yesterday." Galen grinned untroubled. "He seems to have adopted us."

Mentally I placed hat and sunglasses on him and also came up with a match. "Shall we go ask him if he's a weeder or a spy?"

Dan saved us by looking at us through the window. He waved. As he entered, his eyes circled the room. Obviously his habit of being alert didn't retire.

Antonita returned with more coffee and a menu for Dan. We bantered with her as we placed our orders. Dan absent mindedly chose a poached egg, bacon and wheat toast.

When she left, Galen said, "Tell us about Denise, the unabridged version."

"We're here to discuss the bugs."

"They'll keep," I said. "We care about her." It puzzled me that our lives immediately entwine with some people, and we know others for years and never know them at all. A mystery. One of the many.

"Unabridged." He slid his fingers up and down his coffee mug and spoke softly. "She loves to be with people. She perked up when I mentioned going to dinner with you, and really enjoyed our evening at La Fonda. After you called this morning, she woke up for a few minutes and I told her I was meeting you. She asked about us getting together again. She pays for it the next day, but it's worth it to her."

I saw a potential pattern. Perhaps being with friends—even looking forward to it—made a positive difference for Denise. I could help with that. "Would she be up to going out for lunch on a good day?" I could make it a threesome with Amaya Takahashi.

He nodded. "I can tell you care. She feels it too. Unabridged," he said again, then sighed and looked away "I'm thankful for her good days. I worry about her, and she worries about how her illness affects my life." He looked at Galen and shook his head. "Can you believe she worries about that? All I want is not to lose her." He heaved a long sigh, and his voice softened to a soul-wrenching plea. "Oh, God, I wish I could help her."

"You do, Dan, through your presence," I said. "She doesn't have to make this journey alone."

"That's not enough." Abruptly he said, "Back to the bugs."

I noted the change in his eyes. Tenderness a moment ago. Ice now. I pulled the three bugs from my pocket.

He picked up one. Skipped a beat. "They're CIA!" The words were quiet but vehement. "My *friend* went over the line!" He raised his eyes from the bugs to me. "I'm sorry, Lynn." Another beat of silence. "How did you find them?"

"It's a long story."

"More important," Galen said, "is who was assigned to put them there. I'd lay my money on the man in the plaid shirt pretending to be a tourist. Yesterday afternoon he posed as a gardener until we left. I don't know how many weeds he pulled, but he apparently brought in bugs."

Dan grinned at him. "You sound terrified. I commend you for checking the *casita*."

He did check it, I thought, just not for bugs.

Dan turned to me. "Your *protection* is neither skilled nor invisible! I'll take care of that. No more bugs either."

"Have you learned anything more about the poisoner?"

"Like I said on the phone, he's probably the one who called Fay. Not being able to identify the phone number eliminates novices. So far he's made no mistakes. He walks without tracks. Talks without trace. And poisons without prints."

"He may have been watching our *casita* last night," I said.

"Details?" Dan asked.

I shrugged and averted my gaze to the large window.

A man walked by with a beautiful white collie. He glanced in. His sunglasses landed on me.

I smiled at him.

He nodded, returned my smile and walked on toward San Francisco.

As my eyes followed him, the dog got my attention once more. He wasn't wagging his tail and strutting along like collies generally do on walks with their master. I looked again at the man. The back of his neck was thick beneath his gray Stetson. Broad shoulders filled his gray cowboy shirt. He was trim in his jeans, and his gray lizard boots looked custom made. My mind shifted to Monday's balcony scene: watching Polo walk away toward the parking lot, his back to me. I recalled his build, the way he looked from behind, the way he carried himself, the way he walked. Different clothes. The same size and characteristics.

Whoa! A friendly man is out walking his dog on a beautiful morning, and I turn him into a murder suspect!

But I was mesmerized and continued to watch him until he was out of view. My photographic memory clicked in again. My stomach pitched. Dog or not, it was the same man! Passing by just beyond the glass. About four feet away from me!

Galen put his hand over mine. "What is it? You're white as a cotton boll."

"I saw him." My voice sounded like a little girl's, small and shaky.

"Saw who?" He asked.

"The Plaza poisoner."

PART TWO
THE COUNTDOWN
Wednesday, 8:29 A.M.

*There is always a danger
that . . . men will seek simplistic answers;
and there are of course many to provide them.*

—J. Robert Oppenheimer

*Secrecy policies
depend on a vision of the enemy,
an idea of what there is to fear
and the role of information in creating that threat.*

—Alex Wellerstein

1

I stared out the Plaza Café window, still seeing the image of the Plaza poisoner. I felt disconnected from myself, like watching me instead of *being* me.

"You *saw* him? *Where?*" Galen asked.

I watched myself point to the window. "Out there." The words came from far away, a quaver in the voice.

"Tell me!" Dan directed.

I heard my flat robotic words. "A man walked a white collie. His sunglasses looked at me. . . . I liked his dog and smiled. He smiled back. . . . But the collie didn't prance, and his tail didn't wag. It drooped. . . . The man passed on. I recognized him from behind. His walk. His height. His build."

I shuddered. Climbed back into myself, no longer a bystander. Saw his sunglasses aimed at me. Wanted to scream. I folded my arms tight across my chest to keep from shaking. "It was Polo."

"Let's get him!" Galen started to stand.

Dan pressed his palm firmly against Galen's shoulder and spoke softly. "Stay here. He saw you and me too. If we react and follow him, he'll suspect Lynn recognized him. We *don't* want that!"

Galen nodded. Complied.

"Describe him," Dan said hurriedly.

"Gray Stetson. Sunglasses. Long-sleeved gray cowboy shirt. Jeans. Gray snakeskin boots. Black leather gloves—the leash in his right hand."

"Headed which way?"

"Toward San Francisco."

Dan stood. Spoke quickly to Galen. "Get Lynn out of here. Take a cab home. Now!" He headed to Plaid Shirt's table.

><del>}</del>o< ><del>}</del>o< ><del>}</del>o<

Dan pulled out a chair. Leaned in. Spoke softly. "You're no tourist. I'll lay my money on CIA."

The man's sunburned face blanked too late.

"I'm Dan Dickerson."

His eyes widened with name recognition. "Evan Moore."

"The next time you go undercover as a gardener who plants bugs, wear sunscreen."

Moore's startled eyes lowered.

Green as they come, thought Dan. With no knight on the board, he'd have to send a pawn to protect the bishop. "New assignment." He grabbed authority he didn't hold and cut off Moore's protest. "I report to *Director Clifford*. I'm countermanding your orders." He gestured toward the window. "A man just walked past heading toward San Francisco." He quickly described his clothes, mentioned the white collie, gave rushed directives. "Stick with him but don't make him suspicious. Lose him—you're demoted. See heroic visions of catching him by yourself—you're fired because it might get someone killed." He skipped a beat. "Understood?"

Moore gave a quick wide-eyed nod.

"Cell number?" Dan listened and handed him a card. "Here's mine. *Go!*" He looked at his watch. The Plaza poisoner had a 127-second head start.

He texted Juan to call ASAP. When he returned to Lynn and Galen's table, the cab had been called. His cell rang. He noted the number: Evan Moore. "Yes?"

"He's at Starbuck's. The collie is in front."

"Where are you?"

"Across the street in the bank parking lot."

"Stay there. I'm coming." Dan gave Lynn and Galen a thumbs up, mouthed *We got him* and headed out the door. His cell rang. The screen showed *JUAN*. "Our man is at Starbuck's. Gray Stetson, shirt and boots. Jeans. White collie outside."

"I'm on the move," said Juan. "Be there in a few minutes."

"I'm avoiding San Francisco. He probably saw me with Lynn. I'll be in First National's parking lot. A CIA operative is already there."

THE COUNTDOWN

"*CIA!*"

"He's all I had."

The matador unfurled his cape. "*I'll* handle the Plaza poisoner. If he walks out of Starbuck's without me, the Suit can have him."

"Got it." Dan punched *END* and hurried the long way round to the parking lot. On the way he made a quick call to check on Denise.

2

"All will be well," I said as the cab let us out at the *casita*.

"If Dan hadn't said they got him, I would cancel the trip with Chev."

"Not to worry. Dan probably has him in handcuffs right now."

"I like that image." Chev pulled up in a Jeep, and Galen kissed me goodbye.

My mind leapt to Mrs. Martinez. Had Carlos kissed her goodbye that horrible Monday? How quickly life can twist! Someday Galen and I would kiss goodbye for the last time. "I love you." Lightly I added, "Enjoy tromping around in the ruins with Chev."

"Not tromping! Stepping carefully. Walking gently."

"A good way to journey through life, wise professor." As I closed the door behind him, the face of the man with the dog zoomed in and filled my mental screen. I saw his fake smile and imagined malevolent eyes behind the sunglasses. I shivered. "Thank you, Dan," I said aloud, wondering what was happening right now.

I changed quickly into a gray suit and lavender blouse with a lacey collar, a softer touch than episcopal attire. Visiting Marta Martinez, a grieving Catholic widow, was not the time to flaunt women in the episcopacy.

The doorbell rang. It was too early for Matt. I glanced out the window. Two cars were parked in front, a red one with last night's driver inside and an empty silver Lexus. I opened the door.

Hiroshi Takahashi greeted me with a pleased smile.

"Please come in."

"Thank you, Lynn, but I can't."

"Then I'll come out," I said cordially.

"Is it okay to tell a bishop she looks stunning?"

"Thank you."

"Do you see that Juke?"

I nodded. Last night's driver climbed out of it. I waved at him from the portal.

"We never use it," Hiroshi continued, "but now I know why I bought it. Our new friends need a car. It's yours while you're here."

"We can't . . ."

"Of course you can, Lynn. However, I predicted that you would find it troublesome to accept the keys. They are in the ignition. It will be more troublesome, my good bishop, if you leave them there and the Juke gets stolen." He chuckled, and with that he was gone.

3

Juan entered Starbuck's and scanned the coffee-scented room. People sat at small tables chatting together, reading newspapers, using computers. He saw lots of jeans. No gray Stetson, shirt and boots. Restrooms empty.

"Good morning, Juan," said the woman preparing coffee orders.

"Hi, Suzie." He nodded toward the window. "Do you know where that collie's owner is?"

She glanced out. "A white collie. I hadn't noticed him. Isn't he beautiful!"

Juan reined in his impatience. "I wonder who owns him."

"He's mine," came a voice from the table behind Juan.

He jerked his head around. A young man in a St. John's College T-shirt and Texas Rangers ball cap smiled proudly. His black-framed glasses tilted, one stem missing. Juan stared at him for an instant. Expecting a killer, he faced instead a jovial college student with a view of the world skewed toward innocence. Recovering, he mustered a smile and controlled his pace. Patience would save time in the long run, a chat more productive than interrogation. "May I join you?" He asked casually as he sat down. "I'm Juan."

"I'm Ryan."

"Juan de Santiago," he said, hoping Ryan would follow suit.

"Ryan Roberts. My dog is Pal."

"I see you're a student at St. John's."

"A freshman."

Good, thought Juan, I know where to find you. He looked out the window at the dog. "Pal has had a busy morning," he said nonchalantly. "What happened to your friend who was walking him?"

Ryan tried to straighten his one-stemmed glasses. "Not a friend. A stranger."

Juan looked around the room. "Where is he?"

"He brought Pal back to me and drove away in a forest green Dodge Ram. It reminded me of my uncle's back in Texas."

Juan smiled. "I don't suppose you noticed the license plate number?"

"It was covered with mud."

Not surprising. A pro's tag number would either be invisible or fake. Juan reminded himself to appear unhurried. "You wouldn't let just any stranger take Pal for a walk, Ryan." He smiled again. "There has to be a good story behind this, and I like good stories. If I go to the restroom first, I can listen better. I'll be back in a minute."

Ryan nodded.

Juan locked the restroom and called his assistant to put out an APB for a green Ram truck with a muddy tag, the driver dressed in jeans, gray shirt and boots, with a gray Stetson. He doubted the alert would do any good. A pro wouldn't risk the main roads. But maybe he'd make a mistake. He will at some point. Eventually we all screw up. Next Juan called Dan. "The white collie's owner is in Starbuck's."

"Do you need back-up? I'm in the parking lot across the street."

"He's a freshman at St. John's College."

"*What!*"

"Your CIA buddy staked out the *dog*. Not the *man*." Juan heard Dan ask: *Moore, did you **see** our man go in Starbucks?* There was a muffled reply in the background. Dan erupted with expletives Juan wouldn't want his little girl to hear. It was about to become Moore's worst day. The thought brought a smile to his face. "*Amigo*," he said to Dan, "the kid and I will be on the Plaza. I don't want a two-on-one with him, but *after* you shed your buddy, you're welcome to take a seat close by and give us a listen." Juan punched *END* and went back to the table. "Ryan, I bet Pal is tired of waiting for you. Let's go sit in the Plaza so he can be with us while you tell me that story."

"Great idea." He hurried to the door and patted Pal's head. "Good boy." The collie wagged his tail and licked the hand he loved.

"He's beautiful, Ryan."

"That's what the stranger said."

They found a bench. Juan saw Dan sit down on the one across from them and begin reading *The New Mexican*. They ignored each other.

Ryan rested his elbow on the arm of the bench. "Pal and I were walking up Palace toward the Plaza." The dog's head came up when he heard his name, and Ryan reached down to pet him. "As we passed the entry to First National's parking lot, a man in a gray cowboy hat was parking his Ram. I didn't pay much attention until he got out and looked at my dog. That's when he said he's beautiful."

Juan nodded. "He's the only white collie I've ever seen."

"The man said he had one when he was a boy and used to take him for a walk everyday, and he asked if he could take Pal for a walk." The dog lifted his head again and received another pat. Ryan frowned. "I wasn't sure about it. But he seemed really interested. And I felt kind of sorry for him because he spoke with a stutter. I think he was from the South—you know, he kind of had a drawl."

It must have been a heavy one—or fake—to be noticed by a kid from Texas, thought Juan.

Ryan tried again to straighten his glasses. "I guess he could tell I wasn't sure about it. He opened his wallet and offered me twenty-five dollars. That insulted Pal! There was a whole lot of money where that came from. He said he'd just take him on up Palace to the corner and turn on Lincoln Street and then circle back down San Francisco and end up right back in the parking lot. I decided to try for more and told him $50.00 minimum. He paid it, so I agreed."

"For $50.00, what else could a man do?"

"You got that right, Juan. I'm in college and need the money. Pal wasn't so sure, though." Again, the collie's head came up. An automatic pat. "I handed the man the leash."

Fingerprints, thought Juan. He started to interrupt to ask for a description of the man's hands. Large or small. Old or young. Soft or calloused. It was hard to disguise hands.

"I don't know what was wrong. Maybe it was his gloves. Or his smell. Or just that he was a stranger. I even told the man to say, *Heel*."

The collie stood. "Lie down, boy. You just refused to go, didn't you?" He looked back at Juan. "I finally had to order him: *You go on now!*"

Pal ducked his head. Ryan scratched him behind his ears. "It's OK, boy." He smiled at Juan. "You can see how obedient he is. So he went, but he wasn't happy about it. He loves walks and usually prances along and wags his tail the whole time. You know, like he did a minute ago when we left Starbuck's." Ryan frowned. "But with that stranger he tucked his tail between his legs and dragged himself along."

"Collies are loyal, Ryan. I had a sheltie growing up. She was loyal too."

"They weren't gone very long, but it seemed like it. I cut through the parking lot to watch for them. My dog saw me as they turned down San Francisco. He couldn't wait to get back to me. He started leading instead of heeling."

"Was the man trying to slow him?" asked Juan.

"Nope. He seemed to be in a hurry too."

"What happened then?"

"He thanked me and said the walk brought back good memories. But he seemed kind of weird. Anyway, he gave me another five and told me go have a cup of coffee on him at Starbucks. He mentioned that I could tie Pal up outside, but I already knew that." Ryan grinned. "I like that place. I've seen some cute girls in there."

Juan grinned back. "That always makes coffee taste better to us men."

"For sure! Did you see that blond, Juan?"

"It sounds like I missed something special."

"You sure did."

Juan paused an instant. "And that's when he drove off? After he gave you the five for coffee?"

"That's when he got in his truck. He was still sitting there when I tied up Pal and went in Starbuck's. But in a minute or two I saw his truck drive away."

And that, thought Juan, is the story of how the CIA wizard staked out a white dog and let the Plaza poisoner escape in a green truck.

Ryan looked thoughtful. "I'm glad I got my dog back. I don't think I'll risk that again."

You don't have a clue how at risk you were! Juan glanced toward the bench across from them and met Dan's eyes for a second. The slight nod told him that Dan too was satisfied that Ryan Roberts was telling the truth.

4

As the cathedral bells chimed a quarter past nine, Matt rang the doorbell. He wore a black suit, clerical collar and purple episcopal shirt. "You look mighty impressive, Bishop Langham."

"I'm making a pastoral call on behalf of the venerable Archbishop Hannahan," he stated with pretentious dignity. "Appropriate attire is mandatory." He dropped the pompous act. "When my father died it was hard on all of us, but my mother seemed to lose at least half of herself." He, lowered his eyes. "I ache for Mrs. Martinez."

Perhaps the heart attack cover-up was a blessing for her. Murder could make the death of a loved one even more difficult to bear. "I'm glad you invited me to come along, Matt." We walked past the Juke, its keys removed and safely in a drawer. He drove around the Paseo de Peralta horseshoe toward De Vargas Mall and turned by the cemetery. I began to relax as we drove out of Santa Fe, away from a collie-walking killer. I borrowed a TV scene from *NCIS* and envisioned him at an interrogation table, Dan getting answers. Case solved.

Matt's voice faded that scene. "I'm pleased our time here overlaps. Seeing you and Galen last night was my gift for the day."

"You do that also? Note the gift of the day?"

He nodded. "I started it after reading Steindl-Rast's book on gratitude."

"Me too, about a thousand daily gifts back." Matt looked at me, his kind face and compassionate demeanor inviting me to share more deeply. "After the gift of Lyndie was taken from me, his book lit a candle in my darkness. That tiny light showed me life still offered small gifts if I could step out of my despair long enough each day to unwrap one."

He received my words with a comforting reverent silence until I was ready to move on. "I enjoyed getting to know Joe last night. You're fortunate he's your mentor."

"I've been wondering how becoming a bishop might change my life."

"It causes many shifts. Some unpredictable." I listened as he shared his concerns. My cell interrupted. "Hello."

"Dan here. He escaped."

His words struck into me like a double-edged sword. I recoiled in terror.

"Now he knows you can identify him, Lynn. You must be *very* cautious. Where are you?"

"We . . ." I cleared my throat to remove the tremor from my voice. "We're passing the Opera House."

"Who's *we*?"

"Bishop Matt Langham."

"Where are you going? I want to keep up with you until we get that . . . get him."

"We're on our way to Los Alamos."

"*Los Alamos*? Tell me this doesn't relate to Carlos Martinez."

"We're making a pastoral call on his widow, Dan. She's Catholic. Matt invited me to come along." Silence. I waited.

"When will you be back?"

"Probably around noon."

"I'll call Galen about the escape. It infuriates me!" He paused and said firmly. "Be careful, Lynn." Another pause. "I'm . . ." His voice caught. "I'm *extremely sorry we failed*."

I heard his frustration and care. He had little experience with failure. The connection broke. I stared at my phone and sank smaller in the seat, rerunning the terrorizing words. Matt looked at me and back at the road. I was grateful that once again he honored silence, my dark silence. I felt I was in a countdown until they trapped the poisoner.

Or he trapped me.

5

Ariel wound his way to Buckman Road as he headed out of Santa Fe. Officials would question the student who owned the collie, get a truck description and put out an APB. One choice: Stay on Buckman all the way to N.M. 502. A rough, untraveled, at times nonexistent road through the Caja del Rio Canyon, but *untraveled* was the operative word. The rugged Ram should make it. *Should,* less assuring than *would.* Once he reached 502, he'd be vulnerable for a short stretch to Los Alamos, and then on back roads again to his ranch. Once there, he'd be safe.

Safe? His thoughts circled. Prudence required him to avoid an unnecessary death so close to the two on Monday. Yet, his magnanimous altruism of not killing an innocent had placed him in danger. The bishop factor also came into play with his god/God uncertainty. *Ergo* her test. Her *failed* test.

He reviewed the quickly formed plan after the Petersons entered the Plaza Café. A good plan. Park behind the bank. Walk down Lincoln. Pass the café window. Observe her reaction. But when he saw the white collie, he impulsively changed his plan. If she had protection, no one would suspect a man ambling along across the street from where he'd committed murder on a park bench less than 48 hours ago—especially a man with his dog. That impulsive change of plan, however, had cost him the Ram's description. He could repaint the truck, but he'd left a footprint, an unprecedented mistake in his career.

As he bumped along the dirt road, he reran the café scene: When he walked past the window, she smiled at him. Behind his sunglasses he scrutinized her face. No guile. No fear. No hint of recognition. Just a woman smiling at a man walking his dog. He was too skilled at reading people to be tricked. She had a beautiful smile and kind face. In that moment he was glad she passed the test.

But prudence called for extra precaution, so he set up the Starbucks ruse and waited in the Ram to see if anyone took the bait. Bait taken! A man dressed like a tourist in a plaid shirt and shorts skulked into the parking lot. Hid behind the adobe wall. Peeked out at the dog. Made a call. Another Suit without a suit! Test failed! Ariel slammed his fist against the steering wheel.

Something had changed after he passed her. What? It didn't matter. Escape mattered. His Ram bounced over a rock in the rutted canyon road. *Road* was an exaggeration. But it kept him from dozing off. Watching the *casita* all night in his cramped truck had begun to take its toll. *Stay awake!*

Ariel considered the student's potential damage. He can't provide a tag number or a credible description of me. The Stetson hid most of my hair, and the sunglasses my eyes. I know how to talk without showing my teeth. The drawl and stutter were misleading. No valuable information.

But Lynn Peterson is another story. When I left the park bench Monday, did she see me cross San Francisco and enter the Arcade? After I changed my clothes and exited to Water Street, could she tell I was the same man? Surely not. Did she watch me walk to the parking lot and get in the Ford Explorer? The video showed the rest. She appeared to be watching me drive away on Water Street. But it was hard to be positive. None of that mattered now. What matters is that she evidently recognized me this morning after I went by, and she has the power of credibility. She is not just a loose end in the Venom Contract. She is a lethal threat.

The ruts in the road became too deep even for the Ram. He pulled out. Made his own road. And devised the Peterson Plan. Precise and methodical. The strategy came together. He liked it. No indecision. No improvisation. No mercy. He'd had to return his client's tiny speargun to the drop site on Monday. During the few days he had it, he had examined it carefully and taken some photos to create a similar weapon. He knew he could get the kind of poison that would work. He'd used it before. A nice touch to use a poisoned spearpoint on Bishop Lynn Peterson.

6

Matt and I turned off our phones when he parked in the Martinez driveway. I scanned the neighborhood. No ancient adobe houses here. Every residence was built after the Los Alamos site selection in 1943, an instant secret city.

"I'm not sure what to make of this city," Matt said, also looking around. "I read that Los Alamos County is now the third wealthiest in the country based on median household income."

"Small, remote and wealthy—an unusual combination," I said. The beautiful Martinez landscaping showed that someone in the family loved to garden. A variety of rosebushes grew on trellises along one wall, and an interesting rock garden stood between the gravel driveway and flagstone walk.

A young woman opened the door. "I'm Reyna Salcido, Marta's daughter." Laughing eyes would fit her sweet smile and pleasant face, but they held no laughter today. "Please come in, Father Matt." She noticed his purple shirt. "I mean *Bishop*. Excuse me."

"Father Matt first, and always." He smiled warmly at her and stepped back for me to enter. "This is my friend Lynn Peterson from New Orleans."

Reyna's face lit up. "Daddy went to school at Tulane!"
Grateful for the comfort of connections, I added another. "My husband teaches there, Reyna."

"Then you are like family." She led the way to a living area where a small woman sat alone on a floral sofa, her face ashen, her body motionless, her lifeless eyes swollen from crying. Reyna introduced Matt and me, including connections. "Isn't it good that they came, Mama?" she coaxed, like begging her to live again.

I glimpsed Reyna's tears as she turned quickly away to leave the room, probably tears for her mother as well as her father.

Matt clasped Marta's hand in both of his. "I'm so sorry, Marta. Archbishop Hannahan wanted to come himself. He asked me to bring you his love and to tell you that you and your family are in his prayers."

"Thank you." She spoke from a void and closed her eyes a moment.

Matt took the chair near her, and I sat beside her on the sofa, a comfortable silence in the air. I had learned long ago—and evidently so had Matt—that words, though well intentioned and even eloquent, are unimportant during life's grimmest times. It is being present, deeply present, that fosters healing. I recalled a wise saying: *Do not speak unless you can improve upon the silence.* Marta seemed to find solace in being wrapped in a caring presence that required nothing from her.

Reyna returned to invite us into the dining room for tea. The table was filled with baked goods from friends wanting to console. The array of food told me that Marta was surrounded by a community of people who loved and supported her. She would not be alone in her loneliness.

Again Reyna turned to leave rather than join us. I wondered if she felt that her mother needed to talk alone with a priest and rose also. Reyna caught my eye and mouthed, *Please stay.*

Seated at the table with teacup and saucer awoke Marta to hostess courtesies and forced a semblance of life. "Since you're from New Orleans, Lynn, are you a Saints fan?"

"Oh yes!" I recalled the Saints sweatshirt, the reason I so quickly identified with Carlos. . . and then he died. I didn't meet him, but I would never forget him.

"Carlos too. If I had cheered for a team playing against them, he would have claimed grounds for divorce!" She managed a shallow laugh. "He took me to the Super Bowl game the Saints won." The nanosecond light went out of her eyes. Returning to hostess duties, she asked the inevitable question: "Do you have children, Lynn?"

That common question always evoked the memory of ancient words: *My heart is pierced within me.* I took a breath. "We had a lovely daughter, Marta." I made it through that part lightly, then bit my lower lip. "She was . . . in a car wreck . . . at sixteen." Her eyes met mine. Two kindred souls joined by bottomless sorrow, in which never again erased assumptions for tomorrow.

"It is awfully hard." She gazed down at her cup. Much of my life ended with his." Another silence followed. When she looked up again, she sat forward slightly and spoke into the distance. "Carlos had just had a physical." She turned toward Matt. "There was nothing wrong with his heart, Father."

I froze my face, blanked my eyes. Did she suspect a cover-up?

Perceptive Matt enfolded her hand. "Does the medical report trouble you, Marta?"

She hesitated.

"Do not be afraid to say whatever is in your heart. Both Lynn and I, each in our own way, share the same profession. You have our complete confidentially."

She peered at me, her eyes puzzled.

I nodded. "I'm not Catholic, but I'm a Benedictine oblate." I saw Matt's surprised smile. "I have great respect for your church."

Marta studied my face. "I feel . . . I don't know . . . *Safe*. That's it. I feel safe with both of you." She was silent again, then lowered her eyes and whispered, "I want to tell you a secret that I have shared with no one. Not even my children."

7

Zechariah Zeller had driven quickly up U.S. 84/285. The tracking device he had attached to the Ram showed it inching its way on Buckman Road toward N.M. 502, the road's dead end and only exit. Herr Ram's drive would be slow and dangerous. Zeller parked in Pojoaque at the Cities of Gold Casino, conveniently located at the 502 intersection and only a few miles west of the Buckman connection. When the Ram finally reached the highway, he planned to follow the blip like a drone in the distance. So easy.

He settled in for a patient wait, not tempted by the offerings of betting, bingo and bowling. His mind turned to pretty *Frau* Peterson's phone conversation with the man named Dan telling her about the escape. *Ja!* I already knew that, but not that she was in a car with a bishop named Matt Langham on her way to see the victim's widow in Los Alamos. Not good timing. No. Herr Ram was headed to 502, which meant he too was going to Los Alamos. Zeller wanted to get on with the chase, not sit here and wait. Come on, Herr Ram!

Patience! He opened his computer with a fond pat. "We do not have to waste time while we wait, *Mutter*. We have codes to crack and secrets to steal." He hacked into supposedly secure CIA files. First to find something on Andy Bush, an unsurprising dead end. Then he focused on the two searches launched yesterday for *Frau* Peterson. The second search remained within the ranks of the CIA. But the results from the earlier one were emailed immediately, and not even *Mutter* could unblock the address. Did Herr Ram request the report? A case could be made: *Eins*, the secretary's call from fake Andy Bush was made soon after that email. *Zwei*, Herr Ram knew her identity and had learned her Santa Fe address. *Drei*, his skill in surveillance and escape could point to CIA training and a connection that could expedite his information request.

Zeller did not underestimate his shrewd enemy, nor fear him. Hurry up, Herr Ram—a.k.a. Abe and Andy! You'll meet your match on 502!

"He's almost mine, *Mutter!*" He gave her another fond pat.

8

Marta's secret hung over the tea table like a low chandelier with unlit bulbs. Matt and I sat quietly, waiting for her to speak. She set her teacup down and began. "Carlos was a custodial engineer and knew a lot about the Lab." She spoke in a monotone, pulling the words from her soul. I listened with my heart as well as my head.

"There were many changes when the operations management contract was taken from the university and given to a private corporation. You may know that GANNS won the contract."

Global **A**nd **N**ational **N**uclear **S**ecurity Corporation, I remembered from last night's party.

Marta stiffened. "Carlos felt that profit became more important than security. The more he learned, the more concerned he grew. But he was afraid he'd lose his job if he told anyone." She swallowed, and then she managed to say the words that pain wanted to bury. "On Sunday he seemed edgy. Nervous. He invited me out for dinner. A happy memory." She smiled. It vanished. "Our last dinner together." Tears welled up, but she continued. "Afterward he wanted to take a walk. It was a beautiful evening. We ambled along Bathtub Row and around Fuller Lodge. He suggested that we walk on over to Ashley Pond. That's when he began talking. He told me everything as we walked. It replays in my mind like a somber YouTube video." She began to tell his story:

Marta, you know that I was troubled about the changes at LANL. But you don't know what I did. The FBI has always watched for leaked secrets. They hired me to act as an undercover agent, to be alert for anything suspicious and report to them. I thought I could help. All of the staff trust me including the scientists, and as a custodial engineer I'm allowed into many secured places. Gradually I learned how to gain access to the ones beyond my security clearance. I'm not proud of it, but I felt it was for a good cause.

"Carlos looked at me," Marta interjected before continuing. "I saw in his eyes the pain of that decision."

What I learned, Marta, made me even more concerned. The destructive power of LANL secrets reaches science fiction dimensions, and these secrets are managed by a for-profit corporation. GANNS can afford to buy Washington influence that serves its own gain whether or not it's in the country's best interest. I fear we have moved into the danger zone. But all the FBI did was gather information. Nothing changed.

Then the CIA came to me, concerned about potential foreign theft of top secret information. There have been leaks since way back in the beginning of the "secret city on the hill." First Russia during the atom bomb development. Later other countries, including China. I was told that the agencies sometimes withhold information from each other. That makes no sense, and it's dangerous. So I hired on with the CIA too. I thought maybe they would do something. I managed to get every piece of information they requested. But again, nothing changed. Nothing I did made any difference.

Marta stopped and sipped some water. She looked at Matt. "He stopped walking for a moment. I can still feel his hands gently on my shoulders as he turned me toward him."

*Then PAPA wanted my help. The **P**eace for **A**ll **P**eople **A**lliance. That is the answer, Marta. LANL needs to work for the common good of all people. Not for the few invested in it who place profit above people and country.*

I am going to tell you something. Something that you must tell no one. Unless . . .

Unless . . . something happens to me.

Tears came to Marta's eyes. "I need a moment."

Matt reached across the table and took her hand. "There is no need to hurry," he said kindly. "This is very difficult. Thank you for sharing with us."

9

Galen was on automatic pilot as he rode with Chev to the San Ildefonso Pueblo. He couldn't shake Dan's call negating the earlier thumbs-up optimism. A bungled escape. Apparently the only hope was the APB on the vehicle: a forest green Dodge Ram with a muddy tag. *That* was the best they could do? His anger roiled toward Dan, the CIA, this whole game of intrigue that endangered Lynn. Mostly he was mad at himself—he felt powerless to protect her. At least she was with Matt in Los Alamos, not home alone.

He forced his thoughts back to the Jeep. "Tell me about cultural anthropology, Chev. What do you find most meaningful?"

"The holistic study of humanity. Looking at the past: physical characteristics, the origin and distribution of races, the environment, social relations, culture. Considering the impact of global economic and political processes on local cultural realities."

Galen wondered if the impact of global economics or political processes had anything to do with Carlos Martinez's death and the newspaper *Heart Attack* headline.

"I like studying the present cultural variation among humans. Take us, for example. We both have doctorates from Harvard, but our formative childhoods were lived in different cultures. Our paths to the same end were dissimilar, yet equally effective. I find that interesting."

"I do too. And here we are again, my friend, rowing in different streams, yet arriving at the same port." He paused, then risked a personal question. "What was it like when you were growing up?"

Chev glanced at him and began.

Galen listened, fascinated by his stories about the Tewas and growing up in San Ildefonso Pueblo. He tried to place himself in this world he hadn't experienced.

"Bored yet?" asked Chev as they arrived at San Ildefonso.

"No! I'm genuinely interested."

"I sensed that yesterday. It's why I wanted to bring you here," he said as they arrived. Chev parked the Jeep. "Let's begin your education."

"I know a bit about the past," said Galen. He rattled off facts like a student wanting to get an *A* from his teacher. "Spain renamed pueblos after saints. San Ildefonso was named after seventh century Ildefonsus, known as San Ildefonso in Castilian. He rose from monk, to abbot, to metropolitan, to sainthood." He grinned. "I googled all this last night to impress my Harvard brother."

Chev's smile creased the corners of his eyes. "Well done. Our Tewa name came first, of course. *Po-Woh-Ge-Oweenge*—Where the Water Cuts Down Through."

Galen repeated it, trying to pronounce it exactly as he'd heard it.

"Again, well done. My people have been here since the 1300s. Some say 1200s, but I question that."

As they walked through the sand, Galen drank in his surroundings like a desert drifter who'd found an oasis. He thought of little Dosae, the Paleoindian girl he had imagined, and envisioned her walking barefoot here in ancient days, the warm sand clinging to her toes.

Chev stopped beside an aged cottonwood tree. "Have you heard of Maria Martinez?"

"I saw one of her beautiful black pots in a museum. I wanted to hear its story."

Chev waved at a young man standing on a *portal* across the road. "That's her house. Her family still lives there."

Galen waved also. A world-acclaimed potter content with a simple house. When one culture dominates another, he thought regretfully, historians eradicate values the victims could teach.

"The two-story structure abutting it is our new kiva, a meeting place." He shared facts and stories, legends and myths as they walked to the church. He paused. "Bored now?"

"I'm never bored with an opportunity to decrease nescience."

"You engage in hyperbole. Neither of us has to limit ourselves to nikhedonia. We experience success rather than merely anticipating it."

Galen chuckled. "Ah! A fellow lexiphanic." A small cemetery greeted them in the church courtyard. "Bombastic vocabulary aside, I am genuinely interested. Thank you for bringing me here, Chev."

"Our *new* church is a little over a century old. The first one stood here before the Pilgrims landed."

"A point of interest typically omitted in history lessons regarding that era," said Galen. They entered the sacred place of simple beauty and stood quietly. His mind grasped the significance of historical time and sensed the journey of the peoples here over the hallowed centuries.

When they returned to the Jeep and Chev started back toward the highway, he said, "Our heritage . . . spirituality might be a more accurate word . . . regards the Earth and its rhythms as sacred. It teaches us to live in harmony with all creation."

The incongruity struck Galen. Earth's most horrific weapons of mass destruction were developed in the midst of this ancient heritage of living *in harmony with all creation.* He was disappointed in himself for not recognizing it sooner. "I can debate from either side the justification for developing atomic bombs, but why select this area for that project? Why *here?*"

"I've pondered that as a cultural anthropologist and followed the paths of their reasoning—none of them satisfactory to my Tewa heart." He stopped at the intersection before turning west on 502 to go on to the Tsankawi ruins. "But I'll share my version if you'd like."

Suddenly a vehicle bolted from the rugged road across the highway. Shot through the stop sign. Barreled forward. Banked on screeching tires. Careened toward the Jeep.

Chev threw it into reverse. Missed a collision by inches. Chev thundered: "*You execerebrose, apogamic, flotsam dunderpate!*"

The truck skinned past them. Veered into a left turn. Sped west.

Galen sat still for an instant. Tasting death. Breathing life. "Your swift reflexes saved us." Then he grinned. "By the way, that was the best lexiphanic cuss-out I ever heard!"

"That was just a warm-up."

Dan's words flashed through Galen's mind: *A forest green Dodge Ram.* The truck that almost hit them! He'd glimpsed its gray-shirted driver and the muddy tag as it sped away. Toward Los Alamos! And Lynn and Matt and the victim's widow! "Let's go, Chev!" he shouted. "Stick with him!"

Galen tried to call Lynn. "Come on! Answer!" *To leave a message . . .* He left a warning, again feeling powerless to protect her.

10

Matt and I waited for Marta to continue. Our silence together was no longer comforting. We could feel the beat of tension like a tom-tom trio. She poured more tea and began again, her eyes peering into the distance and her words so soft we leaned in to hear:

"He spoke in a tone he'd never used before. I felt his fear, but he was determined."

If something does happen to me, Marta, you decide whether to share all that I am going to tell you. I want you to live in inner peace. But don't trust the police, the FBI or the CIA. And certainly no one connected with GANNS—which means no one at LANL.

She raised an eyebrow. "That seemed to leave only the Holy Mother and the Lord's representatives. He began to talk about what was going to happen the next day. That terrible Monday."

Two weeks ago, Marta, I discovered that a newly developed biowarfare toxin was stolen from the Lab. The theft was covered up. Evidently GANNS cared more about bad publicity than finding the toxin. It is the most lethal ever developed and capable of creating biological mass destruction. They don't even have an antidote yet! It's still in the experimental phase. Who can predict the consequences?

I reported this to the CIA, and they told me to use every clandestine skill I have to obtain the spy's identity and learn how he managed to steal it. I finally succeeded. A meeting with a CIA operative is scheduled tomorrow in Santa Fe to give him my report. They don't trust electronic communications or local operatives with this information.

"I saw his eyes cloud. He was agitated and spoke hurriedly. At one point he literally shook his fist. I had never seen him do that before. Not in all these years."

The CIA leaks like an old septic tank. Someone at LANL may know about me. But what troubles me most is that this lethal toxin is in the hands of one nation, and our nation entrusts its control to a corporation dependent on profit. I fear that some lab employees are susceptible to manipulation. Like offers of promotion if they modify their behavior and ethics. Or threats of job loss if they don't. Small ethical changes evolve into big ones—and lead to the horror of a theft of lethal toxin. **Los Alamos National Lab is no place for tainted ethics!**

There is more. I believe that an antidote to something so lethal belongs in the hands of more than one power. I may have done something terrible, Marta, but I did it to be true to my conscience. I made a copy of the formula at PAPA's request so their scientists can work on an antidote. I have his word that the formula will only be used for that purpose.

I am meeting with two people in Santa Fe tomorrow. One is the CIA operative I already mentioned. The other is a representative from PAPA, and I trust him. Poison is contrary to PAPA's purpose.

So, there it is, Marta. I hope you understand.

She sank back in her chair, the secret told, the burden shared. "I can hardly believe these words I have spoken. But I swear to you they are true."

"We know you speak the truth," said Matt.

She sighed, seeming smaller than before, like a skein of yarn unwound. "*So,* as Carlos said, *there it is.*" Her eyes teared. "Please excuse me. I am very tired."

11

Ariel kept an eye on the Jeep in his rearview mirror as 502 wound upward. He was furious with himself. To doze off like an amateur! Jerk awake at the intersection! Hit the gas pedal instead of the brake! His fury shifted to Lynn Peterson.

The image of her husband in the Jeep's passenger seat hung in his mind. Did he see me at the café? Recognize me now? Have the Ram's description? Call it in? The State Police could be on their way! He slammed his fist into the dashboard. *Years of precise and methodical perfection blown to bits **twice** today!*

Not again! Lose the Jeep! He focused on options.

Take the N.M. 30 exit to Espanola? No! They'd see the Ram turn off and follow me.

Go through Los Alamos on Trinity Drive? No! The truck would be recognized like an RSVP to an APB. I might as well turn myself in!

Think!

He pictured the terrain on the final stretch to Los Alamos. A concrete barrier blocked escape between the 30 exit and the 4 split. Then the road narrowed to two lanes with the ravine on his right. A long curve commenced. A plan unfolded. Yes! He quickly ran through the details, precise and methodical. Dangerous but not impossible. No other options! No more time! No good way out!

First challenge: Gain distance from the Jeep. He pushed the pedal to the floor and sped up the mountain road. A war game to the finish.

><><><   ><><><   ><><><

The Jeep chased the Ram up 502. Galen called Dan. Heard static. Feared they were breaking up. Spoke quickly: "We'reFollowing PoloWestOn502BetweenSanIldefonsoAndLosAlamos." More static. He clutched the phone with white knuckles. "Can you hear me?" Nothing.

Chev glanced at him. "You know that driver?"

"It's complicated, friend." A curve blocked their view of the Ram. Galen leaned forward. "Don't lose him!"

"Not a chance. He's the cowboy. We're the Indians. And we get to win this time!" They came out of the curve and spotted the Ram in the distance. "Keep an eye on Cowboy at the 30 exit!"

Galen watched. "He stayed on 502." When they passed the exit, the highway changed abruptly. A concrete barrier separated the east/west traffic and warnings loomed: **SAFETY CORRIDOR. LIGHTS ON FOR SAFETY. SPEED LIMIT 40.** He read aloud a mileage sign: "Los Alamos, ten miles."

"I have to slow down." Chev tapped the brake until the speedometer fell to 50. "Cowboy wouldn't drive that fast unless he's a crazy man with a death wish!"

)⊙‡⊙⟨   )⊙‡⊙⟨   )⊙‡⊙⟨

Ariel gained the distance he needed. Second challenge: Prepare ruse. His eyes on the road, he felt for his emergency bag, kept accessible and packed for the unforeseeable. He lifted it to the passenger seat. Unzipped it by feel. Fingered various essentials. Pulled out the padded box. Set it beside him. Removed the lid. Felt inside. Found each part. He had practiced the feat blind-folded a million times, completed it successfully twice before. He stilled nerves, steadied muscles, concentrated thoughts. Eyes still glued to the road, left hand on the wheel, his right hand began to connect the parts by feel. Slowly. Carefully. One to two. Two to three. Ready! He brushed his forefinger across the small bomb, satisfied.

Third challenge: Arm bomb. He glimpsed it for an instant, snapped a mental image. Slowed down. Again by feel, he matched his hand movements to his image. Quickly peeked down to be sure. Armed!

His eyes ping-ponged between road and bomb for the final challenge: Set timer for seven minutes. Done!

The countdown began.

Ariel lodged the bomb in the narrow space behind the passenger seat. Floored the gas pedal. Pulled his helmet from the emergency bag. Glanced in the rearview mirror. No Jeep. He gobbled up the last half mile.

Six minutes and counting.

He came to the State Road 4 split. Concrete median ended. Road narrowed to two lanes. He sped along the mini-guardrail between him and the deep ravine on his right.

Now!

Ariel slammed the brake. Set cruise control. Slung emergency bag strap over his head and across his chest. Scooted to passenger side. Fastened crash helmet. Angled steering wheel toward ravine. Opened door. Aimed toward foliage.

Jumped!

He curled in a ball and landed in a roll. Grabbed a *piñon* tree and held firm. *Steady. Steady.*

Stood up. Assessed body damage. Minor bruises. Heard Ram crash into boulders below. Waited. No bomb blast. Its timer held. *Hurry!*

He hid behind a *piñon* cluster. Yanked off boots and gray shirt. Unzipped bag. Removed emergency disguise from shrink bag: long crinkle skirt with elastic waist, long-sleeved blouse fastened with Velcro, ankle-high moccasins, concho belt, silver clip earrings, long dark wig. He put them on. Took the Navajo blanket from the bag. Stuffed boots and shirt inside. Wrapped blanket around bag, held it like a baby.

Four minutes to explosion.

When Chev came out of the next curve, Galen leaned forward and strained futilely for a glimpse of the Ram. "He couldn't have turned off with these barriers."

"They'll end at the 4 split. Look for options a truck could take."

Galen saw the sign. "There's the split. Maybe he took it."

"Not likely. He'd end up in Bandilier and the Tsankawi ruins. Unless he soared over the edge." Chev grinned. "*Thelma and Louise* style, if you saw that old movie."

"You're enjoying this!"

"Could be." Chev's eyes crinkled. "I thrive on adventure. That's why I do what I do and live where I live."

12

Ariel, hiding in the *piñons*, heard a vehicle and peeked out at the highway. The white Jeep sped by, chasing a truck that was now behind it. Dressed like an Indian woman and carrying his emergency bag wrapped in a blanket, he rushed up the few feet to the road. Psyched himself into the role of Indian mother walking with her baby toward Los Alamos. A blue sedan with two older couples inside slowed. *No!* Too many people. The shy Indian mother looked down at the road. Long loose hair hid her face. She shook her head. The sedan drove on by.

A truck came around the curve. Silver semi, dark tinted windows. *Yes!* The Indian mother stopped, lowered her face, lifted her wrapped baby.

The driver stopped and rolled down the passenger window. "I'm going to Los Alamos. Do you need a ride?"

She nodded, shyly looking down, her hair hiding her face. *A nice touch, the Indian mother.*

The driver reached across the seat and opened the door for her.

Head down, she shifted the baby to her left arm. She raised a moccasined foot to step into his semi.

He leaned closer to help her.

Ariel slammed his right fist hard into the trucker's face. Knocked him out. Hauled him from the semi. Bashed his head with a rock—like a blow from a fall. Heaved him down the ravine.

There would be no stolen-semi report from this driver. No report ever again. The discovery of the body would be delayed by the rocks and canopy of *piñons*. When found, officials would connect him with the crashed Ram and assume he'd managed to get out of the truck, too badly injured to wander far. Ariel had bought himself plenty of time. No rush. No worry. No carelessness.

He climbed into the semi. As he drove, he yanked off his wig and jerked the blanket off the emergency bag. He felt inside for his slip-on sneakers and ball cap. Driving carefully, he tugged off the Indian mother costume, traded the moccasins for sneakers, put on the cap, Crammed the costume and blanket back into the emergency bag. Precise and methodical. I'll be at my ranch before they link the trucker's body to his missing silver semi.

One minute to bomb detonation.

>×‡×<   >×‡×<   >×‡×<

Galen's cell rang—Lynn, he hoped.

"Dan here. I notified Los Alamos officials," he said hurriedly.

"We lost him," Galen confessed.

"We've requested a copter from LANL."

Galen looked up at the sky. "Here it comes!"

"Describe your vehicle," said Dan.

"White Jeep. Super driver."

"I'm connecting to the pilot. Hold on a minute."

Galen waited. Watched the helicopter.

"OK, Galen. He sees the Jeep. Got to go."

"That's an *LANL* copter!" said Chev with surprise. "Your friend's influence with GANNS is impressive."

The helicopter's location puzzled Galen. "If the pilot came from Los Alamos, why is he flying toward us? He should have seen the Ram already."

"Good point."

They both heard an explosion.

"Behind us! Let's check it out."

"I'll make a U at the overlook." Chev steered into the turnout and waited for a blue sedan to pass. He started to pull out but stopped. "I don't think I want to lose a race with that semi."

Galen saw it in the rearview mirror. Silver with dark tinted windows.

✴ ✴ ✴

Ariel heard the blast as he drove the semi to Los Alamos. He glanced at his watch. Exactly 10:34. Precise and methodical. A nice touch, the bomb.

He saw the copter fly low, looking for a Ram headed west on 502. He would soon find it on fire in the ravine. Evidence destroyed. Ariel predicted the pilot's report, video attached: *Green truck crashed in ravine. On fire. Survivors impossible.*

Except for the peerless Ace-of-Escape. Driving away while officials focused on the burning vehicle. Looking inside it for a body that doesn't exist. Finding the trucker's body later and incorrectly connecting the disconnected. Once again I walk free. No cops. No cuffs. No questions.

He trailed a safe distance behind the blue sedan that had earlier slowed to offer the *Indian mother* a ride. The white Jeep waited on the pullout, its left-turn signal blinking, its passengers oblivious to the presence of their quarry. The sedan passed the Jeep. So did he, memorizing the tag number. He gave Peterson a triumphant wave, unseen through the silver semi's dark tinted windows.

✴ ✴ ✴

Galen's cell rang as Chev pulled out into a U-turn and headed back toward the blast.

"Dan again. The copter pilot reported a green Ram burning in the ravine!" He skipped a beat. "It looks like our friend lost control and crashed. The truck exploded."

"We heard a blast." Galen moved the phone away from his mouth to tell Chev. "The Ram crashed and exploded."

"The pilot is transmitting the copter's video now. I can see the fire and what's left of the Ram. Survival impossible. Lynn is safe."

Safe. That short word had more power than all the multisyllabic words in every language combined! "Can we do anything to help?"

"Officials are on the way. Where were you originally going?"

"The Tsankawi ruins."

"You'd better head on before traffic builds up at the crash site."

"Amateur help isn't needed?" Galen asked with a smile in his voice.

"It's over! Tell Super Driver thanks."

Galen punched *END*. "Officials are on the way, Chev. He said to thank Super Driver." Immediately he called Lynn with the good news but had to leave another message.

"I heard you say something about amateur help not being needed." Chev examined Galen's face, then smiled.

"What?"

"Your friend's ultracrepidarian gesture is troublesome."

Galen chuckled. "You're right. Intruding in someone else's business is seldom welcome, but he meant well. Let's head to the ruins before traffic builds up. It's over."

Chev's eyes crinkled. "One for the Indians. Zip for Cowboy."

13

Ariel maneuvered through his precise process to unlock the door to his concrete storage unit in Los Alamos. This was not a day of perfection, he admitted to himself, but he had executed a perfect escape. Parking the semi at a Los Alamos truck stop, sanitizing it and sauntering away, an unnotable man with a casual façade in T-shirt and jeans, ball cap and sneakers, toting a gym bag on his way to work out. The Ace of Escape felt confident again.

He liked this safe space. He ran his eyes over the wall-to-wall shelves of well-organized supplies, everything needed for various situations. Precise and methodical. This unit was one of three identical ones in strategic locations across the country. All with adapted locks that required the identical process to open the door. All well stocked with emergency supplies. All contained a black Harley.

He dumped his emergency/gym bag on the table and methodically restocked it. He unlocked the tour box behind the Harley seat. The bike gave him entry to the **H**arley **O**wners **G**roup—HOG, his only group membership besides the NRA. With enemies on both sides of the law, he was safer being a loner.

He finished packing the bag. Zipped it. *Wait*! His pocketknife! He looked carefully on the floor and the shelves. He removed everything from the bag and started over. No knife! It must have fallen out while the bag was open on the truck seat, then burned with the Ram. Or . . . He didn't like the *or*. He saw again the boulders beside Highway 502. Felt the pressure of the countdown. Relived the struggle to put on the Indian woman garb. Once again he looked through the escape bag. *Lost*!

He considered the consequences. Fingerprints were unlikely. He always wiped it clean and closed the blade with the cleaning cloth.

Always? Maybe no one would find it. Or maybe the finder would claim it for himself. *Maybe?* He hadn't built his success on *maybe*. My *third* mistake! A cliché rose like a kite in the wind: *Three strikes and you're out.*

To dwell on the knife would be a mistake. What was done was done. He removed his biker's costume from the tour box. Donned the black leather jacket, pants, boots. Put his black helmet on the handlebars. A nice touch, the face shield that masked him like Darth Vader.

He set the emergency bag in the tour box, tossed in his sneakers, added his ball cap, and thought of his Stetson—his favorite hat burned up in flames. He thought of his Ram—the best vehicle he'd ever owned reduced to a Tonka truck. He thought of the cause: Lynn Peterson! The trucker today made three deaths now instead of two, and she is still alive!

But not for long. Just one more thing to do before he put on his helmet and rode to his ranch: change her life with a phone call! He wanted her to know he was after her. Wanted her days and nights to be filled with terror. Wanted her to walk in fear that he lurked nearby no matter where she was. To take a cab with trepidation that he was the driver in disguise. To dread opening her front door, afraid he was behind it. Or hiding in her closet or under her bed. To imagine she heard his footsteps in the darkness.

And one day soon she would not be imagining it. He would be right behind her, speargun loaded. *Welcome to terror, Bishop Lynn Peterson!*

14

Heavy silence filled the car as Matt and I drove back to Santa Fe. Finally I spoke my troubled thoughts. "Officials need Marta's information about Carlos."

"I agree. But she told us in confidence."

"She didn't actually ask for confidentiality."

"She assumed it."

"I know," I ceded. "But if her doubts about a heart attack are well founded, doesn't confidentiality abet the murderer?"

"They did an autopsy."

And covered up the results, I thought but couldn't reveal. "Carlos told her not to repeat anything *unless*, and I quote, *something happens to me.* He must have known he was in danger."

"That troubles me too," he admitted. "He even warned her whom *not* to tell."

"Something did happen to him, and she told *us* the story. Perhaps she *wants* us to do something, but fears that it might put us in harm's way, and she would feel responsible."

He sighed. "I *cannot* break her confidence, Lynn, without her permission."

"Even asking her permission puts it on her shoulders."

"Your discernment and mine may lead us in different directions."

I wondered what he would do if he knew everything I did. I trusted him enough to tell him, but my commitment to President Benedict locked some things in a vault. "I want to discern what serves Marta and Carlos most effectively—to share this information with an official I trust, or pretend I don't know anything about it." I sighed. "Whatever we decide individually, I know *both* of us will protect Marta as the source."

"Unconditionally, Lynn. It is our sacred obligation." He braked the car behind a long line of vehicles stopped on N.M. 502. "It looks like an accident."

"I smell smoke. I hope no one was hurt." Patrol cars, fire trucks and emergency vehicles blocked the highway. Only a single narrow lane was open. A pilot car led long lines of traffic on it, one direction at a time. I thought about that. "When I grow up, I want to be a pilot car driver, Matt. People follow you without dissension and there's only one lane so you don't have to deal with options and you can't get off track and you don't ever feel lost. No choices, surprises or confusion. And no paradoxes."

"Do I hear a yearning for certitude and the simplistic?"

"Actually that sounds boring."

"We are in for a long wait." He looked at his watch and tapped his fingers on the steering wheel.

I remembered that I'd turned my phone off at Marta's, and checked it for missed calls. Two messages from Galen. *Polo is on N.M. 502 headed toward Los Alamos.* I felt Matt's gaze. My face had spoken unspoken words.

"What is it, Lynn?"

"It's complicated."

"If there is anything I can do . . ."

"No, but thank you for your concern."

He nodded without questions.

The later message startled me even more than the first: *Polo crashed into a ravine off N.M. 502. The truck exploded. A helicopter located what's left. It's still burning. Officials are on the way. To quote: "Survival impossible." You're safe.* I heard a catch in Galen's voice. *I love you, dearest Lynn.* A pause. *Since this is over, Chev and I are going on to the ruins.*

I listened again. Two phrases echoed in my mind. *Survival impossible* and *You're safe.* Polo was dead! My relief left no space for grief.

Matt glanced at me, then back at the road.

Kind Matt. "The second message solved the first problem."

He smiled and quipped, "You know what the Bible says: *It came to pass* . . . It didn't come to stay."

We laughed. It felt good to laugh.

He posed a somber question. "Are you up for further discussion of Marta's story?"

No, I thought as I answered *yes*.

"I wonder whether Carlos met with PAPA before his death. If so, that alliance has, to use Carlos' words, the formula for *the most lethal toxin ever developed*."

"What do you think about PAPA, Matt?"

He ducked the question. "For me *Papa* is a name for the Pope. I see it as an affectionate one."

"You don't get off that easy, Bishop Langham."

"PAPA is a brilliant acronym. The Peace for All People Alliance. Who could be against that?"

"If it has the formula, let's hope that it's as trustworthy as its name."

He glanced at me. "Which makes the acronym effective for an *un*trustworthy group."

"Carlos obviously trusted them. But . . ." I searched for the right words.

"But he might have been duped by a corrupt clandestine entity? And now . . ." Matt cut off the rest. "Listen to me. I sound like a wanna-be 007."

"Me too." Yet, we both know that corruption is not outside the realm of possibility.

The pilot car returned and our line began to move. My cell rang. I answered expecting Galen again.

"I want you to be the first to know."

The distorted voice startled me.

"The rumor about my death is false." Venom spewed through the phone.

"Who is this?" But I knew.

"You do not know my name, but I know yours." A pause.

I felt malice in his silence.

"You know nothing about me, but I know everything about you. I will always know *exactly* where you are." Another menacing silence.

Panic seized me.

"And one day I will kill you." A hideous laugh followed. "And you can join your daughter Lyndie."

My panic morphed into rage. How dare that demonic voice speak precious Lyndie's name! *Desecrate* her! My voice erupted with contempt and malevolence: "*Whatever*!" For a moment I mimicked his menacing silence. "How pathetic to be consumed by chasing me!" I loaded my words like stones in David's sling. "*Get . . . a . . . life!*"

I ended the call and withdrew inside my inner castle surrounded by a moat, into its windowless room with cold stone walls and concrete floor, a room I'd entered as a child when I wanted to hide and feel safe. But being afraid was not helpful. I focused on centering myself and finally entered my true safe haven, my *Living* room. This was not the cold stone walls that protected me through imprisonment. It was the sanctuary deep within that grounded my life, a calm and peaceful place of grace, invulnerable to the darkness. Familiar words came to mind: *The dawn from on high will break upon us, to give light to those who sit in darkness and in the shadow of death.*

My cell rang. Please not *him* again! My hand shook as I looked at the number. "Hello, Dan." I tried to make my voice sound normal.

"The Ram fire is under control, Lynn, but they haven't found any trace of his body yet."

"They won't," I said flatly. "He called me." I turned off my phone, wishing I could turn off the echo of the unkilled killer's words.

15

At first Zeller had followed the Ram like a drone in the distance. The blip sped west on N.M. 502, but suddenly disappeared. Virtual spying can get a job done from a distance with feet up and a stein of beer in hand, *Mutter*, instead of bumping along Buckman Road this morning. But it is not reliable. No.

He heard a bomb blast. Los Alamos National Lab? He thought of his beloved mother, a baby when the atomic bomb was dropped. With a shift in the winds of history, Fat Man's target might have been Hitler's Germany instead of Hirohito's Japan. Berlin could have been spewed with radiation, its landscape littered with mass bodies of women and children. She could have died—and I would not have been born, *Mutter*. He remembered reading about Fat Man. With a shift in the winds of the weather, Fat Man's target Kokura was obscured by heavy fog and smoke and spared "by chance," for the plane diverted to a new target, Nagasaki. By chance? If *by chance* my target was obscured, *Mutter*, I would not simply substitute another target! No! And burn scars, radiation illness, mass killing of innocents are against my code of honor.

Pretty *Frau* Peterson's phone alerted him. As she listened to her messages, his ears stole words intended only for her. The truck's crash and explosion explained the blast and the blip's disappearance. Herr Ram—escapee-turned-corpse. Good news! Pretty *Frau* Peterson is safe, *Mutter*. Our job is done.

Another alert. He added himself to the call, the twosome unaware they were a threesome. The menacing tone punctured his pleasure. He pulled off the road for full attention. Herr Ram—corpse-turned-escapee. Very bad news! I may have met my match.

The distorted voice spewed malice to terrorize her. Her voice showed he succeeded. He threatened to kill her. Then he spat her daughter's name. A gross miscalculation! Instead of shriveling in fear, Petite *Frau* Peterson roared like a lioness. *Get a life!*

Zeller wanted to applaud. Bravo! But this was not good. No. She had scorned and enraged a monster. *One day I will kill you.* "No, Herr Ram! First you will have to deal with a world class sniper in a class by myself!"

He tried to unblock Herr Ram's phone number. Failed. Tried to get the cell's location: Los Alamos. How did he get there without his truck? Zeller zoomed in on the location. The call had been placed from the 4-U Storage Company. *Mutter* hacked quickly into their computer for a list of renters and unit numbers. Success. The name used would likely be false. But which name? First he looked for *AB* initials. Found Art Benjamin, unit 1313. Is that Herr Ram, *Mutter?* It is the best clue we have.

He pulled into the driving lane again and floor-boarded the Volks toward Los Alamos. *Frau* Peterson's cell engaged again. He listened to her terse report to the man named Dan.

When he reached Trinity Drive, he kept the needle on the speed limit. He could speak English with an American accent and his false U.S. credentials were perfect, but he assumed suspicion ran high in the atomic city. This is not a place to attract attention, *Mutter.* No.

He stopped at the intersection to let a black Harley cross heading north, then he turned south toward 4-U Storage. Herr Ram's perfect murders showed meticulous implementation. Zeller envisioned a rigid man who would not deviate from a set of initials, a risk taker who would likely use his real ones. Andy Bush. Abe Buchanan. And now Art Benjamin. Perhaps others he didn't know about. Shadows of his real identity? Do your aliases reveal a personality pattern, Herr Ram? I would bet on it. But the pattern eludes me.

16

I continued to rerun the malicious call, riding with Matt as though alone, my eyes closed, hiding in my cold, dark, self-imposed dungeon. I tried to ebb my rage through Seneca's advice: *Stop. Don't do anything. Don't move or speak. Or rage will grow.* And so will fear, I thought. I felt the car slow and opened my eyes.

Matt pulled into a convenience store parking lot. He turned off the ignition and looked at me. "I couldn't avoid seeing your reactions to the calls this morning," he said gently, his eyes filled with compassion. "It would be dishonest and insensitive to pretend I didn't. The call you received on the way to Marta's frightened you. When you checked your messages after leaving there, the first one also frightened you. The second seemed to bring relief. But the call you last received . . . I saw your terror, Lynn, and heard a *deep* rage foreign to your nature."

My deep rage and terror still roiled.

"I'm concerned for you."

Matt's words knocked on the door to my soul. But the caller's words had machine-gunned my body and mind, driven me back in time to a little girl in a gingham dress, sitting in the dark with my back against the cold stone wall, my legs stretched out on the concrete floor. So alone. But safe. Protected by a moat no one could cross.

"If you ever want a trustworthy listener, I'm here, Lynn."

I longed to dismantle those walls. To cross the moat and run free. Rejecting his offer was like skipping backwards from Easter to Good Friday. But it was the best I could do in the moment. "Thank you, Matt."

He sat in silence, his eyes closed as though in prayer. When he opened them, he shook his head. "You are intensely troubled. You need to call Galen."

"I would have to talk about it, and I don't want to."

"If the situation were reversed, you would want him to call you."

True. With a sigh I turned my phone back on. Dan had left a message and a text. I ignored them and called Galen's cell, hoping for a dead spot so I wouldn't have to deal with questions.

"Hi, Lynn. I tried to reach you this morning. Did you get my messages?"

"Yes. I . . . ."

"We can live in peace again."

"Galen, . . ."

"Chev and I had quite a chase!"

"Listen to me! He's still alive."

"No. He's dead. His truck exploded."

"*The resurrected corpse called me.*" Silence. I waited.

"Are you *sure* he's the one who called?"

"Positive."

"What did he say?" His tone had moved from lighthearted to argumentative to alarm.

"Let's talk about it at home. It's OK, Galen." The more I talked about it, the less OK I felt.

"Where are you now?"

"Matt and I are on our way back to Santa Fe."

"When will you arrive?"

"In about thirty minutes. Please don't rush back from the ruins," I said lightly, hoping he would make a U-turn immediately. "I love you," I added, and disconnected before my voice broke.

Matt and I rode in silence until we reached the *casita*. I dreaded leaving the cocoon of his car. He got out to walk me to the door. "No need," I said contradicting my feelings. "It's OK."

"It isn't *OK* with me, Lynn. You had a conversation that turned your face white and took you from panic to rage. I'll take a quick look inside." He waited beside me on the *portal* while I fished through my purse for the key. He entered first and scanned the living area. He eyed the bathroom on his way to the bedroom. He was back in less than a minute. "*Now* it's OK," he smiled.

I returned the smile. "I think you like the role of *007*."

"It's a new way to do the episcopacy. I may find it suits me. We're a good team, a unique combination of consoling and sleuthing."

"You are a fine bishop, Matt. You care about people."

Serious now, he said, "I intend for one of my guideposts to be the words of St. Teresa of Avila: *The Lord does not look so much at the magnitude of anything we do as at the love with which we do it.*"

"Ultimately that's what it's all about."

"Lynn, don't let that call get the best of you," he said gravely. "No matter how scared you are right now, you have the inner resources to handle the situation. A lot of us care about you," he said, his eyes filled with compassion. "You are not alone."

17

Ariel sped away from Los Alamos on his Harley, his thoughts consumed by Lynn Peterson. *Get a life*! Her words marched in circles through his mind. The craze for revenge vibrated inside him in tandem with the Harley. His fists clenched around the handlebars. His head pounded in fury. She had played with him! Mocked him! Blown off his threat like a feather in her palm! She would rue this day!

He already knew how he would kill her. But when? Their little chat on the phone negated a period of terror first. What terror? *Whatever*, she had mocked. Whatever indeed! He unleashed his imagination and treated himself to visions of cruelty. No respect! No limits! No mercy!

With a will of steel, he stopped his rampage. Shattered her power to control him. Forced her image from his mind. Calmed his breathing. He scanned the road ahead, the area around him. Alert. Cautious. Tense. He saw no one. Heard nothing unusual. Tried to release the anxiety that tainted his confidence. Maybe the trials of the day were catching up with him. *Maybe*? That word again. Like an omen. He had debated refusing the Venom Contract, a lucrative challenge but too close to home. He had known it then, had proved it today. Too late. He wouldn't be safe until he reached his isolated ranch. He topped out his Harley.

The speed refreshed him. He focused on Lynn Peterson's termination. By the time he turned onto the lonely dirt lane of his ranch, his plan was finalized. He smiled behind his Darth Vader shield.

He parked the Harley beside his Chrysler in the empty space for his Ram—his bomb blasted Ram. General greeted him with a hello bark and a wag of his tail. Ariel patted his head. "Be glad you were not with me today!" He poured himself two fingers of Scotch and headed to the portal, weary and empty. He sank into a high-backed cedar rocker and lifted his glass to the dog. Finally, a respite from the day's overload of challenges.

He leaned back and rocked slowly in rhythm to his breath, inhaling the peace of this place as sunlight played on the mountains. Two deer pranced through the meadow. The Doberman sprang forward. "Stay, General!" The dog stopped, his eyes locked on the deer, trembling from the strain of obedience. The deer reached the salt block and grazed unafraid. *Unafraid*. Like Lynn Peterson.

Agitated again, he finished his Scotch and stood. General followed him inside and down the hall to the gunroom, standing guard in the doorway, eyes alert, muscles taut, blaring a silent message: *To get to him, you go through me!* "At ease, General!" His loyal companion lay down—at ease but not off duty.

Ariel eyed the gunroom with pride. A corner room, it basked in light from the bank of windows on two sides. Gun cabinets lined half of one wall, his stellar antique collection displayed behind glass. The other half was steel-lined paneling with an invisible entry that required his thumbprint scan to unlock it. His high tech military arms hid behind it along with the new speargun. "I had to leave the used one at the drop site, General, but I was able to design this one similar to it." His desk faced the arched doorway and to the left was a large painting of a powerful white stallion running free. He envisioned himself galloping the Arabian. Superior man on superior steed, superior Doberman racing after. Free. As free as the wind.

Soon free of Lynn Peterson. He reran his plan. Precise and methodical. He knew exactly when and where and how she would die. "You have a brilliant master, General."

18

I stared out the front window as though watching for Galen would get him here sooner. Scenes replayed through my mind—from murder in the Plaza to the President to Zeller to CIA bugs to PAPA to the resurrected poisoner. Matt was right: I am not alone! Is Zechariah Zeller out there now? How did he know to look for bugs last night? How did he get in? Why did he come to Santa Fe? Yet, his presence brought a sense of protection and comfort—and that realization brought *dis*comfort. He had once saved my life as well as the President's, but he was almost as shivery as the Plaza poisoner.

Galen rushed in. He put his arms around me. We clung to each other until he stepped back to introduce his new friend.

"I told you about Cheveyo Tupatu. Remember? He's a cultural anthropologist, Harvard brother, fellow lexiphanic and super driver. Call him Chev. His friends do, and you don't want *him* for an enemy!"

Chev's eyes crinkled with a smile.

I offered my hand. "I'm Lynn. Welcome."

"It is good to see you, Lynn," both courtesy and concern in his tone.

"I'll get us some lemonade. I want to hear about your adventure today." I also wanted to delay Galen's predictable request for a verbatim report of the sinister phone call.

"The Tsankawi ruins are remarkable," Galen commented, "but San Ildefonso meant even more. It reminded me that we think we know the shape of a culture through distant preconceived images, like assuming we know the shape of water by viewing it in a round glass pitcher. We miss the free-flowing story."

Chev raised his glass to Galen. "There is hope even for history professors. We will send you back to New Orleans a learned man."

"Before we were . . . interrupted," Galen understated, "you were about to tell me your version of why Los Alamos was selected for developing atomic bombs. *Why here?*"

"I've wondered about that too," I said, welcoming a normal conversation on this paranormal day.

"We can thank—or curse—Julius Robert Oppenheimer, our fellow Harvard alum. Before entering college he had an attack of colitis and was sent here to recover. According to one writer, he fell in love with horseback riding and this state."

"Clearly a man of good taste," said Galen.

"Agreed. After getting his Ph.D. and joining the Berkeley faculty, he was diagnosed with a mild case of TB and came here again to recover. He bought a ranch not far from the Los Alamos Ranch School, a prestigious boys' school at that time."

"There was no town?" I asked.

"No. The school was named for the numerous trees on the property—the cottonwoods or *los alamos* in Spanish." Chev swirled the ice in his glass. "Later, when Oppenheimer was appointed the scientific director of the Manhattan Project, he persuaded two colonels and a general to select the school property for the project's site, thus combining two great loves of his life—physics and New Mexico."

"I'm impressed with Oppenheimer's skills of persuasion," Galen commented.

"You asked *Why here?*" Chev's eyes crinkled. "The answer is simple. Our major nuclear weapons city—named after trees—was selected because of colitis and TB."

I laughed with them, but I saw no humor in the paradox of selecting a place of ancient healing as the site to birth catastrophic destruction. *Why here*, indeed.

Galen said, "It's an interesting example of how inconsequential incidents ripple out and affect history."

"My profession causes me to wonder if there are any truly inconsequential incidents." Chev stood. "I need to be on my way. Thank you for the lemonade and conversation." He hesitated, no mirth in his eyes now. "Be careful, Lynn. We chased a brilliant maniac this morning. Unfortunately, in his case that description is not an oxymoron."

Galen followed him to the portal. "Thanks also for leaving the ruins early. I was worried about Lynn."

Chev's voice sparked. "That damn Cowboy was *not* going to harm your wife! Not on my watch!"

"Take care, Super Driver."

"To be honest with you, Galen," he said with a smile in his voice, "I had no idea what I was in for when I invited a staid historian to see some ruins."

Galen chuckled, closed the door and stepped purposefully to me. "Tell me about the call." He listened with horrified eyes as I repeated it verbatim. "How did you respond?"

"I was furious! I . . . I acted smug. Superior, I suppose. I was sarcastic."

"How? Precisely."

I told him what I'd said.

His mouth gaped. "*Get a life!* Oh, Lynn! You launched a missile toward a malicious megalomaniac alpha male killer!"

19

My cell rang, startling me. "Hello."

"I did not capture your resurrected corpse. No."

I gestured *shh* to Galen and put the phone on speaker, mouthing *Zechariah Zeller*. I was surprised to hear the words *your resurrected corpse*. I'd only used that phrase when I called Galen at the ruins. Zeller could freak me out.

"I have information officials need."

I raised my eyebrows at Galen. Could a sniper from a foreign land know more than Dan, Juan, the state police, the CIA and FBI? Actually he might.

Galen circled his hand in a gesture for me to keep Zeller talking. I focused intently on his face to steady my voice. "What is your information?"

"He uses at least three aliases. You know one: Andy Bush."

How did he know about Andy Bush?

"The second is Abe Buchanan, the name used to register the Ram."

Officials couldn't get the tag number. How did he? As though the phone picked up my thoughts, he answered the question.

"I washed his license plate last night while I was watching him watch your little house. This morning he smeared it with mud again."

Galen scrawled hurriedly on a piece of paper: B*ush & Buchanan, last names of presidents: George Bush and James Buchanan.* A nanosecond later he scrawled again: A*be & Andy, nicknames for presidents: Abraham Lincoln & Andrew Jackson.*

I mouthed, Coincidence?

He shrugged.

"Both names have the same initials. The same monogram can be used in every situation. A monogram gives confidence in a stranger's identity." ***Ergo the monogram could be his real initials,*** scribbled Galen.

"He contacted you on a cell phone from the 4-U Storage Company in Los Alamos."

How did he get the calling location? Officials didn't figure it out. A thought creeped me out. I mouthed to Galen: He must be listening to my cell calls. He met my frown with one of his own.

"I obtained the list of renters. There is one AB: Art Benjamin."

Galen scribbled: ***I'm off track.. Too few AB presidential possibilities—only 2 first names begin with A & 2 last names begin with B.***

"Storage unit number 1313."

Of course Zeller knew the number. He knew everything else.

Galen looked thoughtful, the historian in his element. He scrawled again. ***Keep AB presidential initials. One more option: Chester Arthur & Benjamin Harris: <u>Art Benjamin.</u>*** He underlined it. He looked thoughtful, then quickly wrote: ***The Explorer was rented to Abram Baines. 2 presidential middle names: James <u>Abram</u> Garfield & Lyndon <u>Baines</u> Johnson.*** He smiled and whispered, "Beyond coincidence?"

"Are you there?" asked Zeller.

I realized I'd not been responding. "Your information is interesting."

"On my way to 4-U Storage, I stopped at the intersection to let a black Harley go by. The rider wore black from his full helmet to his boots. He was headed north. When I reached the storage company, I saw tracks in front of unit 1313. Shoeprints entered. None left. Tracks the size of motorcycle tires went through the exit lane. None entered."

I was beginning to believe he could be right. The skills this world class sniper demonstrated today were probably the same ones he used to plan assassinations and escapes. I shuddered. Yet, while officials focused on the crash site, he was trailing the poisoner and getting close—light years ahead of them. I thought again of the dotted line between good and evil.

"He is the only one who can open the door because of a complicated process of locks. What does that tell you?"

"I don't know."

"You do not have a suspicious mind," he said softly, almost tenderly. "It tells us *Herr* Art Benjamin has something to hide."

"Yes," I agreed.

"The timing, tracks, lock system and renter's initials point to your resurrected corpse. I was close to catching him. But not close enough. No."

Dan needed all this information.

"Send officials to 4-U Storage to take tire track molds while fresh, and to search unit 1313. I predict it will reveal evidence he wishes to hide. *Eile!* Hurry!"

"I have no power to *send officials*," I said.

"Use your connections."

I paused. "I can try."

"Then you will succeed. I have watched you work."

Another shudder.

"One more piece of information. You were the subject of a CIA search yesterday morning. The report was emailed to an unidentifiable computer. Andy Bush made his call to your secretary shortly afterwards. That tells me he has a CIA connection who follows his orders and reports immediately. I do not like that. No."

"Neither do I."

"The CIA must identify that connection and interrogate him for the caller's identity. A command from your highest ranking connection will speed up that process."

Was he talking about the President?

"When you recognized my voice, you turned on your phone's speaker. I assume you wanted your husband to hear. I *hope* it was no one else."

My resentment for his obvious phone surveillance surfaced. "I *invited* him to hear."

"I am not a voyeur!" He sounded more hurt than offended. "I will only listen in on calls that provide information to help keep you safe. You have my word."

Complex and contradictory Zeller. A man whose word is his bond—but has no problem assassinating people. I softened. And he saved someone at least twice.

"To you, *Herr* Peterson, I say this: My only purpose is to protect your wife. She is not safe. No. He *will* try to kill her."

His words and the agitation in his voice seeped into my bones.

"We must catch him. Soon."

I picked up on the *we*. He saw himself on the good guys' team. "Thank you for your help."

"I saved your life," he said simply and added in that tone verging on tenderness, "Now I am responsible for protecting you." He ended the call.

Immediately I used the *casita* landline to call Dan and Matt and left messages not to call on my cell phone. I gave them the landline number and Galen's cell. I turned off my phone and put it away in the drawer of the lamp table.

The countdown continued.

20

Juan stood at the edge of the highway and stared down at the overcrowded crash scene where law enforcement and emergency personnel looked for a body. A body that didn't exist according to Dan, based on Lynn's information. Juan considered both sources credible. Proving anything would be difficult. Rescuers had treated the crash like an accident instead of a crime scene and contaminated evidence.

He focused on the burning Ram and the chaos around it, then turned around and scanned the highway. No skids where the truck went off. He tracked backwards along the road and came to black marks large enough to match the Ram's tires. *¡Por supesto!* Of course! *Diablo*, as he had dubbed this devil, braked the truck there and timed his jump.

Playing out that scenario, he trekked back toward the crash site. *Diablo* knew exactly where to send his truck over the edge for the safest jump. He must be familiar with the highway, a resident in the vicinity currently or sometime in the past. Or a commuter. Possibly someone employed by the Lab. He reminded himself to restrain conjecture.

Again he scanned the terrain from the highway down to the Ram. His eyes swept right/left in a broad grid all the way to the bottom. He hiked down to the large boulders in the ravine to get the perspective from below. This time his eyes swept the grid upward to the highway. A cluster of *piñons* near the road stood out in the sparse vegetation. He walked up again, angling toward them and searching the ground. He noted the lack of litter—no hikers interested in this area. Near the *piñons* something glinted in the early afternoon sun. He pulled his gloves from his pocket and picked up the object, an unweathered pocketknife. A man in a rush could lose it. Prints might have a story to tell.

He walked on up the few feet to the highway and stopped abruptly. A pair of moccasin tracks led from the *piñons* toward the road. He compared them with his own shoes. Larger than his tens. Maybe elevens. He took photos with his phone.

His friend Esteban, officer in charge, stood on the highway gazing down at the scene. Juan joined him. "*Buenas tardes, amigo.* I need a favor."

"Name it."

Friendship, thought Juan. It's all about relationships. "Let's make it a favor for a favor. To put you in the loop, they won't find a body. There isn't one."

"*Santo Roberto!*"

"What we have here is more likely a crime scene than an accident."

"And what's said between us stays between us?" Esteban asked.

"Until you hear it officially."

"I saw you nosing around the Ram when you first arrived." Chuckling he added, "You weren't as sly as you thought when you sneaked that Stetson into your trunk, Juan."

Caught! "I didn't want the Feds to mess up the DNA."

"Good judgment. I'll keep that little trick to myself if you get me a copy of the results."

"Glad to, *amigo.*"

"What favor do you need?"

"There are a couple of moccasin prints."

Esteban's eyes widened. "*Moccasins*? Where?"

He pointed. "Between the cluster of *piñons* and the highway. We need molds. Can you get it done and give me access to them?"

Esteban nodded. "To put *you* in the loop, we got a call from 911. A man reported that an Indian mother was walking along the highway with her baby a short time before the explosion. He was concerned about her."

Juan's turn for surprise.

"He wanted to give her a ride, but she shook her head so they didn't stop. I thought of it when you mentioned moccasin prints."

"Did you find her?"

"Emergency crews came from Los Alamos and Española, but no one saw her from either direction." Esteban nodded toward the fire. "No sign of her down there either. She probably got a ride from someone else."

"How large was she?" asked Juan, thinking about the size of the prints.

"I don't know, but 911 has the caller's contact information." He gave it to Juan.

"What kind of car was he driving?"

"A blue 2011 Impala LTZ." Esteban's radio crackled, and he said a crisp, "Yes?"

Juan heard the excited voice respond. "We found the body!" He recoiled. Either Lynn Peterson was wrong about *Diablo* being alive, or he had killed three people instead of two.

21

Galen and I were discussing Zeller's call when the doorbell rang. "I'll get it." He unlocked and blocked the door as he opened it.

"Bishop Lynn Peterson?"

Understandable I thought. A historically gendered title and an ungendered first name.

"A package for you, sir. Sign here please."

Galen forged my name and accepted it, closing the door. "Did you hear my new alias?" He grinned and handed me the small package wrapped in plain brown paper.

"It's probably the secure phone from the President." No return address boasting *The White House*. No return address at all. The ordinary looking package delivered in an ordinary way contained an ordinary looking cell phone—with the extraordinary capacity for direct secure communication with the President of the United States. I assumed it had a location device confirming its arrival at the intended destination. "I'm supposed to turn it on and press the star key to activate it."

"Press the star key to activate a secure phone from the President!" Galen shook his head. "A *terrific* renewal leave, Lynn! That is, if we skip the American update to *wonderful* and *marvelous* and go back to the 1667 meaning of *terrific: causing terror*."

I glimpsed the stack of books beside my chair. Pressing that key would fork my path away from the serenity and enrichment I'd envisioned in Santa Fe. It would also affect Galen. But I must help if I could. With a deep sigh, I turned it on and poised my thumb above the star key.

Galen looked at me tenderly and pled again. "Be sure, Lynn! There will be no turning back!"

"I know that. But there was no turning back the moment the President called." I thumbed the star key and listened for the beep, as she had told me, then hit the star again for her instructions.

They were brief. The phone served only as a pager unless activated by its partner phone. A simple system controlled by the President. The remaining instructions related to Dan. I was to answer his questions and get his decision about assisting her. Two sets of directions followed: the first set if he agreed, the second if he declined. So few words to create so weighty a burden!

Galen watched me but asked no questions, merely available if I wanted to share something. We loved each other deeply and were one in many ways, but we were two individuals, not clones. "I know how troubling this is for you, Lynn. I will help any way I can."

"How about now?" I reached for the largest book in my stack. "I don't want to leave her cell laying around. Let's carve out phone-shaped pages." We worked together until we had a *phone*book literally. I tossed the cut-out paper into the kiva.

Galen lit the match, and we watched silently as the paper burned. "Here we go again," he said when we finished.

"Thank you for saying *we*." I tucked the cell inside the book, closed it and set it on my desk. I had touched a star and sacrificed a spiritual book—the first step in this *simple favor* for the President.

22

Dan felt like he'd been in a hit-and-run accident after Lynn told him about the call from the assumed corpse. He was frustrated that she'd hung up immediately and wouldn't respond to his callback or text: *Need details. Call ASAP.*

He was giving Home-Health a break until two o'clock and went in to check on Denise. He found her asleep, a fragile replica of her former self. He sat in the plaid armchair by the bedroom window and watched over her. He thought about the research resources spent to create biotoxins for murder like the one that ravaged his dead friend. What would it mean to Denise and people like her if that intelligence, education and money were invested in prevention and cures instead? He fought back anger and a wave of grief. He longed desperately to transfer his strength to her. To breathe healing into her frail frame. Get a grip, he told himself. Being hopeful and upbeat helps her, not dwelling on the fact that the great protector can't even protect his own wife!

His thoughts turned back to Lynn's call. He left Denise's door open and went down the hall to his office to call LANL. He knew the protection of its secrets mandated mass and miniscule continuous backed-up surveillance. Every street and structure as well as the surrounding area. Eyes in the sky and on the ground. He needed to see that surveillance along NM 502, precisely from 10:24 when Galen spotted the Ram until around 11:10 when Lynn received the call. Forty-six crucial minutes. He ran through his contact list and decided to start with Cliff to expedite the process. He thought of bait to lure his cooperation: an opportunity to lead the pack in finding the Plaza poisoner. He called and tossed it. Bait swallowed. Surveillance forthcoming. But *when*?

He returned to Denise. When she awoke, he moved to the bed and took her hand. "How about some chicken noodle soup?"

"You are thoughtful and kind, Dan."

He put her hand to his lips and kissed it. A brave smile emanating from her fragile body and her dull eyes almost broke his heart. "I'll bring you room service." He left quickly before he lost his battle with tears.

While zapping the soup, he fixed a tray, trying to make it pretty the way she would have done. She would like that. A cheery red placemat, red-checked napkin, plate under the soup bowl. He took time to snip a red rose from the bush and put it in a Nambé budvase, small in his large hands.

She awarded his presentation with her lovely smile. "Five diamond room service." She touched the rose, then his hand. "How sweet of you." Her eyes were more alert now and filled with love.

He propped up her pillows and encouraged her to eat by holding the spoon to her lips.

"It smells good." After a few sips, however, she fell asleep again.

He took her tray back to the kitchen and checked his cell for messages: Lynn *finally* and Juan. He listened to her message first, perplexed: *Do **not** call my cell!* She sounded agitated. *Use Galen's or the casita landline.* Phone numbers followed. What is going on? He decided to see for himself instead of calling. A face has its own vocabulary. Juan's message said he thought our escape artist might be local, and he would share evidence at our four o'clock meeting. Dan checked his watch—almost two. He'd leave when Home-Health returned.

He cleaned up the kitchen, thinking inanely about how a soft warm sponge and a hard cold gun could both cleanup messes. He tiptoed into the bedroom and sat once again in the plaid armchair by the window. He stared out at the mountains with their sunlight and shadows, like life.

23

I heard Dan drive up and walked out to meet him, the President's message acute in my mind.

He climbed out of his white Chrysler convertible and waved. "I hope it's OK for me to come by."

"Anytime. I like your car."

He smiled "I bought it for Denise. She always wanted a convertible." His smile faded. "I should have bought her one sooner, but it wasn't the vehicle of choice in my profession. Too . . ." He broke off and changed the subject. "Do you know anything about that red Juke parked in front of me? We don't need stray cars that close."

"A friend dropped it by for us to use while we're here."

"Someone trustworthy?"

I laughed. "Mistrust charming and thoughtful Hiroshi Takahashi?"

"*Charming* and *thoughtful* are not the same as *trustworthy*."

"And Galen thinks *I* look for conspiracies," I said lightly. "Next you'll want to check it for bugs or a tracking device."

Dan ignored the levity. "Absolutely. How long have you known him?"

Not a good question. "One day shorter than we've known you, and if you loaned us a car, we wouldn't be suspicious."

"We have a long connection through Fay." He glanced at the Juke and back at me. "Trust is a fine trait normally, but in this situation it could be suicidal. *Caution* is your mantra now."

I got his point, but he was wrong about Hiroshi.

Galen met us at the door. "Any news on the escapee?"

"I'm meeting Juan at four." Dan turned back to me. "I tried to reach you several times but didn't get an answer."

"I turned off my cell. I wanted to fall off the planet."

"That's understandable," he said sympathetically. "I'm interested in your talk with Mrs. Martinez this morning. Was it helpful?"

That visit seemed like days ago. I knew what he meant by *helpful* but replied with a bishop-blank face. "It seemed to help her."

He skipped a beat, watching me. "I hope you gained information that will assist the investigation."

I didn't respond.

A long pause while his eyes searched my face. He shrugged. "Let's move on to the corpse's call. Maybe he revealed something useful about himself."

I stalled, dreading to revisit those haunting words again.

Galen spared me, repeating verbatim what I had told him.

Dan stared at me in horror. "You antagonized a killer!"

Enough! I moved to my agenda. "We do have some useful information. He called me on a secure cell phone from 4-U Storage in Los Alamos."

"How do you know where . . . ."

"There's more," I interrupted, avoiding placing myself in the predicament of either lying or revealing Zeller's identity. "The Ram is registered in New Mexico to Abe Buchanan."

"The same initials as Andy Bush," added Galen. "And the Explorer was rented to Abram Baines. There is a renter with *AB* initials at the storage company: Art Benjamin. The aliases could be presidential names, interchanging first, middle and last names. And perhaps they are his real initials."

Dan pulled a small notebook and pen from his shirt pocket and began scribbling notes.

I took over. "Art Benjamin's unit is 1313. A search warrant for that unit might provide a feast of information. He likely left there on a motorcycle, possibly a black Harley."

"Where did you get . . . ."

"Surely the government has some kind of special eyes-in-the-sky surveillance of Los Alamos," interjected Galen. "Can you pull some strings and get access to surveillance that might show a black Harley originating at Unit 1313 around noon today and find out where it went. The driver is wearing black."

"*Stop!* Tell me . . . ."

I rushed on. "One more thing. Yesterday morning someone in the CIA ran a search on me—*before* you shared my name with your buddy. The report was emailed to an unidentifiable computer. Shortly afterward *cousin* Andy Bush called Fay. Possibly—probably?—he has a CIA connection."

Galen's turn again. "I assume the CIA can obtain subject/time reports on their computer searches. An informative little chat with the first techie who ran a search on her would be helpful. For example, who requested it? What's his contact information? Your *buddy*, as Lynn called him, might also like to find out the techie's connection to the requester and why the request was honored."

"That's it, Dan," I said.

"How did you learn all this?"

I procrastinated to give myself time to think. "Would you like something to drink? Lemonade? Coffee? "

"No thanks. But an answer would be enlightening."

I told an abridged version of the truth. "A phone call. No name given."

"The caller had nothing to gain by making all this up, Dan," Galen added. "If we didn't trust the information's accuracy, we wouldn't pass it on."

"But no source?"

Silence.

Dan looked from me to Galen and back at me. "I could ask why the caller is so interested in this case. Or why *you* were called and given this information instead of someone else. Or if you left the message for me not to call your cell because you think the caller spywared it. Or why you want to protect his—or her—identity. We could waste valuable time in that dance." He shrugged, then smiled. "But we won't. Whatever the motives, I'm glad your caller is on our team."

24

I restrained a sigh of relief that Dan found Zeller's information more important than his identity. I thought about how to handle the President's phone message for him. Absent-mindedly I picked up the small colorful box beside Lyndie's photo, fingering the keepsakes inside.

"I'll get the surveillance," said Dan. "Maybe Juan can handle the storage unit search. He thinks our escape artist might be a local man." He stopped pacing and looked down at my box. "Is that from Russia?"

"Yes. I use it for small keepsakes, mementos of special places and sacred moments. You're welcome to open it." I'd brought it simply for the pleasure of its presence.

He smiled. "It's a treasure box. Denise has one too." He glanced inside. Something caught his eye. "May I?"

"Of course."

His large thumb and index finger reached carefully into the box and pulled out a fragment of a spearpoint. The jagged triangle was broken off at the top, its point intact. It was small in his hand, rust colored and shiny. He stared at it thoughtfully.

"I found it a few years ago," said Galen. "We were here for the opera and took a hike on a butte west of here, near the Caja del Rio area. Ancient spearpoints intrigue me and I kept it."

I thought I heard Galen mutter something that sounded like *dosae.* "What?"

He ignored me.

"Do you mind if I take a picture of it?" Dan asked.

"No," I replied puzzled.

He posed it in his palm and clicked. Satisfied with the phone photo, he gave the spearpoint back to me.

As I returned it to the box, my eyes fell on a seashell with wavy blue-gray and ivory stripes. I'd found it at the Black Sea. I picked it up and held it for a moment, then knew what I wanted to do with it. Later.

"Your caller gave us excellent information," said Dan.

I changed the subject. "We need to talk about another matter."

"There's *more*?"

I removed the President's cell from the *phone*book. He watched without comment.

Galen picked up his laptop and headed toward the bedroom. "If you'll excuse me, I'm going to do some more research on *AB* initials."

I smiled at him. Sensitive Galen, giving us privacy. "Please listen to a message, Dan. Then we'll talk about it."

"A message from . . . ?"

I punched in some numbers. "Press the star key."

Dan listened. He was hard to shock, but that did it. He frowned and listened again. "Do you know who is speaking?"

"Yes."

"My initial impression can't be accurate. Too big a stretch."

"It could be."

He shook his head. "I don't like games."

"*This* is not a game. The caller is cautious to protect identities."

"It sounds like the . . ." He shook his head dismissively, then skipped a beat. "Did you listen to it?"

"No."

"Please do." He handed me the phone and sat down.

"Are you sure you want me to hear it?" At his nod, I listened: *I am aware of your reputation. You have served well. Retirement frees you from old chains of command. I need a confidential favor. If you agree to assist, the person with you will serve as my liaison.* No details given. No names used.

"Suppose, hypothetically, you're correct about the caller."

"Then I wouldn't—no, *couldn't*—refuse. I'm a bleeding-heart patriot who would unconditionally assist that office no matter who holds it. Unless," he added somberly, "a foreign country subversively interfered."

"Ah, you remind me of those patriotic days of yore when the people put country before party and the politicians put honor and wisdom before self-promotion."

"Let's drop the hypothetical. Who is she?"

I interpreted his *wouldn't/couldn't refuse* as agreement to assist the President. "You already know."

"She is surrounded by the most powerful people in the world." He frowned. "Why step outside her official circles?"

"Perhaps she needs boots on the ground and it matters who wears them. The lethal toxin theft from LANL could become a national crisis—maybe even international. She can't risk basing decisions on distorted reports. Think about it, Dan. Information gets filtered as it crawls up the chain of command. Sometimes it's erroneously presented, sometimes deliberately misrepresented. Sometimes exaggerated or diluted or skewed to suit personal agendas. Sometimes slanted to fit assumptions about what the next person up the ladder wants to hear. By the time she gets information, how many people have subconsciously or deliberately distorted it?" I paused. "Even in my small episcopal sphere I sometimes experience a similar dynamic."

He feigned shock. "Are you telling me the church has something in common with the CIA!"

"Are you telling me some CIA operatives have personal agendas!" The banter released our rising tension But only briefly.

"But why *me*?"

"You're in the vicinity, experienced, have a proven reputation, and are free from career reprisals and rewards."

He started to say something and stopped himself.

"You are wondering why *me* for her liaison." I shrugged. "We go way back." Enough said.

He eyed me and finally spoke. "She must have complete trust in you, Lynn."

"And in you. She will be grateful for your assistance." I considered telling him about Carlos' story. My mental warning cymbals clanged. He needed the information, but he would easily figure out Marta was the source. I wanted time to think about it. He had revealed me as his source to the CIA director. I understood his reasons but understanding didn't alleviate concern. "One more thing, Dan. It's very important. If she wants the CIA to know you are assisting, *she* will tell the director. Your *complete* confidentiality is imperative."

"I deserve that. I wanted you to have protection, Lynn. I meant well." He skipped a beat. "She has my unconditional loyalty."

I shrugged. "Enough said."

"Tell me, my *messenger* and *liaison*, what do I need to know?"

I filled him in on what little information I had—yesterday's conversation and her phone message to me. "I wish you and the President were in direct communication."

"She's astute. This way both she and I can honestly deny personal contact should the need arise. Please tell her I am honored to serve her." He skipped a bit. "But Denise must come first."

"Of course."

He grinned and saluted me. "So, Bishop Peterson, you are my handler."

"Only if you limit *handling* to handing you that cell phone."

25

Dan looked at his watch. "I'm going to take a walk and think about all this before I meet with Juan." He shook his head. "My calm life has done a 180 since you came to town. Is that unique with me or a pattern with all your friends?" He smiled, then sobered. From up to down in an instant. "I want to check on Denise," he said, calling her as he headed toward the door. "Sweetheart," I heard him say, "be sure Home-Health stays until I get there. I'll bring dinner home." Softly he added, "I love you."

I heard pain in his voice. How many more times would he be able to say those cherished words? May chemo work! He looked so sad. People in pain often asked me to pray for their loved ones. I thought about offering, but a Navajo proverb came to mind: *A rocky vineyard does not need a prayer but a pickax.* I sensed Dan was a pickax man.

He paused at the door, his eyes moistened. "Please pray for her, Lynn."

Evidently Dan was a man of both pickax and prayer. I nodded. "And for you too." As I closed the door, a phone rang. *The secure phone!* "Hello," I said tentatively, more a question than a greeting.

"Is Dickerson willing to assist?"

President Benedict's use of Dan's last name assured me the phone was indeed secure. "He will be honored to serve."

"I appreciate that. He needs full information."

"He's leaving here now. Would you like for him to stay?"

A pause. "Please."

I rushed out the door waving the phone and motioned him. He hurried back and followed me inside.

The President continued. "Yesterday evening the CIA Director gave me his view of the situation." She rapidly repeated the update. She paused.

I didn't respond because they were things Dan and I already knew.

"I assume from your silence that Dickerson was Cliff's source," she said.

It wasn't a question so I didn't affirm it. My mind was on Marta's story. I felt it was imperative to share, but didn't want to reveal her name even though Dan would figure it out. "I have important information from a person Carlos Martinez trusted."

"I have five minutes."

I lowered my eyes, shut out the world and began, careful to avoid gender pronouns. "The night before Carlos died he told my source a confidential story but gave permission to tell it if something happened to him."

"Do you have confidence in your source?" asked President Benedict.

"Complete confidence." My words raced. "Carlos believed that GANNS' powerful influence in DC resulted in corporate interests superseding the national interest. Therefore, he worked undercover for the FBI and CIA. He accessed areas beyond his security clearance to obtain information they requested. But nothing changed, and he saw them as ineffective." I paused for a response. None came. "Then another organization contacted him: PAPA, the Peace for All People Alliance." I hesitated again, wondering if President Benedict had heard of it.

"PAPA," she repeated.

Unable to deduce anything from her tone, I hurried on, the five minutes passing swiftly. "The PAPA contact told him their purpose was to serve the global common good—not to gain profit for the elite. Convinced that PAPA was trustworthy, Carlos agreed to assist them as needed. When he learned that some of the lab's most lethal toxin was missing, he assumed it was stolen and the theft covered up."

The President interrupted for the first time. "Do you understand that the toxin theft poses a national and international threat that could induce panic and must be kept confidential?"

"Understood." I galloped on. "When Carlos reported the theft to the CIA, he was directed to find out who stole it and how. He succeeded, and his report was to be delivered to an operative Sunday afternoon. That's when he was poisoned."

"How do you know he was poisoned?" she asked, alarm in her voice.

"Dan learned it from the local medical examiner's report. After federal officials claimed the body, they changed the cause of death. My source doesn't know he was poisoned but is suspicious about the heart attack claim." I paused briefly in case the President wanted to comment.

"Go on."

"Carlos also learned that the Lab had not yet developed an antidote. Disturbed, he informed his PAPA contact and was told that PAPA had medical scientists who could develop one, but needed a copy of the formula. The contact pledged to keep the formula secure in neutral international hands. Carlos trusted him and obtained a copy, which he planned to deliver last Sunday also."

"Do you know the order? Was he killed before or after meeting with PAPA?" She sounded alarmed.

"It's a crucial question. Carlos would not have realized that the meeting order was important when he told my source all this. I can see only three options—all sinister: PAPA now has the formula. Or the M.E. found it and kept it. Or officials found the copy on Carlos but did not inform proper authorities."

"You know my next question. Who is your source?"

I had expected and dreaded that question. I was unconditionally committed to protecting the grieving widow who trusted Matt and me. I would do everything in my power to spare her from the onslaught of investigators and interrogations. I viewed it as separation of Church and State, as honoring my sacred vows even when it bumped against the wishes of the Head of State. I said what I must. "I'm sorry. With great respect for your office and for you personally, Madam President, I decline to answer. I feel professionally and ethically bound to protect that identity."

Silence.

Dan stared at me dumbfounded.

It was extremely difficult to refuse, but being a bishop had taught me that the first step in knowing what to do is knowing what *not* to do. My responsibility included leaving some words unspoken.

Finally I interrupted the silence. "I trust the source totally. I think it comes down to how much confidence you have in my perception." I hesitated and said painfully, "I am sorry, Madam President. But I just can't tell you."

Another silence. I felt I was standing on ice in a deep cold sea while a black-hooded terminator sawed a circle around me. I began to feel clammy. My chest tightened.

When President Benedict replied, her tone was matter-of-fact and without apparent ill will. "All right, Lynn. I'm going to trust your perception." She paused. "Actually, even though it's problematic, your refusal shows honor, a rare quality."

I felt freed from shrink wrap and breathed again. "Thank you."

"If more information is needed, you will speak with your source again?" It wasn't a question, but the President punctuated it with a courteous rise in her voice.

"Of course, Madam President. I want to be helpful, and I'll do anything I *can*."

"Well, Lynn Marie Prejean Peterson, you have already given me far more information than the CIA and FBI combined. Thank you."

Now or never. "Do you have time for two questions?"

"First?"

"Do you know anything about PAPA?"

"Second question?"

"Would you like to speak to Dan?"

"Never directly. Tell him what I need. First, his mind, experience and confidentiality. The same kind of confidentiality," she added gently, "that you just protected for your source. Second, the agencies will continue to pursue the toxin theft. His help with that is appreciated but secondary. Third, his top priority is to find out what happened to the copy of the formula. By noon tomorrow DC time, his name will be on an elite list that mandates cooperative and efficient assistance from every agency. Would you like for me to repeat all that?"

"No, Madam President. I understand."

"Right now, ask him to choose a codename in case he needs one."

I turned to him. "Dan, please choose a codename."

"Spearpoint," he said spontaneously.

I repeated it.

"Now for your first question. I've never heard of PAPA, and that is not good news."

26

Dan checked his watch. No time for a walk to clear his head before his meeting with Juan. Today had jarred him from Moore's *he's at Starbuck's* to Juan's *he escaped.* And from a truck crash to Lynn's call from the corpse. And most jarring, from a visit with Lynn to the President's personal request: Simply find the missing copy of the top secret LANL formula before it ignites a national or international biothreat! Dread and excitement whirled together. He had put up a good front about retirement, but it didn't suit him. *Denise first,* he reminded himself.

He reviewed the details he'd gleaned from Lynn's side of the phone conversation. He admired her respectful refusal to reveal the source of her information, not only to him earlier, but even to the President of the United States. He'd half expected Navy Seals to descend. It was an easy leap from Carlos' story to her visit with his widow this morning. *Marta Martinez,* unverified source. Lynn had modeled well. He would die with that name sealed.

Dan parallel parked in a small space between a Chevrolet Suburban and a Ford Explorer. His mind turned to Denise as he walked past the O'Keeffe museum. He pictured her standing in front of her easel, brush in hand, painting in her smock. He smiled. Followed by a gut-wrenching *No!* He wasn't sure he could handle losing her.

Juan was entering his office as Dan arrived. The matador looked tired, his notable neatness notably missing: pants earth-stained at the knees, shined shoes covered with dust, pressed shirt limp and wrinkled. "You've had a long hard day, detective."

"It began badly. I had to mop up after a CIA joker spying on a collie."

"He surmised it was safer to target the dog."

Juan pointed to the pine armchair "Do you suppose Moore really is that green? It doesn't fit the CIA."

Dan cupped his palm to his ear. "My hearing's acting up. I thought I heard Juan de Santiago give the agency a compliment."

Juan grinned and removed two Cokes® from the small refrigerator. He tossed Dan one and popped open the other. After a thirsty gulp he plopped behind his well-organized desk. "It's been a long day but not a wasted one, *amigo*."

"Agreed." He relayed Lynn's anonymous caller's information.

"Your friend gets weird but informative 'anonymous' calls."

"Evidently."

"It sounds like you still have a handler," he joked.

"Apparently." *You wouldn't believe!* Dan got them back on track. "I'll get the surveillance information for the 502 chase and the motorcycle. Can you put together a team to handle the storage unit?"

"Consider it done, *amigo*. I'll even get a search warrant." He checked his watch. "They may be able to enter *Diablo*'s unit—if it *is* his unit—before dusk, videos transmitting."

Diablo. Polo. Ghost would fit now. Dan didn't care what anyone dubbed him. He just wanted to catch him. His thoughts shifted to Gary stuffed in the Taurus trunk, his flesh grotesque. Lynn was next on the assassin's list. He had to be stopped! "You mentioned that *Diablo* might be local."

"He knew the highway well enough to select the safest spot to send the Ram over the edge and leap. That familiarity, the New Mexico registration and Los Alamos storage unit point to someone who is, or has been, a resident in the area. Or a commuter. Also, the only options going north in Los Alamos are to stay in town or head on to the national forest." Juan frowned. "I may be overshooting, but perhaps he was riding the motorcycle to a familiar place, one safe and remote."

"Logical but perhaps a bit long on conjecture," said Dan.

"Could be."

Dan exhaled heavily. "We need something concrete."

Juan grinned. "How about this?" He updated Dan on the moccasin tracks. "Molds have already been made—men's size elevens. I found a pocketknife also. It's being examined for prints as we speak."

"You are a great investigator."

"Coming from a CIA hotshot, that means a lot."

"Retired hotshot. What baffles me is that *Diablo* wasn't expecting any of this. He had no opportunity to plan ahead, yet pulled it all off in less than an hour."

"That isn't enough time to be thorough. I'll bet you another lunch—say Tomasita's—that we can find some DNA."

"You're on."

Juan chuckled. "You lose."

"What do you have?"

"I found the gray Stetson, evidently thrown out by the blast. It's in my trunk."

"I can see that it's put on a fast track for results. Let's get it when I leave."

Juan's eyes examined his face, "Surveillance and fast-tracked DNA results? You sound confident."

Dan envisioned his name on the elite list. Tomorrow he would be *directing* others to get information—not *asking* for it *please*. Much more efficient. "Anything else?"

"Could be." More sips of Coke®.

"You do like to build suspense." Dan smiled as he said it, trying to hide his growing impatience to hear the bottom line.

"They found a body."

"A *body!* I'd bet my career it wasn't *Diablo.*"

"What career, *amigo*? You're retired." Juan grinned and took another swig of Coke®. "The body had a nasty blow to the head. They assumed he was thrown out of the Ram and dazed, then wandered a short distance before he died. But they finally found his wallet and ran his driver's license—a trucker without a truck. They contacted his employer, who was less concerned about his driver than his missing silver semi. The semi was scheduled to arrive in Los Alamos late morning."

"A body and a missing semi." Dan began to fit together possibilities.

"After the explosion a man driving a blue sedan—a 2011 Impala LTZ—called 911 to report seeing an Indian mother walking along the highway. He was concerned about her." Juan told Dan what he'd learned from Esteban. "I called the driver. He told me she was walking toward Los Alamos. She was large and carried a baby wrapped in an Indian blanket. He couldn't see her face because she kept her head down. He didn't actually see the baby either."

"Fake baby? Fake mother?"

"Could be. Chev Tupatu is a longtime friend. I called him to check on whether he and Galen happened to see the sedan. He said it passed them while they were waiting to make a U-turn." Juan slowly finished his Coke®. "Chev also had to wait for another vehicle. He couldn't see inside because of the tinted windows. But it was . . ."

"A silver semi!" finished Dan. "*Diablo's* means of escape."

"He is clever enough to swim in the air, as a Spanish saying goes."

"Is he merely clever, Juan? Or trained?"

"By, say, the CIA?"

"You'd dance the *sarabande* if he turns out to be a renegade operative."

"Could be."

Dan glanced at his watch. By now Cliff should have responded about the surveillance. He hadn't asked for an entire country—just the roads into and out of a nuclear lab town with a population of about 12,000! Time to call again and practice his new status. He told Juan he wanted to check out a couple of things and placed the call. Cliff's tone was notably different—more deferential. The elite list clearance must be making its way down the chain of command. Dan used a different tone also—less deferential. He restated his request for the 502 surveillance and added the black Harley. Cliff agreed warmly, like a political candidate at a campaign event. Dan informed him of the poisoner's CIA link who had run a search on Lynn Peterson yesterday morning and emailed back the results—before the official one was requested. Cliff exploded as expected and assured him that appropriate action would follow. "ASAP, Cliff, on the surveillance or we lose this opportunity." Dan punched END and noticed Juan staring at him.

"*ASAP, Cliff*," Juan repeated. "As in CIA Director Clayton Clifford?"

Dan ignored the remark and fingered his iPhone. "I saw this today at Lynn's." He showed Juan the spearpoint photo. "Its jagged point reminded me that the M.E. found a miniscule jagged scratch on the back of Martinez's neck where the poison entered. Do you think something like this could have been used?"

Juan stared thoughtfully at it. "A spearpoint is worth considering. Email the photo, and I'll show it to the M.E."

Dan sent it. "Done."

"And received, *amigo*."

"We're going to get him. It's *make-my-day* time."

Juan grinned. "Sounds like *Diablo* crossed the wrong retiree.

27

I heard the cathedral bells chime half past four. "Carlos Martinez was poisoned a little over 48 hours ago."

Galen looked up from his computer. "It's been a challenging two days."

A countdown, I thought but didn't say. "I like the old tick-tock of time better. Now it sneaks by in digital silence." I decided to make some tea and take a soakey bath. Hot water and bubbles to my chin would make things better. Like cookies.

I took a cup to Galen. "You're working hard."

"I'm trying to locate the man who definitely likes *AB* initials and possibly likes presidents' names."

The menacing phone call echoed. "The way he dealt with me says he thrives on power. The most powerful position in the world would appeal to him."

"Wait! I may be onto something!"

I looked over his shoulder. "What did you find?"

"Dan said Juan thinks our man might be local so I googled maps of the area around Los Alamos. Since private land is scarce, I've been checking online property records for people with *AB* initials."

"You found someone?"

"A man named Ariel Brennan. He owns a small ranch in the Santa Fe National Forest near Los Alamos. The land goes back to a homestead deed granted by Teddy Roosevelt. It was exempted from inclusion in the national forest and deeded to Hiram A. Brennan, who was one of his Rough Riders. It has been in the family ever since, and the current owner's full name is Ariel Hiram Brennan. The ranch is named. . . . Guess what, Lynn."

I didn't have a clue. "The Triple R—Rough Riders Rendezvous?"

"*President's Ranch.*"

"After Teddy Roosevelt."

"Probably." He printed what he'd found. "I know it's a long shot, but it's worth checking him out."

"It's the best clue we have."

"I'll call Dan. Where's your cell?"

For a nanosecond the request puzzled me. Galen knew my cell would alert Zeller and he would listen in. Then I realized that was exactly what Galen wanted—added protection. "You're brilliant!"

He ended his conversation with Dan. "He's still meeting with Juan. They'll have the ranch location checked out." He grinned. "Dan suggested that I freelance as an investigator when I retire."

I smiled and dangled the Juke keys before running my bath. "How about driving to Maria's for dinner tonight?"

"Hiroshi was thoughtful to do that. He's a generous man. I'll call for a reservation—on *my* cell. Around seven?"

I nodded. "We'll celebrate our second careers. Maybe compete with *NCIS* on TV. You can be Gibbs. I'll be Abby."

28

Hiroshi Takahashi greeted the doorman at the Inn of Loretto and chatted briefly with him. On his way to the meeting room, he smiled at each staff person, calling them all by name. At his suggestion the GANNS Board of Directors now met in Santa Fe instead of Los Alamos. It was easier to get to, and the unique pre-Pilgrim arts capital offered a notable contrast to the functional 1940s nuclear capitol. Another of his accepted suggestions was to limit the executive committee to an hour, followed by an early dinner meeting with the full board.

He walked into the room quietly without pretension. No loud greetings or boisterous laugh or quick step of feigned urgency. Hiroshi Takahashi didn't have to pose and posture to gain authority. Soft-spoken and small of stature, he entered every room fully aware of the enviable power of his presence, which he wore with humility. He scanned the room inconspicuously, noting the atmosphere. Board meetings reinforced his determination to retain private ownership of his international shipbuilding business.

He shook hands amiably as people came forward to see him, greeting each by name. The secretary handed him the packet for the meeting, a red Confidential stamped across the front. He scanned the minutes and reviewed the list of directors and staff members. He wasn't the president of the executive committee. He didn't have to be president to take charge; he knew he could rule the floor at any moment he chose. He gave full attention to the words of each speaker, watching for nonverbal clues that painted words in different hues. He listened for tone of voice and searched faces and eyes. He noted individual tics and connected them to psychological patterns that denoted insecurity or anxiety, or foretold a tendency toward distortion. He seldom spoke, weary of people who vied for domination through verbosity.

Both the executive committee and the full board meeting went as meetings go—sparring and starring, opining and whining. The major agenda item was the GANNS contract renewal next year. When the board discussed it, Hiroshi watched the predictable dynamics unfold in exaggerated turf protection and manipulation. A former administration had removed the LANL contract from the public sector and placed it in the private sector, withdrawing it from a university and awarding it to the GANNS corporation. But the Benedict administration's position on renewing the contract was unknown.

"We *must* retain our contract!" said the chairman of the board. "Rumors have surfaced that Benedict questions the wisdom of a private corporation running the nation's nuclear labs. Her bad judgment could prevail."

CEO Perry Pearson stood, folding his arms across his chest as though protecting his image. "It will test whether she puts the country first," he stated patriotically.

Pompous Perry, thought Hiroshi behind his congenial smile.

He looked at Hiroshi. "Mr. Takahashi . . ."

He was the only board member addressed by *Mr.* rather than first name. It was a sign of respect that he found amusing. He smiled at the CEO and nodded his attention.

"The situation is critical! Can you use your influence in this matter?"

"I do not know whether I can be helpful, Perry, but I will look into it if you would like." He'd been seeking an excuse to meet with President Benedict and size her up in a personal setting. This was as good as any. He mentally ran through his broad-based and diverse acquaintances, deciding who was closest to her and could set up a meeting quickly.

"Thank you." Perry sighed with amplified relief.

"Is a motion in order?" asked the chair.

"None needed." Perry's tone dismissed him, and his eyes said *Discussion closed.*

The chair acquiesced. "Once again we are in your debt, Mr. Takahashi."

As Hiroshi gave a humble nod, he wondered what the CEO, and perhaps the chair also, hid beneath the surface. He doubted that he would ever have the privilege of attending a truly transparent meeting of any board, especially this one. He recalled a federal review that found all three national labs to be vastly micromanaged and dysfunctional, and LANL had come out worse than Sandia and Lawrence Livermore.

Hiroshi considered the GANNS meetings to be more superficial than significant, generally the case for boards and committees. He recalled a book about 16th century church reformation divisions and the attempts of various segments to restructure themselves for preservation. History repeats itself, trite but true. The astute author suggested that committees are even more prone than individuals to miss the point of what is right in front of them. But superficial or not, these board meetings were not a game to him. They were essential to fulfilling that passion stirring at the root of his soul, his secret lifelong goal.

After the early dinner meeting he continued to think about that goal as he tipped the parking valet and climbed into his car. He noticed a red Juke passing the Inn of Loretto courtyard. He didn't see the faces, but he knew who it was. Lynn and Galen Peterson would always be easy to spot. They drove the only red Juke in Santa Fe.

29

As Galen drove past the Inn of Loretto to Maria's, I commented lightly about Dan's desire to check the Juke for bugs and a tracking device. "Imagine being suspicious of Hiroshi of all people!"

Galen's piercing eyes cut into mine. He put his finger to his lips.

I thought of asking him *Now who's the conspiracist*? But instead I leaned over and kissed his cheek. He drove the rest of the way one-handed, his other cupped over mine as the brilliant sunset colors spread across the horizon. The reprieve felt good.

All through dinner we kept the conversation light, easy to do in Maria's old informal setting. Our reprieve continued until I mentioned Friday night's big event. "Let's go to Zozobra."

"It will be mobbed with people."

"Translation: *A large crowd wouldn't be prudent*. I want to know what it's like."

"I can tell you. Zozobra is the burning of Old Man Gloom, a 50-foot tall marionette," lectured the historian. "The hardships and despair of the past year—symbolically or on lists—are tossed into the fire and go up in smoke. It started in 1924."

"Since 1924?" I pressed my advantage point, "So, all these years it has been safe."

The professor ignored my interruption. "It precedes *Las Fiestas* which began in 1712, the oldest continuous community celebration in the U.S." He paused. "There. You know about Zozobra."

"To know about it isn't the same as experiencing it. Let's go!"

"I strongly suggest that we see what progress Dan and Juan make during the next 48 hours. OK?"

"OK," I agreed.

He looked at me with surprise, one eyebrow raised. "That was effortless."

I shrugged and smiled, confident that I would go—and Galen would too.

During the rest of dinner we avoided both Zozobra and the day's tense experiences. We carried on a normal table-for-two conversation, offering our best selves to each other. We skipped dessert, eager to get home.

Galen was behind the Juke's wheel when his cell rang. He glanced at caller ID and handed it to me, mouthing *It's Dan.*

"Hi, Dan. Galen's driving."

"Bad news, Lynn," he said hurriedly.

Images of more poison deaths hurtled through my mind. "*What?*"

"Your caller was right. The storage unit door was secured by a complicated lock system."

So the bad news was merely that they couldn't get in. I exhaled in relief.

"When the team tried to break in, they expected an alarm to go off. But the unit was rigged to blow up with a forced entry."

Another bomb! "Was anyone hurt?"

"No one killed. That's the only good news. Two men are in the hospital. No evidence survived." He ended the call.

I told Galen what happened. We rode in silence. I wanted to believe that all people have good in them, albeit sometimes deeply hidden. I was beginning to wonder if Abram/Andy/Abe/Art/Ariel was an exception. The debit column showed poisonings, bombs, a third murder today and a death threat against me. The credit column glared empty beside it. My mind filled the silence with the terrifying call this morning. Like eerie music during a scary movie, his spine-chilling voice reverberated in surround sound. I thought about the countdown. Had it begun at one hundred? Or ten?

30

Ariel gazed through the gunroom windows at the shadows sliding up the mountainside as the sun began to set. He sipped his Scotch and thought about the Venom Contract client. Generally he was able to discover his client's identity. Not this time. He had found not a single clue. The client's directive puzzled him. It demonstrated meticulous planning, which was a surprising contrast to the tedious instructions and uninformed terminology. Due to the client's ignorance? Or a ruse to appear ignorant?

The directive and speargun had been inside a heavy metal box just large enough to hold the palm-sized weapon. He was required to return both the metal box and speargun after the contract was fulfilled. The intricately designed weapon had reminded him of a miniature derringer small enough to hide in his hand, but its barrel was flat with a slot-shaped hole at the end to accommodate a spearpoint rather than a bullet. Instead of a trigger, the speargun had a thumb button to push on top of the handle. After firing, the used spearpoint retracted and lodged in a separate chamber as the second spearpoint took its place. The speargun had to be pressed directly against the victim's neck to pierce the skin, a challenging design flaw.

He turned away from the windows and admired his antique gun collection. Setting his Scotch on the desk, he stepped across the Navajo rug to the steel-lined paneling and scanned his thumbprint to unlock the hidden door to his military arms. He removed the weapon he'd designed to replace the speargun he'd used Sunday. He had replicated the function but not the form. His version fit into a plastic shell-type casing and was smaller and simpler than his client's. "I did a superior job designing this, General," he said to his Doberman as he sat down at his desk. "Later I'll coat the spearpoint with poison and load it."

He lacked access to the biolab poison his client had preloaded in the other speargun. He had an alternative which he had used effectively in a Florida contract. Dying would take a few minutes instead of being instant. However, both poisons shared one necessary commonality: *death*.

"Lynn Peterson will be our test case, General." He raked his chair back and stood. "Listen to this: The burning of Old Man Gloom will be her death scene. Flaming Zozobra flails and moans in the midst of a crazed mob chanting *Burn him!* What an arena to respond to *Get a life!*" He enjoyed this game! No hesitancy. No mistakes. No remorse. "She'll be there, General. Tourists don't miss it." He tipped up his glass and finished his Scotch. "Zozobra burns. Lynn Peterson dies!"

PART THREE
THE DECEPTION
Thursday, 5:47 A.M.

The eyes of men speak words
the tongue cannot pronounce.

—Crow Proverb

The trouble with secrecy
is that it denies to the government itself
the wisdom and resources of the whole community,
the whole country.

—J. Robert Oppenheimer

1

I sipped a cup of white cherry tea and looked toward the east mountains. Dawn waited for the golden ball to roll up the other side of the peaks and grant Santa Fe another sunrise. Thomas Merton's words from *The Seven Storey Mountain* drifted into my mind: *There is not an act of kindness or generosity, not an act of sacrifice done, or a word of peace and gentleness spoken, not a child's prayer uttered, that does not sing hymns to God.* There is a rhythm to the singing, I thought, tempo and tune and interspersed rests along the way. I had viewed my simple favor for President Benedict as a duty. Perhaps it was an act of kindness, a sacrifice, a way to sing a hymn to God. I hoped so. The sun rose in triumph once more. I took my last sip of tea and faced the day, dawn silence complete and my notes waiting to be sung.

One note in today's song would be phoning Denise and Amaya to set up lunch. I wondered if Denise would feel like it and whether Amaya would enjoy it. An invitation was better than a guess. I picked up *The New Mexican* from the *portal* and glimpsed the red Juke in the street. It brought a smile. I recalled that Hiroshi was on the GANNS Board of Directors. Does he know about the toxin theft? Does GANNS know about the stolen copy of the formula? Will President Benedict learn something about PAPA from the CIA or FBI or some other alphabet agency? Will I reach a dead end? My train of thought lurched toward conspiracy and an image of PAPA as a dominant figure dressed in black, wearing a mask with absent eyes and an evil smile.

"Good morning." Galen poured himself a cup of coffee and kissed me on the cheek.

"It's Kwang and LANL day for you."

"Time with him could prove interesting. Perhaps I'll even write the article I jabbered about."

"I should call the Lab and warn them Special Agent Gibbs is coming."

He chuckled, then sighed. "Maybe I can discover another piece of the puzzle."

"What connects the pieces we have?"

He shrugged. "It's like working a puzzle upside down. It's all plain gray, no pattern."

"Maybe a secret connects them. Something not yet revealed."

"But it will be. Human beings are predisposed to tell secrets, especially someone else's. Secrets always come out."

I looked up at him. "Unless the person with the secret carries it to the grave."

2

"Madam President, you have a call from Vice-President Parker."

Dwight would not interrupt without significant reason. "I'll take it, Barbara." Her administrative assistant's pleasant voice and demeanor disguised her impregnable protection of the schedule. President Benedict both liked and trusted her.

Dwight came straight to the point. "Hiroshi Takahashi wants an appointment with you."

"Meaning you couldn't get the request past Barbara."

"Typically astute. Do you know him?"

"I've heard of him." She did a quick name search in her personal contacts.

"He's from New Orleans," said Dwight, "a shipbuilder with international connections."

"I place him now." She scanned her information. "An influential man."

"Very. What's rare is that he's known for integrity."

"You sound like a cynical politico," she said lightly. "Lots of people have integrity." But, she thought, fewer than I assumed the first day I walked into this office.

"True, but the journey toward billionaire can cut that elite group's percentage." In a pensive tone he added, "I hope you can keep your idealism. It motivates us all."

Not idealistic, but hopefully not jaded either, she thought. Not yet.

"He's flying in today, Madam President."

Not once since her election had he used her first name instead of title. She wondered if his flawless respect was because she was the first woman to be president or because he held flawless respect for the office. Or perhaps, she hoped, because he respects the person holding the office. As dancing leaves cast shadows across the carpet, she thought about the political win-at-all-costs misrepresentation and manipulation that shred honor, discourage the people, and lower the nation's esteem internationally. Sometimes she wondered if the great democracy would come tumbling down. *Not on my watch!*

"Hiroshi understands that I will see him if you can't," Dwight continued, "but I think your time would be well spent."

"I know you wouldn't ask unless it's important."

"It could be. He's a person we want in our corner, and he's on the GANNS Board of Directors."

"Perfect timing. I'll ask Barbara to find ten minutes around 5:15 today." She wanted to be armed with information from Dan and Lynn. "Remember the security clearance I requested?"

"I took care of it personally to guarantee its expedition. I checked before calling you. *Spearpoint* is cleared."

She resisted asking him whether the Labrador Retriever or German Shepherd side of his personality had handled it. "Thank you, Dwight. I hope you know how much I appreciate your experience and connections and that I can always count on you." When the door closed behind him, she looked at her watch and gave Lynn a hurried call.

3

The book rang, startling me. I removed the secure phone. "Hello."

"I know it's early in New Mexico, but not for you as I recall."

I heard President Benedict's rushed urgency behind the courteous words. Brief responses served her today. "Right."

"I must have updates before five this afternoon, DC time."

Three o'clock here! Less than six hours!

"I realize it isn't much time. Spearpoint is now on the elite list. I know he will do his best. I need all information he considers significant and some overviews of how it might fit together. Also I need anything you can add and the connections you see. You are good at connecting the dots."

The compliment surprised me. No time for humble rebuttal. "Thank you."

"One more item. Hiroshi Takahashi from New Orleans has come to my attention. Do you know him?"

"We met Tuesday evening." I added what little I knew.

"He has a second home here. He's on the GANNS board."

"What do you think of him?"

"Very charming. Generous. Bright." I moved to a deeper level. "Yet, I sense that he wears conviviality like chainmail protection."

"I've seen that incongruence in others."

"The bottom line for me: I like him." Despite the President's hurry, I asked a critical question. "Has PAPA been identified?"

"The agencies found nothing. They conclude that PAPA was invented as a ruse to manipulate Martinez and he fell for it."

I thought about Marta's story. Carlos' naiveté seemed doubtful. "A logical deduction but, if I may be frank, it doesn't seem to fit. If he were easily misled, how did he succeed in undercover work for three separate entities?"

Silence.

Hesitantly I referred to a previous *simple favor* for her. "Remember St. Sava?"

"Your point is that the ancient society's existence eluded our intelligence sources?" She paused. "Perhaps I accepted the ruse theory too quickly."

Exactly, I thought but didn't say.

"You connected the dots to St. Sava. Maybe you can do it again for PAPA."

Me? Why not a professional!

"You have my trust and confidence," said the President as though reading my silence. "Within an hour the secure phone you are using will be enhanced to leave me messages. The security code is simple— the alphabetical numbers for the nickname of our ancestor."

I translated. We had the same great-great grandparents whose daughter was named Marie-Vincente, nicknamed Vini. Both of us had been given the middle name Marie, after her. I coded the numbers: *V-i-n-i—22-9-14-9.* "I understand."

"I will call again around three o'clock your time. Thank you."

I stared at the dead phone. "I don't have any PAPA dots to connect," I muttered aloud. Merton's statement came again to mind. I feared her request would lead me to something far-removed from a hymn to God.

4

Zechariah Zeller hid amidst the chamisa in the morning light, unseen but seeing. He had found the ranch last night. The road ended at a locked gate that had an ornamental **President's Ranch** designed into the black iron bars. One way into the ranch. The same way out. He parked his van in a secluded space outside the iron fence that surrounded the property. After a long search he found a spot where he could boost himself over the fence without setting off alarms. Wary of alarms he walked stealthily toward the ranch house until he reached a good observation point. Outdoor lights in strategic places were on near the house. The inside was dark. He removed his backpack and settled into the darkness of the still night.

He thought about pretty *Frau* Peterson. She needed his help. She had not said so. No. But he knew. He would not let her down. He also knew that when she and *Herr* Peterson had important information for the man named Dan, they used her cell so he could listen in. They had used it to report their discovery of President's Ranch. It all fit together: the storage unit, the Ram's New Mexico registration, and the motorcycle traveling north up Diamond Drive—the way to nowhere. Despite the day's failures, Herr Ram a.k.a. Ariel Hiram Brennen was now in view. Spy. Killer. Threat to pretty *Frau* Peterson.

When the birds greeted sunrise, he peered through his powerful binoculars into the undraped window of the ranch house. Herr Ram sat at his desk. Guns lined glass cases on the wall. He focused full magnification on the desk and made out a spearpoint that could fit into the small tube-like casing beside it. He moved the binoculars up and down, side to side, sighting in across every article in the study. His eyes rested on the computer, likely the unidentifiable one used for the CIA query regarding *Frau* Peterson.

He watched Brennan swivel his chair around toward the corner windows and stand. He looked out each one. Evidently satisfied, he returned to his desk.

Zeller was not worried. No. He was good at being an unseen seer, a lion attuned to his surroundings. Once again he focused the binoculars on the spearpoint and imagined it loaded into the tube like a shell in a gun.

Ja, Frau Peterson needs me.

5

I picked up the landline phone and called Dan without apology for the early hour. "I received a call from our friend. You're now on the elite list, and she needs an update before three this afternoon."

"Three!" Dan skipped a beat. "Juan and I are going to Brennan's ranch this morning. If the *AB* initials lead is accurate, we'll not only have information but the poisoner himself."

"What a relief that would be!"

"There's another lead also. I showed Juan the photo of your spearpoint, and he discussed it with the M.E.—who thinks a spearpoint could have made that jagged entry wound in the victim's neck."

I pictured it. "An ancient spearpoint with biowar toxin. That's a weaponry oxymoron!" Quickly I moved on. "Her priority for you is the formula copy. "Do you have any thoughts on it?"

"I'm still at square one."

"Could it be hidden in Carlos' belongings?"

"Logically, yes," said Dan. "Realistically, no. *Nothing* could have evaded the officials. And if the M.E. found anything, he would have turned it over to them."

"None of our friend's sources have ever heard of PAPA."

"So that was a ruse."

"They think so, but they've been wrong before about calling an existent entity nonexistent."

"I wonder if his widow overlooked something."

I recalled her detailed story. "She shared everything she knew." Or did she? Maybe there was something that didn't seem important at the time. "I'll talk with her again." The clock raced toward three. "But not in time for the update. I don't want to trouble her before the Requiem Mass."

"I understand." The words were said in a softer voice that seemed to come from a deeper place.

I also understood. A final service would hold dreaded personal meaning for him now.

Dan's get-it-done tone returned. "My former employer has an abundance of confidential information on the Lab. I'll see what I can learn before three."

"I wish you success today."

Galen came in from the bedroom dressed New Mexico style in jeans and a casual shirt. "To whom do we wish success today?"

"Dan. He and Juan are going to President's Ranch."

"I hope Ariel Hiram Brennan is the right man—and he doesn't escape again."

"And I hope you have a dull drive to Los Alamos this morning instead of a chase scene."

He frowned. "You were talking about secrets earlier this morning. The scientists working on the poison project know that some was stolen. I wonder how far that secret has spread."

"I thought they're not allowed to talk about their work or expose anything about the Lab."

"I assume they would honor that with outsiders, Lynn, but being colleagues they likely talk among themselves."

"Do you suppose they know a copy of the formula was made?"

"Not if Carlos was adept."

"I hope you learn something significant."

"It's worth a try. Kwang will introduce me with my highest accolades—putting a feather in his own cap through his guest. That benefits our cause. Also, though I'm in a different field, I respect their areas of expertise and want to do research there. Perhaps they will be a little more open. Scholars tend to be less guarded around other scholars."

"A kind of intellectual tribalism?"

He ignored the gentle barb. "I want time to get the lay of the land before meeting Kwang. I'll grab breakfast in Los Alamos." He held up the Juke keys with a twinkle in his eye. "And you thought we could do without a car!"

Barb for barb. Anxiety clouded over me. But why? He wasn't heading into a threatening situation. As usual, anxiety trumped reason. "Please be careful."

"*You* be careful. Keep the door locked." He hesitated.

"Don't worry. I'm fine here."

"I'll be back around noon." He lifted my chin and kissed me goodbye. "You can count on it."

Anxiety also trumped reassurance.

6

I waited until nine o'clock to call Amaya about lunch. The call went to an automated answering system in which a pleasant male voice repeated the number and invited the caller to leave a message. "This is Lynn Peterson for Amaya. I would enjoy taking you and another new friend to lunch. Perhaps tomorrow. My number is . . . ."

"Hello, Lynn. I apologize for the message. Hiroshi insists on having our calls filtered. Approved numbers are transferred. I added yours after the archbishop's dinner."

"Thank you," I said, surprised by Amaya's response. She had said more in that explanation than the entire evening at Joe's. Maybe one-to-one frees her.

"I would be pleased to have lunch. Who is your other new friend?"

"Denise Dickerson. She's battling cancer."

"*Ohh.* I am sorry."

"You would never know it by her attitude."

"Sometimes the only choice we have is our attitude."

The way she said it made it more than a platitude thrown out lightly. I wondered if it came from personal experience.

"Three is a pleasing number. You may have noticed at the archbishop's dinner that I do not enter well into group conversations. But," she added quickly, "the party was enjoyable."

I agreed. "Do you have a favorite place for lunch?"

"Yes," she said decisively. "Here. It will not be crowded or noisy."

"No, Amaya, I . . . ."

She broke in. "Please honor me by having lunch in my home."

A timely reminder that hospitality is about receiving as well as giving. "Thank you for the kind invitation."

"Today would work well for me, Lynn. At twelve o'clock."

Not *today!* Lunch seemed trivial—but not if Denise feels well and would enjoy getting out. "I'll check with Denise and call you back."

"If she cannot come today, please come anyway."

"All right." *Why do I always say that!* "We appreciate your lending us the Juke. How kind and thoughtful of you and Hiroshi."

"It is our pleasure."

"Please give him my regards."

"He is on his way to Washington for an appointment. That is why lunch works well for me today." Amaya gave the address and directions.

Perhaps it is Hiroshi's absence that frees her. I remembered what the President had said: *Hiroshi Takahashi from New Orleans has come to my attention.* I wondered if his DC appointment was related to her. Or was the timing simply coincidental? I didn't have time to ponder the topic of coincidences.

.

7

Ariel swiveled the sorrel leather chair toward the bank of corner windows in his gunroom. The scenic mountain view was shadowed by a sense of being watched. A deer skittered off into the trees. Predictable deer behavior, but he stepped close to the windows to scan the southern part of his ranch. General rose too. Ariel saw nothing unusual. He glanced down at General, the best alarm of all. The dog stood at attention, alert but calm. Ariel looked at the picture of the powerful white stallion racing across the canvas, muscles rippling, mane and tail flying. Free! Like Ariel Hiram Brennan. No one could take that freedom away! He shrugged off wariness. The ranch was his bastion of safety.

General tagged along when he took the spearpoint and small plastic casing to his workshop. He put on thick multi-fabric gloves with heavy plastic lining to coat the spearpoint with poison. It didn't matter that he had no biolab toxin. For Lynn Peterson he preferred this poison he had used once in Florida. She would suffer for some long minutes instead of dying instantly.

He placed the coated spearpoint into the plastic shell-type casing, then loaded it into the modified Fritz-style cane handle. The hidden triggering mechanism was activated by combined pressure from his thumb on top of the handle and his index finger beneath it. He could strike from a distance up to three feet instead of having to press the weapon directly against her neck, and the spearpoint would remain in her body instead of retracting. He had weapon, target, date and time. Later he would review his precise and methodical plan.

Right now, his priority was strategy. After intercepting the CIA report tucked safely in the *Sports Illustrated* magazine, he had read it on the way to the drop site for his client. It revealed the kind of toxin and the name of the thief. Golden information. "Don't worry, General. I'm too skilled and experienced to leave a trace of tampering." The Doberman tipped his head.

Trained by the CIA but shed of them. An ideal state of affairs. The next task was to invite the poison thief to purchase freedom insurance. "Not blackmail, General. That is beneath us." A nice touch, to have the power to speak a few words and alter a man's life—while improving one's income. "Think about the incredulity, General. The thief pays the assassin for protection from the law! And inferior officials stay on the sidelines shillyshallying."

The reason behind the Venom Contract still nagged him. What could be worth a double assassination and an upper six-digit contract? Both motive and identity remained hidden. No clues. No trail. No links. "The client was meticulous, General," he said as the dog followed him back to the gunroom.

8

Kwang gave Galen the public LANL tour—Ashley Pond, Bathtub Row, Fuller Lodge, the museum. He had also arranged for a pass to additional areas. Secrets, however, were well protected. Galen learned a lot about LANL but nothing useful—except that no one but an insider could have stolen the poison.

Kwang had set up a midmorning coffee, eager to introduce Galen to fellow scientists. As they sat around the table, Galen observed that the conversation dynamics would have been the same at Tulane and in many scholarly groups. The major difference was the approach to their field. His historian friends researched the past and viewed it as a way to understand the present and, perhaps, predict future trends from observable patterns. The Lab scientists focused on research that affected the present and might redirect the course of the future— ultimately fodder for historians to come. He was aware of his propensity to view the Lab's *protective* research as a euphemism for the opposite— escalating risk possibilities and keeping the threat of annihilation alive. He warned himself to examine his view, for he shared the human tendency to see only what reinforces preconceived assumptions.

He tried to imagine a custodial engineer in this atmosphere. In the human tribal pattern of *we/they*, Carlos would have been a *they* among the *we* around this table. Galen better understood Kwang's **just** *a custodian* reference. The same atmosphere at times prevailed at Tulane. As an academician, Galen was part of this morning's coffee klatch *we*. But when they all went back to their projects, the *we* would be filtered categorically, with historians in a *they* field. He was enjoying himself, but he was wasting time. Nothing here was helping him get closer to the poison thief.

Kwang's phone rang.

Galen noticed that he answered it without apology, as though all his calls were of utmost importance.

"Kwang-Sun Rhee." His eyes circled the group, the star on stage as he listened. . . . His expression of self-importance shifted to shock. "*No!*" . . . "I don't know what you are talking about." . . . His face went ashen as he rose from the table and moved away. . . . "That is impossible. . . ."

Galen could barely hear him now.

Silence again and then Kwang responded with a passive weak, "Yes." . . . "That is im—" He broke off before finishing the word and listened. . . . In half a minute he removed the phone from his ear and stared at it. He straightened his shoulders and turned back around, his face even paler. He scanned the table again and laughed with bravado. "A crank call! He had me going for a minute." He looked at his watch. "Galen, it has been a pleasure to show you around. I must get back to my project now."

"Thank you." Galen imitated Lynn's polite nod-bow at the dinner party. "I appreciate your time." As he walked to the Juke, he thought about Kwang's revealing phone monologue and the gamut of his emotions. Now *that* made his visit worthwhile.

9

I called Denise about lunch. Despite the time crunch, it felt good to hear her voice come to life. "I'll pick you up about 11:30."

"That gives me time to get gussied up. It takes longer now than it used to."

"For all of us, Denise. It seems to take more and more for less and less."

She laughed. "I'll see you later."

My cell rang as I hung up. Surprised, I dug it out of the drawer. Caller ID displayed Galen's name. Ah. He wanted Zeller to hear this call. "Hello."

"We need to check out Kwang-Sun Rhee," he said in quarterback mode. "I just left him. He received a call this morning that transformed him from arrogant to ashen. I think the call needs to be traced."

I clutched the phone as though holding it tighter would bring Galen closer to me.

"I may be making wild leaps rather than logical links," he continued. "But it's worth a try."

"What leaps?"

"First background. After seeing the Lab's security regarding who's admitted there, I'm convinced only an employee could have stolen the toxin. Also at Joe's party Kwang showed excessive interest in the Plaza death. He received a phone call this morning. From his agitation during it, I leaped to considering what topics might be so disturbing to him. From there, to wondering if the call related to the thief's identity. Then a huge leap to wondering if Kwang was the thief. And if so, how the caller knew that. Another leap: Did the poisoner read the intercept before delivering it? Then a wild one: Could the poisoner be talking to the thief?" Galen paused. "A lot of leaps."

I heard his doubt and could identify with watching thoughts unravel when spoken aloud. "Do you want to call Dan?"

"I don't know. He doesn't strike me as a leaps man."

"But he'll listen. And he might be able to trace the call to Kwang."

Galen nodded. "OK. I will."

With the update crunch, I decided to get Zeller in on trying to find PAPA. "To change the subject, no one seems to know anything about PAPA."

"The Peace for All People Alliance," Galen added, evidently understanding and wanting also to catch up their listener. "Maybe it's a dead end."

"But maybe Kwang won't be. If he turns out to be the thief, he might have some information about the person who hired him. At least he'll know the drop off site for the poison, and some evidence might be found there."

"That's a big *if.*"

"Don't dismiss your leaps lightly. When we don't have any dots to connect, we have to start with wild leaps."

10

Ariel's call had gone exactly as planned. He'd slammed the cell door on Kwang-Sun Rhee's arrogance and financial lifestyle. "His behavior changed, *General*, when I enlightened him on his choices: *Before one o'clock today go to your bank and withdraw the initial premium of your freedom insurance in the amount of $5,000 in cash and follow instructions. There is one alternative: I provide LANL with proof of your guilt as a traitor against the United States of America.* That got his attention." Ariel pictured him scurrying to the bank at noon to withdraw the cash and then waiting with angst for the second call providing instructions. After researching Rhee's financial worth, he had chosen a manageable sum, barely—a bimonthly premium totaling $30,000 a year. "Rhee walks free, General, but we condemned him to ten-years in financial prison. Then we will extend his sentence."

His *Art Benjamin* cell rang and identified the caller as the 4-U Storage Company. "Hello."

"Mr. Benjamin?"

"This is Art Benjamin."

"I have been trying to reach you," he said in a tone that suggested Ariel owed him an apology.

Ariel removed the phone from his ear and checked—a missed call last night and earlier this morning. "And you are?"

"Kenny."

"Kenny who?"

"Kenny Whiteside. I have unfortunate news for you." He paused.

The words evoked anxiety and the pause irritated Ariel. "Get to the point."

"You rent unit 1313 at 4-U Storage?"

"You obviously know that or you wouldn't be calling."

"I'm sorry, Mr. Benjamin. That unit blew up last night."

The image filled Ariel's mind. His tidy well-stocked safe space blown to rubble!

"I overheard one of the officials say that it was apparently a bomb. Someone must have planted it."

A permanently planted bomb set to be triggered by forced entry. *Officials* had left empty-handed. All evidence destroyed. Necessary, but costly.

"Are you there, sir?"

"Go on."

"I am very sorry, sir."

The invasion of his privacy enraged him. Only his cycle was left, safely protected here at the ranch. He controlled his tone. "I am in California for three weeks, Kenny. I'll deal with this when I return." He disconnected. How did officials manage to connect Unit 1313 to him? If they figured out the storage unit, could they also connect him to the ranch? No. Different names, different addresses. Impossible.

But he'd also thought the discovery of his storage unit was impossible. He couldn't take a chance. "Let's go, General."

11

Zeller's phone vibrated an alert while he watched the ranch house with his binoculars. He listened to *Frau* Peterson answer her cell, a call from her husband. Not a private call. No. It pleased him that they used her cell to include him. He remembered the conversation verbatim and would act on the information: *Eins*, call the man named Dan at the number *Herr* Peterson called. *Zwei*, find a safe place to park the Eurovan for research on something called PAPA and also on Kwang-Sun Rhee. Though *Herr* Peterson's leaps are big, *Mutter*, we will do thorough research as always. But Brennan is our priority here and now.

To try to take Brennan by himself risked an escape—again. The man named Dan had adequate information from *Herr* Peterson's call yesterday to bring a team and take Brennan legally. They should have arrived by now. Their continued delay risked another escape.

He watched Brennan pick up the phone at his desk. Agitated gestures ensued. He took the phone from his ear and shook his fist at it. He jumped up. Grabbed the laptop and a gym bag. Rushed out of the room with his dog.

He would have to take Brennan alone. He yanked his camouflage shirt and pants on over his night blacks. Warily he started toward the ranch house. Crouched low. Pulled his Glock 31 .357. Stepped with caution. Alert for sensors . . . for movement . . . for reflections. He neared the house.

"Let's go, General." Ariel grabbed his laptop and escape bag. He rushed to the garage. Unlocked the hidden door with his thumb scan. Rushed down the stairs. Thumb-scanned the door to the fetid tunnel "Run, General!" He reached the camouflaged Jeep. Drove up to the exit road. It surfaced under a canopy of trees that provided cover until he reached a hidden entry onto the remote mountain road. A nice touch, an escape route invisible to manned and unmanned eyes in the sky. "The ace of escape is free again, General," he said. Just a man and his dog innocently Jeeping in the mountains.

>◦‡◦<   >◦‡◦<   >◦‡◦<

Zeller sensed emptiness in the house. He peeked in through the windows. No noise. No activity. No Brennan. He ran zigzag to the barn. Made it! Entered. Smelled hay. Scanned the rough walls. Stepped toward the center. Heard a dog bark once, growl briefly.

He stopped. The growl came from beneath him. He aimed at the sound and shot a hole through the floor. Silence beneath him. A miss? Or an instant death? He searched for a floor exit. Nothing. A wall door. Nothing. He scanned the barn again. Began to examine the walls by feel. Nothing. He heard vehicles. Doors slammed. Voices shouted. The man named Dan was not leading a sneak attack. No. He had opted for overwhelming force—and arrived too late.

It was time for his own escape. Zeller slipped out of the barn and into the trees behind it. He swung in a wide arc and worked his way back toward the hidden Eurovan. Climbed over the high iron fence. Removed the camouflage that hid the van and the blocks against its tires. Jumped into it. Rolled in silence down the steep road for half a mile. Officials had blocked the entry to the ranch house but left the road toward Los Alamos wide open. He turned on the motor and drove away.

>◦‡◦<   >◦‡◦<   >◦‡◦<

Dan was agitated. Using Juan and his team required too many legal hoops. The delay could be costly. His cell vibrated. A blocked number. "Dickerson here."

"You are too late," said a distorted voice.

"Who is this?"

"Brennan *is* the man you are after. I recognized him."

"You have seen him before?" Dan's second question was also ignored.

"He left in a hurry with his computer and dog. I heard the dog growl beneath the barn floor and took a shot. Find the bullet hole and cut open the floor around it. You should find his escape route."

"Who are you?"

"A temporary friend. You need me on your team." He shot a warning like rapid-fire bullets: DO-NOT-SEARCH-FOR-ME! DO-NOT-TRY-TO-IDENTIFY-ME! I make a life-shortening enemy."

Even with the voice distortion, Dan heard the steel of truth.

12

The *casita* phone rang. "Hello."

"Dan here. He got away."

Again. Nausea roiled.

"But I have some good news."

I borrowed his to-the-point phrase. "Tell me."

"I got a semi-friendly call from a man with a distorted voice and blocked number."

I thought of Zeller.

"He had good information. We're working on it now. I'm optimistic." He skipped a beat. "Your *anonymous* caller seems to have added me to his contacts."

"Are you looking for him?"

His tone changed. "Do you want us to?"

"No! He might be able to help us again."

"He's resourceful. I'll give him that. Do you trust him?"

"I am ambiguous, Dan. But I believe he would do anything in his power to help me. So, in a strange way, I trust him."

"That's good enough for me. Is Galen with you?"

"He's probably on his way home from Los Alamos. Did he reach you about Kwang-Sun Rhee?"

"Yes. I'll check on Rhee when I wrap up things here."

"Thanks, Dan."

"You have nothing to thank me for yet. All I report are continued escapes." He skipped another beat. "My take on Brennan is that challenges whet his appetite instead of scaring him off. He sees himself as untouchable. We have underestimated him." He ended the call.

Am I underestimating him also? Unrealistic about his power over me? Without question! I'm living one step removed from Life because of fear. It hovers even in good moments. I'm weary of worry! Weary of a sense of powerlessness! Weary of fear! *Enough!*

As I hung up the phone, I looked out the window and wondered if anyone was out there looking in. My determination already waning, I turned away, sympathizing with alcoholics.

13

Bishop Matt Langham found a seat amidst the crowd gathered for the second day of the regional ecumenical conference in Albuquerque. Archbishop Joseph Hannahan held the audience in his hands during the morning lecture. He was charismatic, articulate and not afraid to be direct. The painful things he said about the lack of social conscience were expressed with an eloquent charm that left people reluctant to disagree because they would risk appearing disagreeable. The master, thought Matt.

Following the lecture, Matt and Joe had red pepper corn chowder and cobb salad for an early lunch in a private room to plan the final details for Carlos' Requiem Mass the next morning. When they finished, Matt reported on his visit with Marta, confident that she would have shared her husband's story with Joe had he been there. "So there it is. I'm having trouble putting the pieces together, but your network reaches into all walks of life around here. What do you think?"

"I hear things. None of it especially meaningful in itself. But when I put all the pieces together, sometimes I come up with a fairly clear picture of what's going on in various places."

"Including LANL?"

Joe shrugged. "Several parishioners work there. I listen with my eyes too. Observe things." He paused. "Like at dinner Monday evening. I invited Hiroshi and Amaya partly because he is a benefactor, but mostly because they live part time in New Orleans and I thought the Petersons might know them. I invited Kwang-Sun and Sue Min because she does research at SAR and I thought Galen might have met her there." He frowned. "But something puzzled me. Did you see

Hiroshi's expression when I introduced Kwang-Sun to him? It was reflexive, I think, and covered immediately, but it wasn't favorable."

"I missed it."

"Ah, my good bishop, you must learn to take note of nonverbal details. They tell us more than words."

Another teaching moment, thought Matt with appreciation.

"Since Kwang-Sun works for the Lab and Hiroshi serves on the board of directors, I wondered if he had some problematic information about the scientist." Joe shrugged again. "On the other hand, maybe my perception was incorrect."

Matt doubted that.

Joe checked his watch and rose. "I need to look over my notes for the afternoon lecture."

"Of course." Matt stood also.

"Thank you for driving down to finalize preparations for tomorrow and for telling me about your visit with Marta. Bless her! Her husband tells her he's involved with the FBI and CIA, that he discovered a poison theft at LANL, and that he stole a copy of the formula for PAPA! All of it well intentioned, I believe, knowing him." He shook his head. "Pray for Marta, Matt. And," he added softly, "pray also for the cruel lost soul who murdered Carlos."

Matt stared after Joe, mentally fingering a corner piece of the puzzle. He hadn't told Joe that Carlos was murdered. He didn't even know it.

14

I was walking out the door to put Amaya's address in the Juke's GPS when the landline phone rang. "Hello."

"Hi, Lynn. It's Matt. I'm driving back from Albuquerque. Do you have a moment?"

"Sure." Why do I always say that?

"When we talked about Marta's story, you strongly supported sharing it with officials. I'm guessing you were aware then that Carlos was murdered."

I wondered how he knew but didn't ask. "I wanted to tell you but couldn't."

"Joe mentioned it in passing this morning. He probably thought I already knew."

"I wonder who told him."

"He didn't say, and I was too stunned to ask. Probably not Marta. I think she would have told us if she'd known."

I agreed.

"Carlos is dead, whatever the cause. You and I—and Joe, of course—may be the only ones who care first and foremost about Marta."

"I'd like to talk with her again, Matt. Carlos may have said something that seemed inconsequential at the time."

"Let's give her some time after she gets the Requiem Mass behind her."

I felt the same way despite the President's three o'clock update. "Of course."

"On the other hand," he continued, "she might see it as a way to show care for Carlos. His Vigil is tonight. I may—though I doubt it—

ask if she's thought of anything else she would like to share with me. I'll get a feel for what is best."

A thought flipped my stomach. "Marta is my major concern. I wonder if she would be in danger if someone learns that Carlos told her about PAPA and the copy of the formula."

"Or perhaps in danger from PAPA if it has the copy. If PAPA actually exists."

"It might also be dangerous for her if PAPA didn't get the copy and thinks she knows where it is."

"She told only us, Lynn, and we will protect that information."

"Unconditionally," I said, repeating Matt's word the last time we discussed her protection.

"There's another option. Perhaps PAPA exists and Carlos was duped. What if it has the formula in hand and malice in mind?"

I didn't want to think about that.

15

I rang Denise's doorbell a little early, eager to give her the seashell in my pocket. I had decided the day Dan looked in my keepsake box that I wanted her to have it.

She opened the door quickly—makeup, denim dress, cute red scarf where hair used to be, matching red shoes, necklace and earrings.

I forced the day's tensions aside and gave her center stage. "You look great!"

"I feel much better." She grinned. "After you called, I even told Home-Help to bugger off. Do we have time for you to come in?"

"Sure." That word again. We entered the foyer. I looked over an adobe half-wall into the open living space with fourteen-foot ceilings and the casual warmth of southwest décor. Across the room another adobe half-wall partially hid a small kitchen. A breakfast nook extended beyond it with three windows in the curved wall. I imagined that Dan brought function and Denise brought form and harmony. My eyes circled back to a dining area with a handcrafted table. In the center stood a Nambé vase holding red roses. "I love roses."

"I do too. They come in many colors and have both beauty and thorns, a metaphor for humanity."

"That's exactly how I see them, Denise."

"We're kindred spirits."

I smiled. "Yes we are." We walked past the hall table with geometric carvings, and I noticed the striking painting above it. A beautiful Indian maiden wore a fringed, beaded white leather dress. Long black braids framed an unsmiling face. Her reflective dark eyes stared at a snow-capped mountain. Her arms were lifted toward the sunrise song of vivid hues. She stood near a stream that looked so real I could hear it ripple. A spearpoint was half-buried on the bank beside it. "What a powerful painting!" I looked for the signature: *Denise Foster Dickenson.* "It's yours! It's magnificent!"

"Thank you. Painting is my gift."

"How talented you are!" She led me down the hall. When we stopped, I pulled the seashell from my pocket. "Something in my keepsake box reminded me of you, Denise. I like to stick my toe in the seas around the world and bring home a shell." I opened my hand. The shell's wavy blue-gray and ivory stripes were vivid in the sunlight. "This one is from the Black Sea at Varna. I want you to have it."

Her eyes lit up. "How did you know?"

"Fay told me that your grandfather grew up there. She said he used to tell both of you stories about wading in that sea when he was a little boy. I gave her a shell also."

"Let me show you something," she said excitedly, leading me to a gallery of family photos at the end of the hall. She pointed to one. "That's Grandfather. I *loved* him. He told me about wading in the sea as a child." She brushed her finger tenderly across the shell. "And this is from his sea! It's like I'm there with him. I can see him walking along the beach. He squats and picks up this shell. Then," she said, miming his gestures, "he brushes off the sand and smiles as he admires it in his hand."

"I'm glad it brings him close. For me, seashells are a symbol of healing waters."

"This one will be a symbol of healing for me also." A tear rolled down her cheek, and she gave me a hug. "Thank you."

I had experienced, though rarely, the sense of souls touching. This was one of those beautiful moments of connection. As we hugged each other, I longed for my strength to pour into her. *Oh God of Many Names, may your healing flow into Denise*, I prayed silently with blinked-back tears. The moment ended, and life moved on.

16

"What a beautiful home!" said Denise as we S-ed up the high winding driveway toward Amaya's house.

I admired the curved simple beauty of the three-level adobe house sprawling across the hillside like part of the earth. Impishly I wondered how the Juke felt about its temporary demotion to a *casita* and street parking. Two security cameras brought me back to the real world when I parked. A third stood above the arched adobe gateway. Before I rang the bell, its wooden door swung open to a flagstone courtyard with a three-tiered central fountain surrounded by pots of geraniums. We walked across the courtyard and up the steps to the double doors with stained-glass panes. Beauty abounded. Yet with each step I felt watched. A casually dressed muscular man opened the door immediately. Butler? Bouncer? Guard?

Muscles smiled. "Welcome. Please come in." He waited in the spacious *entrada*. It had a polished walnut floor and high ceilings supported by log *vigas* a foot thick.

I glanced through the entry hall's wide archway, intrigued by the view. Identical open archways, spaced about 25 feet apart, progressed all the way to the back of the house, the same polished floors and high ceilings with *vigas* trailing along.

Muscles disappeared when Amaya entered, graceful and smiling. "Welcome!"

I smiled at her and introduced Denise.

"Lynn and Denise," she said, each of her hands reaching for one of ours. It pleases me that we can have lunch together." She walked beside us through the long wide hall with commodious rooms on both sides. All of them had open entries that mirrored the hall's wide archways.

First we passed the *sala* or living room to the right, the library to the left. The next room on the left was a masculine study that also opened into the library—Hiroshi's, I assumed. A large collection of spearpoints, framed without glass, hung on the wall behind the tidy cherry desk. A matching credenza held his computer. The room across from it on the right was a more feminine space, Amaya's I supposed as we walked past. Next to it was a dining room so large it dwarfed the ebony banquette table with sixteen chairs. I noticed the cozier breakfast room on the left. Closed wide doors toward the back likely led to a kitchen and other service rooms. Oriental rugs and fresh flowers decorated every room. None was overcrowded with furniture and table tops weren't cluttered with objects. In this home, less was more.

The last area was a beautiful garden room that ran across the back of the house. Its massive windows looked out over a spectacular view. The midday sun lit mountains that seemed to touch the azure sky. A single puffy cloud sailed slowly across the horizon. Two separate conversational areas were arranged to take advantage of the view. On the far left I noticed an artistic adobe stairway curving upwards, probably to guestrooms and private areas. On the far right glass doors opened onto a colorful garden.

Amaya gestured to a round glass table. Three tall delicate orchids rose in the center, matched by lavender placemats and standing yellow napkins folded like candles. "It pleases me that you are my guests. It is peaceful and quiet here. Homes are scattered, and our closest neighbors come here only two weeks a year."

"This is lovely," said Denise. "I could spend the rest of my life . . ." She winced faintly at the common phrase, ". . . standing at these windows, painting the mountains at different times of day in different seasons of the year."

"You paint!" said Amaya. "I sculpt. My studio is upstairs." She lowered her eyes. "Not that I am good at it. I do it because it pleases me, not for fame or compliments."

"That is why I paint! It pleases my soul."

"What pleases your soul, Lynn?" asked Amaya.

Time in my inner sanctuary where my intellect rooms in harmony with my mysticism, I thought but didn't say. "Being with people I enjoy. Reading good books." And playing around with a novel I want to write someday—another thought I didn't say.

"Not serving the Lord as a bishop?"

I laughed. "It is questionable whether some aspects of being a bishop serve the *Lord!*" I laughed with them and added seriously, "There are many ways to serve. Like sculpting or painting. Or being generous to good causes." I smiled at Denise. "Or being courageous when life throws us a curve."

"Courage is important," agreed Amaya resolutely.

"So is forgiveness," said Denise. "We've all been hurt at times, some people much worse than others. But harboring grudges erodes our joy."

Amaya frowned. "Some things are unforgiveable."

17

After Ariel played them with another Houdini escape, Dan drove from President's Ranch toward Los Alamos. His mind was on the report to the President. Less than 24 hours on the job—and another escape. Failure was new to him.

His cell rang. "Hi, Cliff."

"I heard a rumor yesterday about the elite list. I see that it's confirmed. Congratulations." He sounded sincere. "I've arranged for you to see the surveillance you requested. LANL is expecting you."

"I can be there in about ten minutes. Thanks."

"I'm curious. Friend to friend, Dan, how did you get on that list?"

"Not by request."

Silence. "You'll need help. I have a good man in mind I could assign."

To keep eyes on me, thought Dan. "Thanks but I'm doing fine." *Right!*

"Let me know if I can be of further assistance."

"Thanks," he repeated.

A pause. "I want to be kept in the loop, Dan."

And first to the President to interpret the info to your advantage. Sorry old friend, but I'm retired. "I appreciate the surveillance, Cliff. I'll be in touch. Thanks again."

At LANL Dan was treated like Gen. Groves or even J. Robert Oppenheimer back in its beginning days. Red carpet instead of red tape. He watched the surveillance unaccompanied, uninterrupted and unquestioned. It told the whole story: The Ram speeds in a left turn onto 502, almost crashes into a Jeep. The chase begins. Brennan leaps out and rolls out of sight seconds before the Ram goes off the road into the ravine. A semi heading toward Los Alamos stops for a hitchhiker—a large Indian woman carrying a wrapped bundle like a baby. The driver reaches across the seat to open the door. *She* starts to get in. Suddenly drops the baby. Drags the driver out. Slams his head with a rock. Heaves him into the ravine. Climbs into the semi and drives on. Dan backed up that scene and reran it. Soon the semi passes a Jeep by the roadside with its turn light blinking. The semi reaches Los Alamos and parks at a truck stop. *He* gets out and walks away, a man in T-shirt, jeans, ball cap pulled low, carrying a gym bag. The surveillance supported Juan's scenario and Galen's report about the semi with tinted windows passing Chev's Jeep.

Dan moved on to the motorcycle surveillance: A black motorcycle leaves a storage facility and travels through residential neighborhoods toward the National Forest and into the mountains beyond satellite range. That information supported Lynn's anonymous caller's scenario. Who is that caller? Why is he involved? Why does Lynn protect his anonymity? Dan decided to let it go—for now.

He drove home to the quiet empty condo. It was unusual to be here without Denise. *Without Denise.* Don't go there!

Immediately he called a friend from the agency. "Dan here, Tony."

"Dan! It's been a while."

"I would appreciate a favor. I need to clear up some loose ends."

"Shoot."

Dan chuckled. "Dangerous thing to say to an operative."

"You'd miss anyway. Everybody—even the great Dan Dickerson—has to miss sometime."

"I need everything you have on Kwang-Sun Rhee." Dan was glad Tony didn't ask for a reason. All he had was hearsay regarding Rhee's shaken demeanor during a phone call—laughable to anyone who didn't know Galen. Juan was probably questioning Rhee right now, hopefully getting cooperation. The detective was skillful at exposing tiny crevices that widened into a cracked door. "He works for LANL so he's been through a security check."

"You need it immediately, I suppose."

"Like yesterday."

"Hang on. I'll do it now."

As Dan listened to the silence, he decided to try to clear up some other loose ends. The escape from the ranch confirmed for him that their target was trained. Also, Cliff had not yet responded to his request regarding the first computer search on Lynn.

Tony came back on. "Kwang-Sun Rhee—clean as a whistle."

Dan frowned. "OK. Also I need information about Ariel Hiram Brennan. Was he ever in the CIA? If so, why did he leave?"

"OK. Same urgency?"

"Absolutely. It's related to national security."

"It always is. I'll do my best."

"One more item. Could you check out who did a search on Tuesday for Bishop Lynn Peterson . . . ."

Tony interrupted. "That's a coincidence. The same request came from the Director's office this morning. They are interrogating him as we speak. I'm working on identifying the receiving computer. I'm getting close."

"When you succeed, I need the names on both ends."

For the first time Tony hesitated. "I don't know, Dan."

"I'm on an elite list encouraging cooperation. But check it out. Don't take my word for it." He meant it.

"Your word is enough for me."

"Unwise, my friend."

"Still the same old Dan. Retired or not."

"Thanks for your help, Tony. He ended the call, and the update for the President began to take shape. But he had nothing concrete. He wouldn't even have the Stetson's DNA results in time.

His cell rang, an incoming call from a blocked number. "Dickerson here."

The familiar distorted voice said, "One, Kwang-Sun Rhee received a call this morning. The number was blocked, but a call with the same start and end time was made from the ranch house you stormed. Two, Rhee was born in North Korea. He spent time in China. Three, my research indicates that PAPA does not exist. No." The call ended.

18

"Thank you, Kei," said Amaya to the petite woman who entered with a tray of soupbowls. She nodded toward the lobster bisque. "We have a simple lunch."

"Beautifully presented," I said.

"Worthy of a painting," added Denise.

"I am pleased you think so."

When Kei left, I said, "We were talking about forgiveness. I am fortunate to have so little to forgive in my fluffy life." Instantly my mind slammed to the drunk driver and precious Lyndie. I willed myself to refocus on the present moment.

Amaya said softly, "I guess Hiroshi received your share, Lynn. He has much to forgive." She looked away.

"What happened?" asked Denise with concern.

"It is a long story."

I smiled at her. "We have time."

"Before Hiroshi was born, his father helped his grandfather run the small family business. They did well until terrible World War II forced them into a Japanese internment camp in Arizona."

I winced at the injustice of that shameful chapter of U.S. history.

"His father, grandfather and their whole family lost all that they had—their business, their homes, and everything else they were unable to carry with them on the bus taking Japanese Americans to Arizona."

My mind flashed to a departure scene in *Schindler's List*, when the Jews were forced to leave on trains with only what they could carry. The Takahashi family's situation was different, of course. This wasn't Germany and they weren't Jews who would ultimately face extermination. But *this* happened in the United States of America, a democracy with *liberty and justice for all!* Minus the except-for footnotes from generation to generation.

"They had done nothing wrong," Amaya continued, "but that was not the issue. Being *Japanese* Americans was the problem." She looked down and when she spoke again, her intensity was gone. "I am sorry. I did not mean to be rude." She smiled and changed the subject. "Let me tell you about my grandbaby."

"Please do," we affirmed simultaneously.

Amaya laughed. "I won't bore you with that. We don't have one. But isn't that the topic that everyone dreads except the speaker?"

I smiled. "You may be right—until they also become grandparents." We all laughed. I forced mine. I would never have that privilege. Precious Lyndie. Again, I pulled out of my dive.

Light conversation lasted until Kei entered again, following soup with crab salad.

"I know that wasn't the end of your story about Hiroshi," said Denise as she picked up her fork. "Tell us the rest."

Amaya sighed. "Hiroshi's father joined the military." She looked away from us toward the garden. "Their extended family still lived in Hiroshima. I cannot imagine how his father felt when that city was bombed and the fatality rate ultimately reached 200,000. Sometimes I don't understand how Hiroshi can abide the genocide of his ancestors. He must not have a single bone of vengeance in his body."

I was struck with a thought I didn't like: Or perhaps he hides it well.

Denise shook her head and said sympathetically. "They didn't trust Japanese American citizens with *freedom*, but they trusted them to *fight* on the *right side*. That is a logic challenge!"

"Agreed," I said.

"His family did not complain; they worked hard. The experience taught his father—and therefore Hiroshi—about injustice through the internment, but also about compassion through the Pennsylvania Quakers who eventually took in the family and found his grandfather a job."

"The faithful Quakers!" I said.

"There was also a Methodist minister who helped them and many others while they were in the internment camp. That minister lived his faith."

Denise looked thoughtful. "Living out faith seems to be a piece of cake until it requires courage or forgiveness."

"When was Hiroshi born?" I asked.

"Not until fifteen years after their internment. They were still struggling to reach the financial level that had been taken away from them." She sighed again. "No more talk of that!" she said with authority. "Do we need to make up grandchildren stories?"

"Let's get ourselves married first," said Denise. "How did you meet Hiroshi?"

"He came to Kokura on ship-building business. It's a port city. We met and married." She smiled. "My wedding day was a happy day."

"Is your family from Kokura?" asked Denise.

"Not originally." Amaya paused. "My mother was orphaned at five years old and lived there with her aunt. It is where she was married. I was born there. Being an orphan was difficult for my mother." Amaya looked away and said softly, "She often talked to me about it."

Kie brought dessert and coffee.

"Key lime pie!" said Denise. "That's my favorite. And it's yellow, not that green stuff imitators try to push."

"Once I was considering ordering it in a restaurant," I said. "I asked the waiter if the key lime pie was yellow or green. He said, 'Green, of course, Ma'am. It's *lime*. But we have lemon pie too if you prefer yellow.'" Easy laughter, a respite from internment camps. "I understand his reasoning," I added in support of him, "but logic doesn't always triumph even in simple matters."

"Better a confused waiter than chef," Denise commented.

We chatted on, heavy conversation behind us. I enjoyed the time together but was beginning to feel anxious about the President's report. I should have spent lunch time getting information. I checked my watch, antsy to leave. "This has been lovely, Amaya." Denise and I thanked her and said sincerely how much we enjoyed it.

I drove the Juke out of the driveway back toward its temporary humble surroundings. "Amaya is interesting, isn't she," I commented.

"Very. I have never been in a more beautiful house."

"Neither have I." Yet, it seems to ring of beauty without peace, I thought but didn't say.

"Did you happen to look into any of the rooms as we walked down the hall, Lynn?"

"All of them."

"Do you remember the masculine one—probably Hiroshi's office?"

"It could introduce a bishop to coveting." I glanced at her and grinned.

Her brief smile ended in a frown. "I automatically notice anything framed. Did you see the spearpoints?"

"Yes."

"They clicked in my mind because Dan showed me his cell photo of the one you and Galen found." She paused. "I think two spearpoints were missing from Hiroshi's collection."

"I didn't notice that." I wished I'd been more observant.

"Every decorative item in his study is symmetrical and meticulously aligned—except for the framed spearpoints. It has space for 42 spearpoints: seven rows with six points in each row. But the bottom row only had four. The two end spaces were empty."

"Maybe he only has 40 in his collection."

"Think about it, Lynn. Since exact symmetry is obviously important to him, if he only had 40 spearpoints to begin with, why didn't he have it framed with eight rows and five spearpoints in each one? Or vice versa?"

"But if they are missing, wouldn't he notice?"

"*Two theories*, as Dan would say. First, when I'm used to something on my wall, I don't really look at it anymore. I see what I expect to see." She paused.

"And second?" I asked, glancing at her troubled face. The Juke's motor filled the silence. I waited.

When she spoke, her words were said in an unnerving tone. "Maybe, Lynn, he found a use for them."

19

I parked the Juke and was getting out when Dan pulled up. I waited for him.

"Hi, Lynn. No news on Brennan's escape. He seems to have vanished. Again."

Again and again and again, I thought but didn't say. No one but Zechariah Zeller seemed able to keep up with him.

"We were there! We had him! *No way* it could be blown!" He lowered his eyes. "So I left to keep my LANL appointment to look at yesterday's surveillance of Brennan's truck and motorcycle. I wanted to have that information before the President's report—which is going to be a non-report." He shook his head in self-condemnation. "I'm sorry, Lynn. I should have stayed at the ranch."

"The *President of the United States* requested you to make that report a *priority*. You're too hard on yourself, Dan." I unlocked the *casita* door, offered him a chair and changed the subject. "Did Denise have time to tell you she thinks two spearpoints are missing from Hiroshi's collection?"

"Yes, briefly. No details. I trust her eye, but it's a stretch to call it a clue." He looked at his watch and shifted back to the report. "Thirty minutes to go—and I don't have enough solid information to give President Benedict a reliable overview."

"Were Galen's leaps about Kwang-Sun Rhee helpful?"

"Interesting conjectures. A lot of *leaps*, as you called them. Yet not beyond possibility. I agree that only an employee could have stolen the toxin, and we know Kwang has access to the Lab's biowarfare research." He frowned. "Do you concur with Galen's observations of him at the Archbishop's dinner party?"

"I was less observant, but something about him was amiss. It's a feeling, not a logical deduction."

"IF Brennan read the report he intercepted, and IF it named Kwang as the thief, and IF Brennan was the other person on the phone this morning, and IF he was threatening blackmail, that could explain Kwang's agitation during the call." He paused. "Too many IFs to bet on it, but I'll keep all those points in mind when I have a crack at interrogating him."

"Not exactly helpful to the report for the President," I said. "Any non-IFs?"

"IF you trust your anonymous caller. He phoned me today with information. Mainly, he accessed phone records for Kwang's call. The start and end times matched a call from Brennan's ranch. Coincidence? He added that Kwang was born in North Korea and had ties with China. But my friend at the CIA who checked him out for me said he's 'Clean as a whistle.' I wonder where your guy found the contradictory information." Dan paused. "Would he make it up?"

I passed. But I trusted Zechariah Zeller's accuracy.

"Regardless, it doesn't fit that China would have Kwang steal the toxin and then use it to poison two CIA men—like putting the theft on Facebook. Someone else hired him." He skipped a beat. "Your guy also found no existence of PAPA."

"That seems to make it unanimous," I said. "Matt told me the archbishop knows Carlos was murdered. It's a longshot, but maybe he has other information too." While Dan paced, I looked up Joe's number at the cathedral and called on the landline.

"Archbishop Hannahan's office. This is Camila. May I help you?"

"I'm Lynn Peterson, Camila. I had dinner with the archbishop . . . "

"Yes, Bishop Peterson," she said warmly as though we were old friends. Her cordiality reminded me of Fay. "He asked me to put you on his *Favorites* list. I have your cell phone number, but our caller ID doesn't recognize the phone you're using. Which do you prefer?"

"My cell phone developed a problem." A Zeller problem, I thought but didn't say. "Please list this number and ask him to call me. It is important."

"Your timing is excellent. He is between lectures. I'll contact him immediately, Bishop Peterson."

"Thank you, Camila." I hung up and looked at Dan. "She'll have him call."

He moved on. "We have feelers out, but the President needs concrete facts. I feel like a little boy whose homework isn't complete and he wants his mommy to call him in sick."

A scared little boy was so far from my image of Dan that all I could do was laugh. It was contagious. A tension release for both of us.

His cell rang. "Hi, Juan. How is it going with Kwang-Sun Rhee?" . . . "Smug and superior," Dan repeated for my benefit. "He's guilty but admits nothing." . . . "He made a $5,000 withdrawal?" Dan looked at me.

Maybe Galen's leaps weren't as big as we thought.

Dan continued. "Try this, Juan. *Speculation*: Well trained, Brennan reads the intercept before delivering it to his client and gets Rhee's name. *Fact*: Today Rhee gets a midmorning call, visibly shaking him. *Fact*: A call is made from Brennan's ranch house, beginning and ending at the exact time of Rhee's call. *Speculation*: The call is to initiate blackmail. *Fact*: Rhee withdraws $5,000 from his bank at noon. . . ."

"Here's what I learned about him from the CIA and our anonymous caller." Dan repeated the contradictory reports. "Also I think it's time to admit that PAPA doesn't exist. That leaves a ruse."

When he hung up, I said, "I still don't think Carlos would fall for a ruse."

"You didn't even know him, Lynn. You only saw him through the eyes of his loving and grieving wife."

True—the person who knew him best. But time to move on. "If Kwang could steal toxin for a client, why couldn't he steal a little extra at the same time. Maybe sell it to China later. Or to a terrorist organization."

"Let's not condemn him of too much too fast. But LANL should know how much toxin is missing. That's a start."

The landline rang. "Hello."

"Lynn, this is Joe. Camila said it is important that I call you." He sounded concerned. "Is everything all right?"

"Galen and I are fine."

"Good." Relief filled his voice. "Matt told me about the conversation with Marta. He said you were sensitive and helpful. Thank you for going with him."

"I enjoyed getting to know her." I came to the point. "I would appreciate some information if it doesn't break confidentiality. How did you learn that Carlos was murdered?"

"It isn't confidential at all. One of the cathedral volunteers is a good friend of Will, the medical examiner. They had lunch together yesterday, and Oliver told me about it."

Joe's voice went into his sonorous story mode, imitating Oliver:

About an hour after Will submitted his report and was getting ready to go home, officials came and took over. They treated him like he didn't know anything about being a medical examiner. I told him he should have taken them into his office and shown them all his degrees and awards. Will said they probably can't read. We both got a chuckle out of that. They said it was a heart attack, not murder, and told him he didn't know what he was talking about. While they were saying that, they were very busy searching Carlos' clothes. Every piece. Every lining. Every pocket reversed. All that for what they called a heart attack! They didn't find a thing. Will said he could have told them they wouldn't. He'd already searched—found one gum wrapper.

Joe relinquished his story-hour tone. "Oliver told me they took Carlos' personal possessions—wallet, cell, pen. They even took off his wedding ring!" He raised his voice. "That was Marta's decision to make, *not theirs!*"

"I feel so sorry for her, Joe. Thank you for telling me about this." I hesitated then asked another question. "Is there idle chatter about the way Carlos died?"

"No. His friends wouldn't want murder to reach Marta's ears and trouble her. People tell me all kinds of things they wouldn't normally say."

"I know how that is. Do you have confidence in the medical examiner?"

"Will is a man of honor and integrity, and he's very good at his job."

"And so is the man in this phone conversation right now. Thank you, Joe." He had answered all my questions without asking why I wanted to know. I hung up and looked at Dan.

"Well?" he asked.

I shook my head. "No copy of the formula found on Carlos."

"So he met with PAPA first." A deep sigh. "That means the people behind the ruse now have the formula for the latest biowarfare toxin!"

The book rang. "Here we go." I reached for the President's phone.

Dan frowned. "This is an embarrassing report."

.

20

"Hello, Madam President," I said.

"I know you had little time to prepare an update. Do you have anything new?"

"Not as much as we'd hoped."

Dan tore a sheet from his legal pad and handed it to me. His cell rang.

I looked at his neat hand-written notes. "Regarding the formula: No good news. Both the M.E. and officials who claimed the body did a thorough search. They found nothing. So he had already transferred it before he died."

I overheard Dan say Thanks, Tony, and glanced at him. He was scribbling more notes. I turned my attention back to the President. "Regarding PAPA: No dots to connect. Officials found nothing helpful on Carlos' computer. No communication with the FBI or CIA or anything called PAPA." I remembered to refer to Dan as Spearpoint. "Spearpoint affirms that PAPA was a ruse."

"It is crucial that we find out who has that formula," said the President. "I know Dan is doing his best, and his best is *the* best. Tell him finding the formula continues to be my top priority."

"Yes, Madam President. Regarding the toxin theft: A suspect is in custody in Santa Fe—a scientist at LANL named Kwang-Sun Rhee. But the evidence against him is thin, and he has not confessed. Spearpoint will have an opportunity to question him later this afternoon. The CIA's background check when he applied at the Lab was satisfactory, but that has been contradicted by an outside source who discovered that he was born in North Korea and spent time in China. However, Spearpoint excludes China from the poisonings, assuming that if

Kwang provided China with the toxin, they would keep it secret, not use it to kill someone on the Plaza." I paused.

"I consider a suspect this soon to be very good news."

I moved on. "Regarding the assassin: Strong evidence points to Ariel Hiram Brennan. He used a CIA contact to search for information about me, and the agency identified the contact and interrogated him earlier today. We don't know the results. Brennan was almost caught this morning at his ranch in northern New Mexico, but he escaped. He may have tried to blackmail Kwang, but that is unconfirmed." Dan handed me his new information from Tony. I scanned the note. "Brennan was formerly with the CIA but dismissed. Unfortunately," I tossed in on my own, "they trained him too well in escape tactics."

"Ask Spearpoint to give Cliff the assassin's information and get his assistance. Anything else?"

"You asked about Hiroshi this morning. I was with his wife today and have one more detail if you're interested. By the way, she told me he is in DC for a meeting, but it's probably a coincidence."

"Ah, yes. Coincidences." She neither affirmed nor denied a meeting, but there was a smile in her voice. "What is the detail?"

"His parents and grandparents were in an internment camp in Arizona during World War II, and his father was one of the Japanese Americans who served our country during that war."

"We prefer to forget the internment pages of our history," she said, her sadness palpable. "That's easy for us. But for people like the Takahashis, it's an integral part of their family heritage." She paused. "Please tell Spearpoint he has done a remarkable job."

I repeated her words to him. He smiled—the first I'd seen since he had agreed to help her.

"So have you," she continued. "This is the most informative and fastest report I've received in a long time. My thanks to you both." She ended the call.

Dan and I bumped fists like a couple of teens, our fear of an embarrassing report replaced by affirmation from on high.

21

Dan paced the *casita*'s small living area as we reviewed the President's call. "We have zip on the copy of the toxin formula. Nothing fits." He paced faster. "One track is that Martinez stole it, gave it to PAPA, left no clues, and he's dead. The other track is that there is no formula theft and PAPA is a ruse. I don't even have any instinct about it, let alone a clue."

"I see one possibility, but I'm not very hopeful. Matt will be with Marta throughout the Vigil service. He may talk to her about whether she remembers anything else Carlos said. He's going to feel his way and won't do it if he thinks it might upset her."

"Understandable. *Not very hopeful*" he added, "is better than hopeless."

"Do you think the same person hired both Kwang and Brennan?"

"Yes, and I'm frustrated that we have nothing. It's someone skilled enough to leave no leads, or someone extremely detail-oriented who could foresee and handle all the facets. It was very well planned. But for what purpose? What was the motive?" He stopped pacing and looked at me, his eyes thoughtful.

"What?"

"I heard you tell the President that Hiroshi Takahashi's parents and grandparents were in an internment camp. I wonder how that family experience affected him."

"What do you mean?"

"It was probably the most defining moment in their lives. Their stories as he grew up would be embedded in him."

"Come on, Dan. I know you were suspicious of the Juke, but I hope you're not leaping to suspicion of Hiroshi because of conjectured family stories."

"Whoa, Lynn. There's a big gap between *wondering* about family impacts and *suspecting* someone of hiring bad people to do bad things."

"I'm sorry."

"I'll have more to go on after I question Kwang-Sun Rhee." He pulled out his car key. "Right now, despite the President's priority for me, my major concern is your safety and catching Ariel Hiram Brennan. He is walloping all of us, including the CIA!"

"Maybe he's scared and running and I'm safe now."

His look mirrored *the Galen look* of total exasperation. "I need to call Cliff." He pulled out his cell, and I watched him walk fast to the white convertible, phone to his ear.

22

Hiroshi, respectful but unawed, entered the Oval Office with the vice president. He'd been here before with presidents of both parties. Wealth had its privileges.

Dwight introduced him with that big sincere smile Americans loved. President Benedict rose from her desk and extended her hand. Hiroshi, aware of her small hand that seemed to enlarge his own, gave a humble nod. "Madam President," he said warmly, returning her smile while registering her expression, eyes, body language—aware that she was probably doing the same with him.

"Welcome, Hiroshi."

She too was respectful and unawed. No *Mr. Takahashi* here. He liked that.

She sat again and gestured to the dark leather chairs across from her desk.

He got it. This was to be a brief to-the-point meeting, not a cozy little conversation around the coffee table. He liked that too.

"Dwight is highly complimentary of you."

"Thank you for warning me. It means he will seek a contribution before I leave." He smiled congenially at the vice-president.

Dwight chuckled. "What a good idea!"

It was easy to smile here. Hiroshi also liked that. His eyes swept the Oval Office. No citations of honor, image-enhancing pictures, mementos. He found only two personal items. One was a scuffed old saddlebag in the display case. He wondered what secrets it held. The second was a sculpture he recognized as *The Shy One* by Alan Houser, a Chiricahua Apache who was awarded the National Medal of Arts and had lived in Santa Fe. Hiroshi nodded toward it. "I see we both appreciate Alan Houser—nee Haozous. He brings life and movement to cold hard bronze."

"I like him very much." Her warm Katie Couric voice caressed the words.

He had connected. His primary purpose for coming was achieved.

"You wanted to see me," she said.

Watchful, Hiroshi tiptoed into GANNS' concerns. His mind was on reading her response—a difficult task. Her blue-green eyes were alert but remained cautiously blank, offering no clue to her thoughts. She was as good at masking self-revelation as he was. Even her clothes—tailored yet feminine, with simple jewelry—offered few hints to her personality. It was her presence that struck him. She was confident without an air of superiority. She wore power comfortably, neither passive nor aggressive. She was already developing the reputation that she would listen and weigh but not be bought. He sensed that serving another term was less important to her than serving this one well. Surely not! Yet he trusted his trustworthy intuition. The President before him was a ship that could hold her own on stormy seas as well as shallow waters.

He came to the GANNS bottom line. "Madam President, the Board of Directors is unsure whether your administration will renew their contract."

Her eyes flashed from blank to spearpoint sharp. She lowered them and picked up the worn Mont Blanc pen on her desk, fingering it tenderly.

Hiroshi had read that it was the one her father had used, old Senator Morgan Heffron III, who had lived long enough to attend his daughter's inauguration.

"I can understand their concern." She looked at Dwight.

From his peripheral vision Hiroshi saw a slight nod.

President Benedict put the pen down and leaned forward. "As a member of that board, Hiroshi, you may or may not know of the potential danger LANL has brought to our country—and perhaps the globe. Some corporate boards operate mostly in the shadows."

He chose silence and blank eyes.

"The Biological Threat Reduction Program developed a top secret toxin and did not secure it adequately. Some was stolen, creating a biothreat, and the theft was not reported immediately." Her eyes seemed to scan his thoughts. "That disaster is compounded by their corresponding lack of antidote development. So far two people have been poisoned. One in the Santa Fe Plaza, as you probably know. It was called a heart attack. However, the rats of rumor are gnawing away at that cover-up."

Hiroshi did not react or respond. He knew all of this except that the cover-up was not holding.

"We now have a strong lead on the identity of the traitor who stole the toxin."

That was a bomb. Mask intact, Hiroshi restrained himself from asking questions.

"In addition we have learned that a copy of the formula was made. It is missing." She paused, then the ship sailed full speed ahead. "GANNS wonders about its contract? They are building a strong case against renewal."

He liked her directness. "I will report your concerns, Madam President."

"They should also know that the decision has not yet been made. Efforts to redeem the dysfunction that causes things like this would be timely and could be helpful."

He nodded. "Thank you, Madam President." He added sincerely, "I am glad you sit behind that desk."

She smiled. "Sometimes I am glad, and sometimes I'm not, Hiroshi. I have been told that you are charming. I was also told you are a *3-I* man, known for influence, integrity and international connections. It is good to get a face on the fine reputation."

"If you ever need a well-built ship to navigate stormy waters, I will assist you." He rose and bowed his head to her. Safely behind his unreadable mask, he recommitted himself to his lifelong goal, that secret passion stirring at the root of his soul.

"So, Madam President . . . you've met Hiroshi Takahashi," said Dwight in Labrador retriever mode. "What do you think of him?"

She weighed her response. "He seems genuine."

"*Seems?*"

"If he is who he appears to be, he could be a helpful member of my Inner Circle." She chose carefully the twelve members of her advisory team, placing knowledge and integrity above party affiliation and political opinions. All members were unpaid, nongovernment, and had expertise in various fields: a widely acclaimed national historian, a retired general with diplomatic skills, an environmental scientist, four international relations scholars, and specialists in the fields of health-care, education, poverty, and cyberspace. She expected members to state concerns in their areas of expertise, followed by a discussion based on penetrating questions. Opinions within the circle clashed, an asset not only for making good decisions but also for recognizing points of disagreement that warned her to explain those points carefully in public and political arenas. She withheld her personal ideas and opinions to prevent being told what they thought she wanted to hear. Her task was to listen, learn and draw holistic conclusions. The death of the twelfth member had left an opening in the financial area, a position that could offer insight regarding how potential policies could impact the corporate world nationally and internationally.

"Hiroshi is respected in the corporate world," said Dwight. He observed her a moment. "However, I understand your caution. You must be able to trust every member of the Inner Circle. You cannot risk an egotistical manipulator hiding behind a mask!" Dwight gave her his all-American smile. "I've been around politics a long time, Madam President, and you have done an extraordinary job to be so far along in these few months."

"Thank you, Dwight. You serve both as coach and cheerleader." She looked out the window at the sunlight that would soon be dusk, another day joining the past. She thought about the Takahashi family in the internment camp for Japanese Americans. "Do you think Hiroshi would be a good choice for my Inner Circle? I always appreciate your input."

"I trust him." He straightened his tie.

She'd noticed he did that when he was unsure whether he should temper a comment. She recalled Lynn's words about Hiroshi: *I sense that he wears conviviality like chainmail protection.* She agreed.

"But my opinion," Dwight continued, "doesn't guarantee that he's trustworthy in every way."

"I'm glad you gave me an opportunity to talk with him."

After Dwight left, she decided to weigh the Inner Circle decision when she had more information. She was puzzled by Hiroshi's neutrality about LANL. GANNS had sent him as their liaison, and he had served that role. Yet, she wasn't sure that he supported their contract renewal.

23

Galen and I sat at the kitchenette table and reviewed the day over Earl Grey tea and banana bread. Brennan filled our minds mentally, but by tacit agreement his name wasn't allowed to desecrate this time together. The landline rang. "Hello."

"Hi, Lynn. It's Matt. How are you?" Not routine and trite, but a question of genuine concern.

"I'm fine, thank you," I replied, determined to make it true.

"I talked with Marta this afternoon."

"How is she doing?"

"It is very difficult. They had many plans. Now it's too late. But I think she's strong and will get through this as well as anyone can. She has a lot of support."

I wanted to interrupt and get to my bottom line: Does she have information that will help us understand whether Carlos fell for a ruse? But instead I listened.

"Marta appreciated your coming with me to visit her. She feels you sincerely care and asked me to give you a special invitation to come to the Vigil service for Carlos tonight in the cathedral chapel —if you wish."

"Of course I'll come."

"She will be pleased. Galen, of course, is invited also."

"I'll check with him. Carlos has become part of our lives even though we didn't know him. Matt, do you know whether Marta is aware of the talk of murder?"

"She hasn't mentioned it. Who would tell her? It's enough now to bear his death without adding the violence of murder."

I agreed. The truth wasn't timely. Perhaps learning that one's loved one was murdered—even if perhaps she suspects it—is never timely. "I'll see you tonight."

I rejoined Galen at the table. He refilled our tea cups as I shared the conversation with him.

"Someday they will catch Brennan," he said, "and Marta will know the truth."

"But she is spared right now."

"Usually the whole bomb is dropped at once on the victim's family, and they have to hear about the murder every hour on the news."

I winced. Galen and I had experienced a lot of news coverage about the crash that killed Lyndie.

"Matt said Marta asked him to invite us to the Vigil service tonight." I looked at him.

"I want to go. Primarily so you can support Marta, but also we might learn something."

I thought of Carlos on the Plaza bench, meeting an obligation he felt to his country—never again to hug Marta or Reyna. Or cheer for the Saints.

24

Hiroshi waited in his Challenger for his pilots to take off. Home this morning. Home again tonight. In between a meeting with President Benedict. His excuse was LANL; but his real purpose was to foster a connection and size her up in a personal setting. He had found her only smallness to be physical.

Back to work. First he called Friedrich Streiff in Switzerland about the envelope the Challenger had flown to him. "Wait one more day, Friedrich. I'll provide instructions tomorrow."

The next call could be the most important he would ever make. He focused his power of intellect, experience and charm and called LANL CEO Perry Pearson. Hiroshi reported succinctly to him what the President had said about GANNS and the LANL contract renewal. He listened patiently as Perry countered her words with angry arrogant blithering—as expected.

When it seemed timely, Hiroshi calmed him. "You are in charge, Perry. But I have a couple of alternatives to offer, and also what I consider to be the likely outcome of each one. Would you like to hear them?"

"Of course, Mr. Takahashi. Your ideas are always welcome."

Now for the crucial part of the call. Hiroshi paused to focus clearly. He stated both options somberly, expressing no preference. He paused. "I invite you to spend the evening thinking about the bottom line and what you consider to be the best way to proceed." He paused again. "I want to warn you that words alone will not cut it with President Benedict." He strategically concluded with hope. "Her decision has not yet been made. In my judgment GANNS' leadership can be saved, but it requires change—*real* change—toward security, stability, competence and cooperation. It is not too late. It is in your able hands, Perry." He ended the call and made another.

This one was to Bob Benbrook, a successful reporter and trusted friend originally from Louisiana. He could count on Bob when he wanted a story on the front page of *The New York Times*. Hiroshi gave him the details and asked him to hold the story. "I'll call you back tomorrow to confirm in time for you to meet the deadline for Saturday's paper." They spent a few moments bantering and catching up on their lives. Hiroshi drew the conversation to a close. "Thank you, Bob. You'll be receiving season tickets for the Saints games, my friend. Maybe we can get together after one of them."

He put his phone away, sat back in the comfortable leather seat and watched the plane leave Earth behind. Done! He savored the aroma of his dinner, the best three-course cuisine a blip 9,000 feet in the air could provide. He was served on blue china with sterling silver. As he ate, he thought through the whole situation, beginning to end. It was like origami, folding the paper into a form, each fold the right length and made in the right order, each significant to the whole. He thought of the difficult folds in the origami green pheasant, the national bird of Japan. Again he felt the secret passion that stirred his soul. Close to fruition.

25

Galen and I arrived at the Cathedral Basilica of Saint Frances of Assisi and signed a guestbook before entering the chapel. Our names followed Hiroshi's. Marta and Reyna and the Martinez family greeted people. Some of the mourners mingled, softly whispering. Others sat in pews, waiting for the Glorious Mystery of the Rosary. Archbishop Hannahan circulated around the chapel, offering blessings and genuine interest. Matt stood near Marta. I was relieved to see her doing notably better than when we visited her yesterday morning, perhaps buoyed up by the comfort of all these caring people.

We stood behind Hiroshi in the line of friends slowly moving up the aisle toward the family. I realized he was unaware of our presence. Perhaps his mind was still on his business in DC. I wondered again what took him there.

Galen tapped him lightly on the arm. "Hello, Hiroshi."

He turned. "Lynn and Galen! I'm glad to see you." His smile ebbed to a deep sigh. "I wish it were under different circumstances."

I heard genuine sadness in the timeworn statement.

Galen picked up on it too. "It sounds like Carlos Martinez was more than an acquaintance."

"An old friend and a fine man. He grew up in New Orleans and worked for me. I provided his scholarship to Tulane. He didn't know it, of course. That was a long time ago. He paused, his eyes gazing on old memories. "Later I helped him get his maintenance engineer position at LANL."

Janitor. Custodian. Maintenance engineer. A classic example, I thought, of how word choices paint different images of the same thing.

"I didn't realize that you knew Carlos," he continued.

"I know Marta," I said.

He sighed again and changed the subject. "You could probably tell how dismayed I was by Kwang-Sun Rhee's remarks at Joe's dinner party."

I wanted to apologize for Kwang's insensitivity when he lauded the atom bomb's death rate, and to express admiration for his and Amaya's restraint. But I didn't.

"The Plaza seemed more important to him," Hiroshi continued, "than the man who died."

I agreed, but I didn't want to go there. "I had lunch with Amaya today. It was lovely. How kind of her to invite us to your beautiful home."

"I was there for a few minutes before coming here. She told me how much she enjoyed it." We continued to chat softly as we made our way up the aisle to the front.

As Hiroshi stepped forward, he nodded at Matt and hugged Marta, and began to lift up memories of Carlos' life.

I wasn't trying to listen to their conversation, but I couldn't help overhearing.

"When it happened, Mr. Takahashi," Marta said, "he was wearing a New Orleans Saints sweatshirt. You probably don't remember—you do so many nice things—but he took me to New Orleans for the Super Bowl when the Saints won it. He told me you got the tickets for him." Tears came to her eyes. "It was a very special trip. Thank you."

"My pleasure, Marta."

"Our last goodbye was at 11:30 Sunday when he left for Santa Fe. He looked very nice."

Hiroshi smiled at her. "Yes he did."

She shifted her gaze for an instant. "I keep wondering why he changed into his Saints sweatshirt." Her soft voice rose like a delicate solo above the hummed murmurings in the chapel. She looked small and frail, her sad eyes as dark as her black dress. Her hand was in Hiroshi's, drawing comfort. "Carlos was really looking forward to your lunch together." Her tears spilled over. "It brings comfort to know he was with you when he ate his final meal on Earth."

Matt caught my eye, both of us aware that Marta had omitted a significant detail when she told us Carlos' story. Surely Carlos did not give the toxin formula to Hiroshi Takahashi! I hoped without hope that their lunch together was not a guilty verdict.

26

It brings comfort to know he was with you when he ate his final meal on earth. Marta's words rang in my mind as the cathedral bells chimed eight o'clock this Friday morning. I cupped my hands around my coffee, troubled about Hiroshi. Charming and generous? Yes. A hidden side? Perhaps.

Galen set his cup down and called Dan. "We need to talk. . . ." "Thanks." He ended the call. "Dan will be here in twenty minutes."

He arrived in fifteen. "Tell me."

"First, how is Denise?" I asked. "I hope yesterday didn't wear her out."

His anxious face eased into a smile. "I think it was good for her. She's doing well."

"Coffee?" I asked.

"Please. Black. Tell me," he repeated to Galen.

"It's about Hiroshi Takahashi. Perhaps trivial, possibly vital."

"You wouldn't have called if you think it's trivial."

Galen told Dan about being at the Vigil service and overhearing a conversation between Marta and Hiroshi. "We've all been trying to figure out whether Carlos met with anyone before his Plaza meeting at 4:00. He did." Galen paused. "He and Hiroshi had lunch together Sunday noon."

Dan's face convicted Hiroshi. "So he has the copy of the biotoxin formula."

"Maybe the two old friends were simply having lunch together," I suggested, longing to believe it.

Dan moved on. "Carlos trusted Hiroshi. That's why he fell for the PAPA ruse. We need hand-off evidence. Mrs. Martinez probably knows where they ate. Let's ask her . . . ."

I interrupted. "Her husband's service is this morning, Dan. No probing questions on this difficult day of grief." His eyes softened, and I wondered if he was thinking of Denise and that his own difficult day might come.

"Of course, Lynn. You're right."

Galen broke the silence. "We're stymied on Hiroshi for the moment. Did you question Kwang-Sun Rhee?"

"Last night. Successfully." Dan wondered how many times he had lured a fish to stray from the path of denial. His interrogation streamed across his mental screen:

I watch through the glass. The interrogation is going nowhere, blocked by Rhee's cocky confidence. His smirk says he's home free.

I step in and take over. Look at his face and see the image of Gary's body. Rhee deserves back alley tactics! I start to lunge at him. Restrain my rage. I could kill him!

I cool down. Play the game I'm skilled at. Use legal tactics to ensure legal revenge. This one is for you, Gary. I take a breath. Silently eye Rhee for a long hostile moment. See a hairline crack in his confidence.

And I go fishing. I play him like a rainbow trout in a mountain stream. Loosening and tightening the slack. Gradually I sense how to reel him in. He is wary, weary, wastes energy splashing around.

I am patient, gradually wearing him down, moving from his denial to his understanding of his situation. We both know he is a thief, a traitor and an accomplice in two murders by providing the means—poison. And one of those victims is Gary, right beside me in this boat. He tries to wiggle out of the theft. No deal. I suggest that he may have partnered with killers before and we're looking into other poison murders His smirk is long gone.

Raising my rod and tightening the line for the catch, I remove a sheet of paper from my pocket. Slowly unfold it. Study it. "Interesting. First your theft. Then your blackmail payment." I stare at him, shake my head. Eye the paper again. "A large recent cash withdrawal."

His guilt is written in bold caps across his face. Confirmation. "There is one way you can help yourself."

Rhee slumps and confesses in hopes of a deal. Caught!

Dan took no pride in the fact that he had misrepresented a few things to Rhee. Like waving a piece of paper that had nothing to do with a bank withdrawal. But I would do it again, he thought. The guilty opt for a deal.

Lynn's voice brought him back to the present. "Who hired Kwang?"

"He said he doesn't know, and I believe him. No clues have been found. He's playing it like one of the good guys now, hiding nothing, trying to get a deal. But all he could do was give us the drop site."

Galen leaned forward. "Where?"

"Here in Santa Fe. Not far from our condo." Dan gestured up toward the ski area. "A large secluded house that is used only two weeks a year. Cedars and *piñons* surround the patio, and it has an outdoor kiva. Investigators found an empty metal box hidden among the trees near a walking trail not far from the house. One of his prints was on it, and he said the box had been hidden behind logs in the kiva. He had been directed to leave the toxin inside it and remove the cash. He assumed his client was observing from a distance within rifle range."

"Do you know how much toxin was stolen?" I asked.

Dan nodded. "He told us, and it matches the amount LANL found missing—a very small amount. He wouldn't have kept any for himself—it would be evidence against him." He turned to Galen. "You did well to pick up on his behavior during that blackmail call. Thank you."

"I'm glad I happened to be there when the call came."

"President's Ranch gave us a lot of information about Brennan. For starters, the black Harley in the satellite images is in his garage, a bathroom glass and comb yielded DNA results matching the Stetson found at the truck's crash site, and we have his photo as a CIA operative. Ariel Hiram Brennan is definitely our man."

"Our *escaped* man," noted Galen.

I felt sympathy for Dan who was trying so hard. "You've learned a lot in 24 hours, and you've been really close twice."

"Thanks, Lynn. But *really close* doesn't cut it." He looked at Galen. "We *will* get him. I promise you that."

27

Hiroshi sat reverently in the cathedral as Archbishop Hannahan officiated over the Requiem Mass for Carlos Martinez. Flowers, symbols of transient beauty, scented the mourning air with an aura of hope. Amaya had begun crying as soon as they took their seats. He put his arm around her as she continued to weep silently. When she fumbled in her purse for more tissues, he handed her his custom monogrammed handkerchief. The gesture carried his mind back through the long Takahashi family journey from internment during WWII to his own success as a shipbuilder. During the ancient low-voiced *oratio secreta*, now simply the "Secret," Hiroshi thought about his own secrets, none of which would ever be orated.

At the conclusion of the Requiem Mass, the cathedral bells pealed over Santa Fe. Each time he heard them—whether here or in New Orleans—he hoped that cathedral bells would ring for him when his time came.

"A fitting service for Carlos," he said as he took Amaya home. He drove with his left hand and placed his right over hers. "It was difficult for you." Extraordinarily so, he thought. She seldom showed emotion at funerals.

"I will be all right," she assured him.

Though more tears contradicted her statement, he opted to accept her words. He had a meeting with Perry Pearson and wanted to arrive first. He walked her to the door and gently kissed her goodbye.

Hiroshi parked his Jaguar in the Municipal Parking Lot and waited for the LANL CEO. Perry had driven in early from Los Alamos to attend the service for Carlos. Not one to miss an opportunity to make points, he'd had a PR photographer in tow to record his consoling presence for newsprint and social media.

Alone and right on time, Perry parked beside him. Hiroshi motioned for him to get in the car. His disappointed face was not a surprise. The CEO would rather be seen in a restaurant with *Mr. Takahashi* than meet in the car, but he opened the door and climbed in.

"We must talk in complete privacy," Hiroshi explained, omitting that their conversation would be taped.

"I understand. That is a wise decision." Perry, as predicted, opted for affability over yesterday's arrogance and anger. "Thank you for telling me about your conversation with the President." He looked down at the floorboard. "I apologize for my response yesterday. I was taken by surprise." The humiliating apology behind him, he went into defensive mode. "I did not expect her to be so well informed."

"I was surprised also." Hiroshi tossed him a compliment. "You have an important position that calls for wise judgment in difficult circumstances." He paused as though weighing the import of what he was about to say. "Have you reflected on the alternatives I mentioned yesterday after meeting with the President?"

"I have thought about nothing else."

"Have you reflected on their potential outcomes?"

Perry waited, searching Hiroshi's face.

Hiroshi remained silent, watching him try to read the blank face before him. He wondered what the CEO would decide. Truth? Lie? Half truth, half lie?

Finally Perry spoke. "To be honest, which in this situation is uncomfortable and humbling, I didn't even know the formula was copied until the President told you."

Hiroshi returned truth for truth. "Your honesty is commendable, Perry, and to wear humility is an attribute."

"Would you mind reviewing the two alternatives you suggested yesterday?"

"I will reiterate them, but the decision is yours to make. You are in charge." He held out his left hand. "On one hand is the option to assume that the theft of a copy of the formula is true. If so, you would put your energy and resources into catching the persons involved and getting it back." He frowned and shook his head. "Of course, two thefts so close together—poison and formula— could leave the impression that LANL is poorly run."

Perry nodded.

Hiroshi extended his right hand. "I also see a second alternative. Perhaps the formula theft is rumor. Obviously, if supportive evidence existed, you would have discovered it, just like you discovered the toxin theft." He paused and frowned again. "Actually, Perry, I see the timing as suspect. A formula theft is rumored, discrediting GANNS at precisely the time when your contract is coming up for renewal. Can that merely be coincidence? Or is it more likely to be a false rumor created by a competitor? If the rumor is false, you would put GANNS energy and resources into refuting it. GANNS is too important to our country's security to be sidetracked or derailed by unsubstantiated rumors."

"GANNS will *not* be taken down by rumors!" Arrogance and anger returned. "We have the power to destroy any part of the world we choose. We can certainly handle malicious competition!"

"I want to repeat that you are in charge, Perry, and the decision is yours. I will be helpful to you any way I can, whatever you decide."

The meeting had taken less time than expected. Hiroshi rushed home, parked in the garage and made the calls he had promised yesterday while on his Challenger. He phoned Friedrich Streiff in Geneva regarding the envelope flown to him and gave him instructions. Then he called Bob Benbrook at *The New York Times*, finalizing the story they had discussed. Bob thanked him and said it would run in tomorrow's paper.

28

The landline rang. I answered.

"Dan here. Tonight should be a good opportunity to catch Brennan. But it involves you."

"So you have a plan?"

"Maybe. Maybe not."

A predictable response.

"Shall I come back over now?" he asked. "Time is a factor."

"Sure."

When he arrived, he came straight to the point, pacing. "Zozobra is tonight, a huge Santa Fe event for tourists and locals alike. Brennan's style indicates that he likes an audience. I think he will assume you both are there and will try to spot Lynn."

Galen frowned. "Obviously he'll be wrong."

"I understand your concern," said Dan softly, evenly. "But the best way to protect her is to catch him. We'll keep her covered."

Galen shook his head. "You'll know exactly which person in that mob to nab?"

"The crowd is the gift. He won't be able to maneuver nimbly."

"This killer posed as a mother with a baby and it worked! Tonight he'll just saunter in looking like his CIA photo? Come on, Dan!"

"I know how to do this."

"If you get it wrong, you and I aren't the ones who pay!"

Silence.

I broke it. "I'm in the room, gentlemen. Talk *to* me instead of *about* me. It's *my* decision." I looked at Galen. Then Dan. And back to Galen. "I will risk it," I said, using my *nonnegotiable* tone.

Galen's eyes reflected the ancient male instinct to haul me over his shoulder and carry me to the rear of the cave for protection. "Brennan wants to *kill* you!"

I stared back. "*I'm* going to Zozobra tonight. You are free to stay home if you wish."

Neither of us blinked, like always. And, like always, I knew we would make up before going to sleep. The only new dynamic in our standoff was an audience. Not good. I turned the tension down a notch and tried to explain. "Please understand. I *want* to do this. Not only for Carlos and Marta and their family, but for me. Yes, Ariel Hiram Brennan does want to get me. And I don't want to spend my days wondering whether he is around the next corner."

Another silence. "Are you *sure*, Lynn?"

"Yes."

A heavy sigh followed. Then eyes filled with love met mine, and he put his arm around me. "OK, Dan. What's the plan? We must make it perfect."

"I've inspected Fort Marcy Park and selected the best place for us." He was strictly business. Straightforward. Strategic. "Let's do a verbal pre-run. We're at Zozobra. All our troubles are burned with Old Man Gloom for another year. Think super party. Like *Mardi Gras* in New Orleans."

"Tonight may be more about bullets than beads," Galen countered.

"We play this calmly," said Dan. "Be natural. No glancing around or nervous tics. Lynn, wear your bishop's mask tonight. You're very good at hiding your thoughts and feelings behind it."

Compliment or accusation? Possibly both.

"Who will be close to Lynn?"

"You," said Dan.

"Of course me."

"Fay has talked a lot about you. You're a major asset tonight. If you want to be armed, I can arrange a Beretta 92A1."

"I'd like a little help."

"I'll be right there with you. So will Juan and his team. We'll have plenty of police on duty, which always happens at Zozobra, so it won't send a warning signal. And we'll have every undercover cop and detective team we can get, plus some well-placed marksmen. Also Lynn's 'invisible protection' team provided by Cliff has worked shifts around the clock since Tuesday afternoon, and they all will be there tonight except for the one watching this *casita*. It's a good team," he added, "since Moore was dismissed. Brennan can't get to you, Lynn, without getting through all of us."

And what can I do, I wondered. No gun or knife. I still don't know karate. I'm just a words-woman. "I'm not sure what to expect, Dan, but I'm not helpless."

"No argument from me."

"*All* of you there tonight? It's overwhelming."

"We are committed to keeping you safe *and* to catching Brennan. It is *imperative* to put that man away!" He paused. "But think about it again, Lynn. Are you sure you want to do this?"

I nodded.

Galen's pupils moved back and forth, thinking, evaluating. "Any special assignment for me?"

"You're the last line of defense. Get her out of there if something goes wrong." Then he smiled, shifted the mood, and spoke lightly. "Your role is simple tonight. All you have to do is be your logical/egghead/marksman/kick-boxing self."

It felt good to laugh.

Dan moved toward the door. I need to get going and make sure everything is in place. A few plainclothes cops will be out there this afternoon, nonchalantly wandering around and scoping for any suspicious behavior. I'll pick you up at 6:00 in a black Range Rover CAV."

"CAV?" I asked.

"Custom armored vehicle."

That was scary. I tried to picture myself at Zozobra. Fear blocked the image. I opted to add the additional protection of a man loyal personally and proven professionally. "Can you give us a couple more minutes, Dan?"

He nodded.

"Just play along. OK?" I removed my cell from the drawer and said, "Call Dan." *Oh, please be listening, Zechariah Zeller. This call is meant for you.*

Dan looked puzzled but answered on the second ring. I told him we planned to go to Zozobra tonight and invited him and Denise to come along. He agreed. "See you tonight around six." I ended the call.

Dan put his cell in his pocket. "*That* was weird!"

"You'll get used to her," Galen said fondly. Abruptly his demeanor changed. "I still see Zozobra as inordinately risky for Lynn. I want the Beretta." His piercing dark eyes met Dan's. "*Not* getting him tonight is *not* an option."

"*We'll get him,*" Dan vowed.

A simple handshake. A life or death pact. "*So be it.*" said Galen.

29

Galen and Dan, both armed, stood beside me in Fort Marcy Park. "Don't forget," said Dan. "Fun on your face, not fear."

Behind a facade of nonanxious presence my tension built like a race horse at the starting gate. I stared up at Zozobra to distract my mind from my real purpose tonight. The massive animated marionette, annually doomed to go up in flames, stood about five stories tall. Seeing him surpassed my imagination. His head twisted, his eyes rolled. He flailed his arms, roared his threats. The surreal and grotesque scene was set in a party atmosphere, back-dropped by evening sun and ageless mountains.

Galen craned his neck to view Zozobra's huge ears, red mouth and ghoulish eyes. "He's built of wood sticks, chicken wire, and muslin. And," added the historian, "bushels of shredded paper that traditionally included divorce papers, outdated police reports and paid-off mortgages."

I wondered if he too was focused on Zozobra to ward off anxiety. I turned my attention to the park. It bloomed with people dressed in rainbow colors. Smells wafted from burritos, roasted corn, cinnamon almonds and other crowd-pleasers offered by a dozen vendors. High school clubs sold drinks and candy, joking and laughing while they counted out change. Children ran around chasing each other, laughing and free. Strollers were banned because they slowed the long security lines, so Daddies and Grampas toted the toddlers, and Mommies and Grammies carried the babies. Ensembles played, soloists sang. Dancers danced. The crowd clapped to happy music. I could feel the energy of a gathered body. Celebration. Ritual. The power of community—as old as the human race. Beneath the colorful scene, I felt an undertow.

Anxiety. Apprehension. Fear. The power of a death threat—also as old as the human race.

"The Zozobra atmosphere is puzzling," Galen said to Dan. "But it's festive. I see why you mentioned *Mardi Gras*."

"Both are big parties," I agreed, pretending we were engaged in a normal conversation. "But shouting *Throw me something, mister!* casts a different spell than *Burn him! Burn him!*"

Galen donned a smile. "Your comment is revealing. It says you're not into violence—practicing avarice is your thing."

"And that comment tells me you're not much for silence. Practicing prideful analysis is your thing."

He put his arm around me and forced a laugh, but I felt his ready-to-spring tautness. My own edge of fear seeped into my nerve endings. Keep the façade, I reminded myself.

"There's Hiroshi," said Galen.

We waved at him. Amaya wasn't with him. Understandable. This was not the place for a person uncomfortable in crowds.

He waved back. The man beside him looked familiar. I realized it was Perry Pearson. *The New Mexican* had run his photo with an article about LANL this week.

I scanned the park and saw a few people I knew. I smiled at Ramon from La Fonda. Waved at Chev Tupatu, who gave me an encouraging nod. The police officers chaperoned the party in a jovial low-key manner. Some of them skirted the edges of the park. Others mingled with the people. Among the minglers were the three officers who had rushed to Carlos' bench in the Plaza. They were nearby and seemed to be keeping me in their line of vision.

Young Ian walked by with his partner Vernon. "Have you found any bodies in a trunk lately?" he asked me with a wink.

I smiled at him. "I hope you're there if it ever happens again, Ian."

"I'll assign you to crowd control." He lowered his voice. "I was told what might go down tonight. We'll keep you safe, Ma'am."

A bolt of fear surged through me. I masked it. He'd meant to be comforting. "Thank you." I tried to add *I'll be fine* but couldn't shape the words. I continued to scan the park. Matt and Joe were making their way through the crowd. Matt saw me and waved. Popular and beloved Joe progressed slowly, greeting his greeters.

Matt finally left him behind and made his way to us. "Joe will join us. First he has the daunting task of speaking to everyone he knows. Which is just about everyone here."

Dan eyed him.

I introduced them. "Bishop Matt Langham. Dan Dickerson."

Straight-to-the-point Dan said, "You visited Mrs. Martinez with Lynn."

"Yes." Matt donned his own bishop-blank face. "Lynn was kind enough to join me in a pastoral call on a widow."

I heard Dan mutter something that sounded like *Two of a kind.* But the crowd's chant was too loud to be sure.

Matt bent to my ear. "*Burn him! Burn him!* Are we back at the Roman Coliseum?"

"We've made a little progress. Zozobra is only an effigy."

He smiled. "And there are no hungry lions."

"The chant troubles me too," I confessed. "Perhaps I take some things too seriously."

"Maybe both of us do. Let's join the party."

The only gloom in the park was Old Man Gloom—and my own, hidden beneath my mask as I pretended to be oblivious to what I knew to be true. This setting would work well for the man with the menacing voice who had spoken Lyndie's name and threatened me. Regardless of Dan's intentions, Galen was right to be concerned. I am bait for Ariel Hiram Brennan in a *Burn him!* scenario. I wanted to step outside myself and watch from the bleachers.

30

Dan was alert to everything around him. Scanning the crowd for a disguised Ariel Hiram Brennan. Zooming in for incongruence, wary demeanor, suspicious actions. Trusting his instincts. Keeping his face frozen in party visage. Wired. Ready.

The question in his mind was not *if* but *when*. He banked on a character flaw indicated by Brennan's previous actions: Arrogance overshadowed wisdom. Confident in his ability to escape, he murdered a man on the people-filled Santa Fe Plaza on Monday afternoon, and Wednesday morning he walked blatantly down Lincoln past the crime scene to see if his potential target could identify him. Altruism? Dan doubted it. He would have been drawn by the challenge of returning and was playing the odds that she wouldn't recognize him. He would come tonight to terminate Lynn, not only because she could identify him as the poisoner, but also because she had demeaned and eluded him. He was like a bulldog tasting the prey in his mouth, shaking his head ferociously from side to side, never letting go. It fit his ego to play before a large audience, as he had in the Plaza. Dan's instincts told him the escape artist was a man who thrived on challenges.

So much ground to cover! So many people to observe! Dan scanned the broad perimeter and saw Juan and Esteban by the fence. Both watchful, skilled, experienced. The trio had developed tonight's strategy together. An excellent plan that called for a lot of good people whose competence and silence could be trusted. Many in uniforms, many not. All willing to give their lives, including him. But deep down Dan knew proficiency, commitment and strategy might not be enough. Ultimately, total protection was impossible in a setting like this. He recommitted to stick to Lynn like Velcro.

Juan was talking to a young man outside the fence, stopped from entry by the *No Dogs* rule. Dan recognized Ryan Roberts, whose hand rested on a white collie—better outside the fence with Pal than inside it without him. Dan caught Juan's eye and motioned for him and Esteban to join him near Lynn. It was time to begin the dance with fate.

><del>×</del>×⊀ ><del>×</del>×⊀ ><del>×</del>×⊀

Zechariah Zeller parked his vehicle along Artist's Road and ambled toward Fort Marcy Park. He was dressed to be invisible— white T-shirt beneath an unnotable jacket, faded jeans, old sneakers. An Albuquerque Isotopes baseball cap covered most of his hair, dyed blond, and the brim shaded his face. Normally when he walked into a crowded area, the power and intimidation he exuded parted the sea of people. Not always helpful. No. Tonight he transformed himself into an invisible entity. His role was not to part the sea, but to blend in unnoticed with the crowd and kill Brennan in time to save pretty *Frau* Peterson. He knew he could do it. He had always been able to do what was necessary. *Except save you, Mutter.*

A man alone would get a second look from security, so he stayed close to the family ahead of him as they drew near the checkpoint. He laughed and talked with them in American English as though part of their group. The versatile multi-lingual shooter wanted by the FBI passed through security without a glitch.

He meandered through the park toward a trash can near the fence and tossed in a wadded piece of paper. He missed and bent down to pick it up. Reached for his Glock 31 .357 sandwiched between two rocks, hidden there this afternoon immediately after listening to *Frau* Peterson's call to the man named Dan. His roomy opened jacket dipped to the ground and hid the gun while he retrieved it and stuck it safely inside his belt in one smooth gesture. The Glock was made in Austria, his home country, by a company that had first made curtain rods. Both rods and guns shaped into hollow metal—one for décor, the other for death. He picked up his wad of paper, stood and threw the litter in the trash can. So easy.

At first he stayed his distance from *Frau* Peterson. He needed to focus and listen and learn, to figure out the *who* and the *how*. He scoped out every man in her vicinity, noted details that told a story about them and gave him a glimpse of the whole person. He had seen Brennan several times, but knowing what he looked like would not help. No. He was superb at disguise and would not be recognizable tonight. Yet two distinguishing traits could not be changed: height and build. Though that helped eliminate a good portion of the crowd, it was still like looking for a pet goldfish in the Adriatic Sea.

He changed focus from *who* to *how*. If Brennan's weapon of choice followed his poisoned spearpoint pattern, he would stand very near his target. Hiding in the distance and using a sniper tactic seemed unlikely. The crowd was in constant motion. Small *Frau* Peterson would be a difficult target in their midst, and only one shot could be fired. I could do it, he thought, but I do not miss. No. With only one chance, he doubted Brennan would risk missing. He is thorough and methodical, close up and personal. But I must still watch for a red laser dot on pretty *Frau* Peterson's head.

He began to make his way toward her. *Herr* Peterson stood to her left. The man named Dan would be the one on her right, the man I've spoken to on the phone and given helpful information, the man *Frau* Peterson called on her cell this afternoon. She wanted me to hear their conversation. Wanted me to know she would be here. Wanted me to come. He smiled to himself. Oh, yes. Pretty *Frau* Peterson needs me. He liked knowing that.

The man waiting in the security line looked older than he was. He walked heavily on his black wooden cane, hatless and white-haired, with white eyebrows and a tidy white beard. He was hunched over so severely that his back and neck were parallel with the ground. His shoes were scuffed, his pants an inch too short, his wrinkled shirt peeked out from a roomy jacket with worn elbows and frayed sleeves. He saw pity in the eyes of the people around him when he lifted his face to look up. He said nothing but offered them a brave smile.

He felt he deserved their pity, but for different reasons. Inferior agents of the law had stormed President's Ranch, his old family home. Their attempted forced entry to his storage unit in Los Alamos had set off the security bomb and destroyed his well-stocked safe haven.

All because of Lynn Peterson. That debt would be paid while Zozobra danced.

Ariel Hiram Brennan, stooped and needy, made it easily through security. No questions. No search. No problem with his cane.

The crowd was larger than he had expected, but his precise and methodical plan should still work. *Should*! That word again. It *would* work! It had to.

He saw Galen Peterson. His height made him an easy target. There she was beside him! They were surrounded by people. But that meant nothing. Everyone here was surrounded by people. He made his way through the park easier than expected. He found that their awareness of his cane and bent back, subconsciously if not consciously, caused them to give him space. Their courtesy benefited them—this cane was lethal.

He felt his rage grow as he drew close to Lynn Peterson. But not too close. He stooped and caned his way until he had staked out his place in the crowd. *Get a life* she had told him. He was about to do exactly that. Get a life—*hers*!

31

Burn him! Burn him! thundered the crowd in unison. Zozobra's eerie eyes glared down at us. He twisted his head from one side of the crowd to the other. His wide-lipped mouth roared rage. His arms flogged the smoky air.

Burn him! Burn him!

As the blaze rose in full force, I watched Zozobra's gyrations, heard his moans and groans. I turned away from him and glanced at Galen and Chev on one side of me, Dan and Juan on the other. I looked back at Matt and Joe behind me. Flickering light and shadows moved across their faces, mirroring the flames of Zozobra. *Old Man Gloom, take our troubles with you tonight.*

Burn him! Burn him!

Zeller melted into the shadows, unnoticed in the chanting crowd. So easy. He edged toward pretty *Frau* Peterson until he was near enough to close the gap quickly. She would not recognize him tonight because he had altered his appearance and kept the Isotopes ball cap pulled down close to his eyebrows. He avoided eye contact with everyone and remained silent, an unnecessary precaution because his voice would not have carried over the din.

Burn him! Burn him!

Still trying to locate Brennan, he carefully scanned the mesmerized crowd. Archbishop Joseph Hannahan, a man often pictured in the newspaper, stood behind her. No worry there. Zeller scanned the next row back and noted a man in worn clothes leaning on a black cane.

His back formed a right angle to his legs, and he had to force his face upward to see the people around him. Zeller felt pity for Cane Man, and his eyes moved on. Then flicked back. Canes could be weapons. Or conceal weapons. They could pass through security lines without suspicion if cane and contents were made of the right materials. His height was not detectable. Neither was his build in the baggy coat. A bent man or a brilliant disguise?

Burn him! Burn him!

Zeller shifted positions and watched him through his peripheral vision. Cane Man did nothing suspicious. Naturally, because he was innocent? Or contrived, because he was guarded?

Burn him! Burn him!

Grimacing, Ariel took a step forward. He tried to wedge gently around Archbishop Hannahan, sure he would assist him.

"We can make room right here," said the archbishop with a smile, scooting closer to the priest beside him to make space.

Ariel nodded his thanks and stepped feebly into the spot. A nice touch to have the archbishop's help with the final step in the Venom Contract. Without looking at his cane, he brushed his thumb across the top of the handle. His index finger slid backwards on the bottom of the handle. Slowly he turned the cane until the handle aimed at his target. He paused to savor the moment of victory.

Burn him! Burn him!

Do not be so helpful, Archbishop! No! Zeller saw Cane Man come to life like a dead robot with a new battery and position himself too close to pretty *Frau* Peterson.

Zeller focused on the black cane with its elongated Fritz style handle. He recalled seeing the spearpoint weapon through binoculars on Brennan's desk in the ranch house. Mentally he snapped that image into the cane handle. A fit!

He saw Cane Man's thumb move along on top of the handle. Saw his index finger slide beneath it. Saw him turn the handle. Zeller's hand flew under his jacket to his Glock.

Burn him! Burn him!

The cane handle pointed at *Frau* Peterson! "***NEIN***!" Zeller roared. Aimed. Fired. Lunged toward the cane. He spread his arms like a crucifix. His body her shield.

32

I saw Arial Hiram Brennan sprawled on the ground. His disguise askew and cruelty unveiled. The Plaza Poisoner was dead. A single shot to the head.

Then I saw the second victim. The one who had shot Brennan and shielded me. I looked past his dyed blond hair and recognized him. The poisoned spearpoint penetrated Zechariah Zeller. The spearpoint intended for me.

Galen had caught him as he fell and laid him gently on the grass. I dropped to my knees and cradled his head. I felt so very sad. Once more he had saved my life. This time, giving his own. I didn't know whether he could hear, but I drew close to his ear and whispered, "Thank you, Zechariah. Thank you for saving my life. Again." Tears filled my eyes and dripped down my cheeks. I tried to hold back my sobs.

>◇✦◇<   >◇✦◇<   >◇✦◇<

Zeller saw pretty *Frau* Peterson kneeling beside him. He wanted to reach for her hand. To run his palm across her cheek. To say he was glad he had saved her again. He tried. He could not speak. He could not move.

Her face began to blur into his dear *mutter*'s face. He morphed into the helpless little boy of six, strapped in a chair and forced to watch three men torture her slowly to death. "*NEIN!*" He snapped the ropes that bound him to the chair. Leapt in front of her. Spread his arms like a crucifix to protect her. Killed her torturers. A single shot to the head of each one. *Mutter*, you are safe now.

He heard her words: *Thank you, Zechariah. Thank you for saving my life.* The face he saw before him was not the beaten and bloody one in his last memory of his mother, but the face she must have had before that, the face of a smiling beauty. There she was. Kneeling beside him. Calling his name. Waiting for him.

Burn him! Burn him!

The thunderous chant drowned out the silenced shot. It had happened so fast and the mesmerized crowd was so focused on flaming Zozobra that only the people close by seemed to notice, most of them officials. They formed a tight circle protecting the bodies from view.

I heard Dan take charge, his voice ringing with calm authority. "Crowd control is our priority. Keep it contained. Avoid panic. It's over. The victims killed each other."

The victims killed each other. Matt knelt beside me, his quiet presence comforting. I was conscious of the words around me but centered on Zechariah Zeller, his head still resting in my lap.

Burn him! Burn him!

Dan looked at Juan for help. "Officials *must* keep the atmosphere calm. Panic in a crowd like this would be a disaster!"

"You're in Santa Fe, *amigo*. We know how to handle crowds." He motioned to Vernon and Ian. "Congenial crowd control. Spread the word."

Vernon gestured to the three officers from the Plaza scene and explained. Word spread and all the officers on duty donned the charm and low key demeanor well-taught for crowd control in Santa Fe. They knew how to decrease tension and increase a sense of comfort and security. If something had happened, it was minor. Give a little smile. Make a little joke. All is well.

"We need the M.E.," said Dan.

"He's here," Joe said, reaching for his cell. "I'll call him."

Dan looked down at the body killed by a single shot to the head. He sprawled on the ground near Joe, his back straight, beard askew and white wig absorbing red. Dan compared him to the photo of CIA ex-operative Ariel Hiram Brennan. "Take a look, Juan."

He nodded. "It's over, *amigo*! No escape this time."

Burn him! Burn him!

33

Dan came close. "Is that the anonymous caller?

Galen answered for me. "Yes. He is Zechariah Zeller."

"Mr. Zeller was our chief investigator," said Dan.

"It's the second time he saved her life."

"He deserves a medal."

Galen didn't respond.

Burn him! Burn him!

The M.E. reached our inner circle and greeted Joe and Juan.

"I'm sorry you are needed tonight, Will," said Joe.

"But I am needed, Archbishop, and I thank you for calling." He pulled on the ever-present gloves of his profession, then knelt beside Zechariah. Will checked his eyes. His gloved hand probed the four-inch plastic shell-like casing protruding from his heart. "A spearpoint."

I felt sick, averted my eyes. Distanced myself from this horror scene.

Juan nodded toward the cane. "Intriguing weapon."

"Homemade and effective," Dan agreed.

Effective. I looked over at lifeless Brennan for an instant and began to shake with rage. Not because he had tried to kill me, but because he had killed Marta's husband on the Plaza. And Dan's friend and left him in the trunk. And now Zechariah Zeller instead of me. I looked down again at my strange protector. My strange . . . *friend.* My tears spilled over and dripped on his forehead.

Galen bent down to me and said tenderly, "He doesn't need you now, sweetheart." Gently he raised me to my feet.

I leaned against him.

"Was he poisoned?" asked Dan.

"Yes," said Will. "But I think this toxin is different from the one that killed Carlos Martinez. This body isn't showing the same reaction. I'll know better when he's taken to my lab. Was death instantaneous?"

I forced a reply. "No. It took a few minutes."

"You're *sure* he didn't die instantly?"

"Yes. I'm sure. He seemed to want to speak, but he . . . he couldn't."

Will looked up at Juan and Joe as though wondering about the statement's credibility. Both nodded. "Then it *is* a different toxin." He examined the body further and looked puzzled. "I'm surprised the killer attacked his heart instead of his neck."

The height difference between Zechariah and me, I realized. Ariel Hiram Brennan was aiming for me. A mental image flashed of the spearpoint penetrating the nape of my neck. I almost threw up.

Burn him! Burn him!

34

I still felt numb when Dan brought us home from Zozobra. We all climbed out of the CAV and walked up the path to the *casita* for a recap. Galen unlocked the door. No hiding watchers tonight.

"It's over," Dan said as he sat down.

I sank into the white chair, my inner reserves spent. No energy even to offer coffee.

"Zechariah Zeller grasped the situation." Dan's voice was filled with admiration. "He knew who to go after and how dangerous it was. He was *totally* committed and competent. I've never seen a man behave more bravely." He turned to me. "All the rest of us were doing our best, but *he* saved you, Lynn. I don't know what else he did in his life, but in my book he's a hero."

The poignant image of Zeller shielding me resurfaced. I knew it would flash for the rest of my life.

Galen broke the silence that had filled the room. "Brennan is dead, and Kwang confessed to the toxin theft and ultimately to his link to North Korea." He paused, then voiced the unasked question hanging in the air. "Are there any leads to the person who hired them?"

"We had hoped to take Brennan alive and question him," said Dan. "Kwang knows nothing. He was interested in the money—and in *not* knowing anything about the source. Juan found his drop site for the toxin. But not a single clue. *Nothing!*" Dan shook his head. "Frankly, I see no way to proceed since we can't question Brennan." He looked at me. "You are safe. The two people who actually committed the crimes have been dealt with. On this one we may have to be content with that."

Again silence filled the room. *Content*, I thought. Which meaning? *Satisfaction? Pleasure? Unquestioning acceptance? Acquiescence?* I decided on *acquiescence: passive assent.*

"Cliff resolved the other loose end," said Dan. "They caught Brennan's 'Sclavus' who did the research on you, Lynn. He confessed everything, including that while working for the CIA, Brennan discovered that 'Sclavus' had sent classified information to China. Brennan traded his own silence for a permanent link to any information he wanted—classified or otherwise. Cliff told me that the email connection helped the experts gain access to all of Brennan's 'secure' computer files." Dan paused. "That sounded good until Cliff got to the bottom line. Quote: *Nothing in those files relates to this contract. It's a dead end.*" Dan skipped a beat. "He's right. We're left with no leads, no clues, no place to turn for information. Zip."

Back to being *content*, to *acquiescence*, I thought. *Passive assent.*

"So the instigator goes free," said Galen. "I suppose I should care, but Lynn is safe and that's really all that matters to me."

Dan winced. "Yes, I understand that," he said in a pain-filled voice." He recovered. "It's time to call it done and move on."

Galen nodded and changed topics. "Have you learned any more about a connection between Hiroshi's lunch with Carlos and a copy of the formula?"

"Nothing there. I jumped to conclusions. As Lynn suggested this morning, Carlos and Hiroshi were friends and could have simply had lunch together. LANL admits that the toxin was stolen but denies any theft of a copy of the formula, and there's no proof. Words to the contrary would be considered hearsay or malice-induced rumor to hurt GANNS' chances of contract renewal. Again, zip."

Everything appeared to be settled in everyone's mind but mine. On one hand I doubted Marta's confusion about Carlos' story. On the other hand I felt relief for Hiroshi, whom I didn't want to suspect of contracting the theft of biowar toxin or of being involved with a copy of the formula . In so many areas I found myself living not with a two-fisted *either/or*, but with the open hands of *this/and*. Aristotle spoke to me from across the centuries: *About some things it is not possible to make a universal statement which shall be correct.*

35

When Hiroshi arrived home from Zozobra, he followed their custom of removing shoes at the door, then walked through the wide hallway to his study. Amaya's presence there was unexpected. She stood in front of his spearpoint collection, her back to him and her fingers pressed against a spearpoint on the bottom right corner, apparently until glue adhered. He stood in silence, his mind flashing scenarios. None of them reassuring. His controllable world began to tilt. "It is unusual for you to be in my study, Amaya."

She jumped and turned around, an expression on her face that he'd never seen before.

He smiled casually. "May I help you with something?"

"I'm finished, thank you."

"Finished?"

"When Lynn and her friend Denise were here for lunch today, I noticed that your spearpoint collection is visible from the hall and that two of them were missing. They must have fallen off. I guess the maid threw them away. You are so busy you probably didn't notice. I bought replacements this afternoon. I hoped to have this done before you came home tonight. It was a surprise for you." She took a breath. "How was Zozobra?"

During all their years of marriage, she had never uttered so long a monologue to him or spoken so rapidly or appeared so nervous. "When you bought the spearpoints, did you explain why?" he asked cautiously, his tone direct but gentle.

"No, Hiroshi." She looked scared. "I said nothing."

"I was unaware that you are so attentive to my collection." He frowned. "When did you get interested in spearpoints?"

"It pleases me to know about things you like."

His mind created options. Again, none of them reassuring. "When did you notice they were missing?"

"Today, as I said."

He could tell she was lying. "Why were the spearpoints important to you, Amaya?"

"I thought this collection should be put back like it was."

"Why?"

"You are fond of it."

Again she was lying. "Do you know what *really* happened to the ones that are missing?"

Her eyes flashed. She said nothing.

Her eyes and silence revealed the answer. He must handle this conversation with utmost caution. He took a breath and asked, "Did you replace the spearpoints because of the two deaths this week?"

She nodded. Tears filled her eyes.

He recalled the beautiful woman he fell in love with the first time he saw her, still lovely. He could smell her perfume, the scent she had worn throughout their marriage. He glimpsed the light of the half-moon through his study windows and foresaw their future, a future severed from the past. Nothing would ever be the same again. A coyote howled. "How did you know the deaths were caused by poisoned spearpoints?"

"Rumors," she stammered. She stared at him, tears overflowing. "No matter what terrible thing has been done, I still want everything to be the same between us." Her chin quivered. "I would always help you if you need it, dear Hiroshi. I will always love you. *For better or **worse**.*"

36

For better or worse.

Amaya began to sob.

He took her in his arms and drew her close, feeling her familiar softness. He lifted her chin and kissed her forehead and the salty tears on her cheeks. She buried her face against his chest, the deep heaves of her sobs unstoppable.

Now he understood her day of weeping. As he held her, he debated what to do. His mind went back to the story he'd heard Amaya tell many times, a story about something that occurred long before she was born, a story her mother had told her repeatedly, a story about August 9, 1945:

My mother visits her aunt in Kokura, excited to be with her cousins. They spend the morning playing in their usual way. Unaware of the secret plan against their city on that day, a plan developed far away. They play in the ground haze that sometimes comes. Unaware that the B-29 called Bockscar makes three passes over Kokura, but the weather prevents a clear target, and Bockscar is diverted to Nagasaki. She and her cousins talk and tease as they eat lunch. Unaware that at 11:50 A.M. Bockscar drops Fat Man. Unaware that the fatality rate in the central part of Nagasaki is 20,000 people per square mile.

Unaware that the death toll includes everyone in her family.

From that day forward my mother bears the guilt for being in Kokura instead of in Nagasaki with her family, the guilt of being alive. The horror of the mass deaths, destruction, and radiation stays with her as she grows up, marries, and I am born. She carries the horror into my bedtime stories.

As Hiroshi held Amaya, he silently reprimanded himself for not seeing the warnings. Each August 9, she followed a ritual of repeating that story and lighting the large black memorial candle: *With this candle I honor my mother, and also her family and all the children and grandchildren that would have been born to them if they had not been killed.* Her mother had transferred to Amaya her deep-seated obsession for revenge against Fat Man's creators: Los Alamos National Lab.

His heart ached for her as he gently stroked her glossy hair. He recalled that she had urged him to serve on the GANNS board, and her interest had surprised him. Now he realized that his *yes* had given her access to the inside information emailed to directors. He kept the email password and other important items in the locked hidden drawer of his custom-built desk. He wasn't concerned that she knew about that drawer and where he kept the key. Writing down the email password was careless, but it was not a serious mistake because the reports to the directors provided less information than was available on the internet by googling *LANL* and *Biowarfare*.

Her rhetorical question echoed back to him after her August 9 ritual a few weeks ago: *Oh, Hiroshi, why do governments research horrible ways of mass killings? The people—the citizens—aren't aware! Like in 1945 the people of Japan—and America—didn't know about the atom bomb. Death from biowarfare weapons would outrage the national and international community! The people need to **know** about this!*

With a heavy heart he realized that she had learned about LANL's move into biological weapons research—another means of mass killing, again justified by protection—and had been greatly troubled. He had not heard sadness as he thought, but justification for her plan already underway. A plan that she naively expected would make front page news and spread across the internet and bring change through local and global outrage. Instead, the plan had resulted in the death of a good friend and a silent cover up.

His wife, his sweet Amaya, could not undo what she had initiated, nor the horrible unpredictable consequence that Carlos was the victim. *I have so much power,* he thought, *but not enough to change any of this.* Tears came to his eyes as he held her. He had not foreseen—would never have believed—that beloved Amaya was capable of what she had done.

Finally her sobbing ceased. She looked up at him with dead eyes. Her body trembled. Her voice shook. "I didn't mean . . . I just wanted . . . Oh, Hiroshi. What have I—?"

"Shhh!" He put his finger over her lips. "If you have an agonizing secret, it is *imperative* that you tell *no one*. Not even me." He enfolded her close against his heart, loving her dearly, wanting to protect her. "*Listen to me, Amaya.* This is the most important thing I have ever said to you." He stated each word like a single drumbeat at an execution: "***You—must—take—your—dark —secret—to—your—grave.***"

For better or worse.

37

After Amaya went to bed, Hiroshi returned to his study. He sipped a glass of wine and stared at his framed collection of spearpoints. He was painfully aware that he had unknowingly provided her access not only to the two spearpoints, but also to crucial facts. He mentally reran the scenes.

First the call from Carlos and the walk together.

"I am very much concerned about a matter at LANL. You are a trusted friend, Hiroshi, and on the board."

I listen to his concerns about the latest biowarfare weapon, a highly contagious toxin with lethal effects. "Is there an antidote?" I ask.

"They aren't working on one yet."

"I might be able to help with that if you can get a copy of the formula."

"It would be difficult. It is carefully guarded."

"I understand." We walk a few steps in silence.

"Perhaps it would be possible," he says hesitantly. "I would need some time."

"Of course."

"I am also concerned about one of the lead scientists working on the toxin—Kwang-Sun Rhee. I am beginning to wonder if he is disloyal to the United States."

Now, Hiroshi chastised himself for the second biggest mistake of his life: When he returned home from that walk, he wrote a two-word note about their conversation: *Kwang—biowarfare toxin.* He locked it in the secret drawer, again unaware that Amaya would access it—and he would not have been suspicious of her even if he had learned that she opened that drawer.

Then, ten days later Kwang requested another meeting and suggested Tesuque, between Santa Fe and Los Alamos.

We get a cup of coffee to go and stand under a tree away from the café and others' ears, and appear to chat casually, carefully guarding our words.

Carlos smiles, and his nonchalant demeanor does not change as he moves to the point. "Some of the lethal toxin has been stolen."

I force a smile in return. "Are you sure? It wasn't in the news."

"It won't be. They are covering up the theft." *He chuckles as though he had told a joke.*

Unable to muster a laugh, I shake my head and say lightly, "My friend, that is a bad joke."

He sobers slightly. "If I get the recipe you mentioned, what would you do with it?"

Very softly I tell him about PAPA—Peace for All People, a medical organization that deals with developing antidotes against biowarfare threats.

Now, Hiroshi could see some of the pieces and put part of the puzzle together. Amaya had met Kwang at LANL parties with staff and directors and perceived him as sly, arrogant and greedy—as I do, he thought. Evidently she had made an offer he couldn't refuse—a small amount of the new toxin for a large amount of money from her funds. Hiroshi had access to them and could find out the fee, but what was the point now? No wonder she had been so uncomfortable at the archbishop's dinner party! Kwang didn't have a clue that the unknown person who contracted him to steal biowarfare toxin was sitting at the table with him.

Then a week later a cryptic call came from Carlos: "Maybe we can bump into each other when I leave the early weekday mass tomorrow."

At 7:30 the next morning I sit on the park bench near the cathedral front doors, as though contemplating walking the labyrinth. As people leave mass, Carlos greets me with a friendly handshake and suggests we have lunch on Monday. "By then I'll have a copy of that recipe you were interested in," *he says with a nonchalant smile, and hurries off to get to Los Alamos in time for work.*

When Hiroshi reached his car, he read the note Carlos passed during their handshake, with a brief *keep this—just in case.*

1. Toxin thief: Kwang

2. Mon. 2:00: CIA op. ETA ABQ

3. Mon. 4:00: Handoff of full report > SF, Plaza bench

He found it interesting that Carlos' CIA contact for the handoff was flown in instead of local. Was mistrust a factor? He went home and locked the note in the hidden drawer, unwittingly giving Amaya the last piece of information the contract killer needed: times and places. He pictured her reading that note, not knowing she was looking at Carlos' handwriting.

Now, fury at himself gripped him. "Keeping that note," he said aloud, "was the biggest, most unbearable mistake of my life!" He could hardly restrain his hands from yanking the framed spearpoint collection off the wall and hurling it out the window.

He settled down and poured himself another glass of wine. He tried to climb into this unknown part of Amaya's mind, possessed by her mother's venom. She had planned each meticulous detail and managed to follow through in this completely foreign realm. She had been driven toward revenge—and left without vindication. No widespread publicity. No national and international outrage. No LANL shut down. The cause of the deaths was covered up. And, he thought, I abetted that cover up. I had my own obsession—organizing PAPA and getting a copy of the formula to Friedrich Streiff. Hiroshi faced their new reality. Cover-up or no cover-up, Amaya will live the rest of her life with the horror of the death of Carlos Martinez.

Even when she cried all during his funeral this morning, he thought, I didn't put it all together. Not until I walked in tonight and saw her replacing a spearpoint that I hadn't even noticed was missing. Far too late to stop the deed and the damage. If I had noticed it in time, could I have prevented all this? Perhaps. All I can do now is try to protect her from confessing.

Marta's tearful face filled his mind. "GOD! Oh GOD!" he cried out from the depths of his soul. He bowed his head, longing for the power to reverse it! To prevent it! But the only thing he could do was merely care for her financially. What a hollow recompense!

Justice, Amaya had sneered long ago in her mother's voice. In Hiroshi's experience justice depended on one's point of view, which was partly—mostly?—influenced by childhood formation, the media and those in power. Was the destruction of Nagasaki and Hiroshima justice? It was viewed so by some and condemned by others. Would the imprisonment of Amaya for instigating a crime that was born of Fat Man's ripples be justice? That too would depend on one's point of view. He picked up her photograph from his desk, memories swirling.

"Oh, Amaya," he said aloud. "Naïve. Loyal. Revenge-obsessed at your mother's knee! You will spend the rest of your life in the self-imposed prison of guilt and grief.

He emptied his glass and thought again about justice. Was it justice for me to persuade Carlos to make a copy of the LANL toxin formula? To have my pilots fly it to another country? To entrust it to Friedrich under the auspices of PAPA? That too depended on one's point of view.

But how else could an antidote be developed and made available globally to victims?

EPILOGUE
Saturday, 6:30 A.M.

Just as the unconscious affects us,
so the increase in our consciousness affects the unconscious.

—Carl Gustav Jung

The opposite of a correct statement is a false statement.
But the opposite of a profound truth
may be another profound truth.

—Neils Bohr

I open my eyes as the sun peeks above the mountains. Immediately last night's tragedy tumbles in on me. I see Zechariah Zeller's head in my lap, his goodness of heart present beneath his shell of destructiveness. I see the scattered disguises around the body of Ariel Hiram Brennan, his menacing words on the phone still reverberating through my mind and soul. I yearn to believe that all people, no matter how bad they seem to be, have good somewhere inside them. That is clearly true of Zeller. But Brennan? Juan's sobriquet comes to mind: *Diablo*. I found nothing good in him. Perhaps because I didn't look. Or perhaps because he had let the space for good be snuffed out, and evil had filled the void.

I pour a cup of coffee and watch Galen reading *The New York Times* on his iPad. It is one of those tender moments when my heart overflows with love for him. I kiss his cheek and join him at the table. "Good morning, love."

"Look at this article!" He passes me the iPad.

I begin reading:

ANTIDOTES DEVELOPED
TO DETER BIOWARFARE
International cooperation initiated
By Bob Benbrook

The Peace for All People Alliance, known as PAPA, is a previously undisclosed unit of the United Nations. It counters international biowarfare labs by obtaining copies of illegal toxin formulae so that medical research teams can develop antidotes and make them accessible to any attacked nation. Both overt and covert means are used to obtain these formulae.

PAPA's purpose is 1) to promote protection and world unity, 2) to deter the effectiveness of biological warfare, and 3) to prevent any nation or terrorist group from obtaining the power to mass murder through biowarfare. The medical research team is based in Geneva, Switzerland under the direction of Dr. Friedrich Streiff. PAPA is endowed by anonymous nonpolitical donors.

The team is led by seven medical research doctors whose names were withheld. They represent each continent except Antarctica, and two are from Asia because of its large population: **Africa**: Cairo, Egypt; **Asia**: New Delhi, **India**, and Hiroshima, **Japan**; **Australia**: Sydney; **Europe**: London, England; **North America:** Edmonton, Canada; and **South America:** Lima, Peru.

Four were trained at top medical schools in the United States.

I looked up at Galen. "Well, there it is! Both made The *New York Times*—the nonexistent PAPA and the nonexistent copy of LANL's biowarfare formula."

Galen reviewed the situation. "Marta tells Matt and you that Carlos trusts PAPA and is going to provide them with a copy of LANL's new biowarfare formula, and he has lunch with Hiroshi on Sunday. Today we read about a*nonymous nonpolitical donors endowing* PAPA for global protection against any single world power, and about PAPA obtaining *copies of illegal toxin formulae* by both *overt and covert* means in order to *develop antidotes*."

"Thanks to Hiroshi and Carlos."

"You are a good judge of character, Lynn."

I smiled. "My choice of husband proves that."

"I'm serious. Despite all that Dan and I said, and the CIA and even the President's sources, you trusted Marta's view of her husband, and you trusted that Carlos was a man of integrity."

I didn't feel deserving of this compliment so I ducked into flippancy. "Of course I did! He had on a Saints sweatshirt!" I pictured him on the Plaza bench and my frivolity faded. "And," I added softly, "he tipped an imaginary cap to me." That image struck a soft place in my heart, and my eyes teared with reverence for his life.

"You also pegged Hiroshi. I should have trusted you about him."

"I was beginning to have my doubts too." I remembered what Amaya had said about him during our lunch together in her home: *Sometimes I don't understand how Hiroshi can abide the genocide of his ancestors. He must not have a single bone of vengeance in his body.* "I admire Hiroshi, Galen. Instead of continuing harm by transferring his hurts onto others, he takes the path toward doing good and attempts to transform the globe in his small way."

"I'd call PAPA a big way."

The phone rang—the President's phone. I removed it from the book. "Good morning."

"Have you seen the article in *The New York Times*?"

"We just read it."

"Interesting. You are right, Lynn. An organization's eluding our intelligence sources does not preclude its existence."

I waited for her to say more about PAPA.

When she spoke again, she changed the subject. "A report came in from GANNS late last night. They refuted a rumor that a copy of a top secret formula was stolen from LANL. They state that their security is too tight for that to happen and there is no evidence to support the claim. They assume the false rumor was started and spread by a competitor trying to discredit GANNS in order to affect their contract renewal."

I realized that she hadn't actually changed the subject. She assumed, as I did, that a highly respected GANNS board member was behind that report. Carlos had left no evidence behind, so there was no proof that a copy of the formula existed. Matt and I were the only ones who knew that Marta was the source of the copy story, though Dan had made the leap. What mattered was that the copy—via Hiroshi—was now in the hands of a medical team tasked with creating antidotes to distribute for international use as needed. I recalled all the formula scenarios that had run through my mind. This was not a bad ending. Justice has some untidy rooms. I responded simply, "I see."

"Yes, I imagine you see clearly." The President paused. "By the way, I thought you might like to know that I'm inviting Hiroshi Takahashi to be the business representative in my Inner Circle."

"He will serve well."

"I also have the report about what happened last night. The Plaza poisoner is dead, and that difficulty is behind us. The LANL toxin thief—Kwang-Sun Rhee—will be charged with theft and espionage. Spearpoint's job is done. Please express my appreciation to him."

"I will. It gave him pleasure to serve his President."

"This simple favor really was simple in the end. Thank you for your help. I'm grateful to you."

"Thank you."

"If you don't mind, hang on to the phone you're using. For a while. Just in case I need you or Dan again."

Don't do it! "I'll be glad to, Madam President."

Her tone lost its Commander-in-Chief timbre. She spoke softly, warmly. "Zechariah Zeller saved both our lives before, and this time he sacrificed his life for you, Lynn."

"Yes," I said, also softly. He was rightly a wanted man, but he was also more than that. The two of us talked about him for a few moments. I realized that if ours was his only eulogy, it would have made him proud.

I returned the phone to the drawer and joined Galen at the table. "I keep thinking about Zechariah. Do you remember the morning we were walking to the Plaza Café and talking about him?"

He nodded. "I'm indebted to him. Again."

"Do you remember that I said I wouldn't help take his life?" Tears filled my eyes and my voice broke. "I did, Galen. I took his life."

"No, my darling Lynn. He gave his life for you."

🔷 🔷 🔷

The cathedral bells tolled ten o'clock as I walked down San Francisco and upstairs to the coffee bar balcony. I sat again at the corner table overlooking the Plaza and looked down at the park bench. I pictured Carlos Martinez in his New Orleans Saints sweatshirt. My mind replayed these few days here, then turned to writing a mystery someday. I had only written the first sentence of my dream novel: *Secrets take us on a journey.* Where? Why? Now I longed to write The Santa Fe Secret. But I couldn't tell this story. I contented myself by adding the second sentence.

Secrets take us on a journey. A journey where good can be bad and bad can be good, and God holds the paradox in the Mystery of grace.

APPRECIATION AND ACKNOWLEDGEMENTS

To P. David and Jan Smith for their care and personal interest in the quality of each book published. Western Reflections is a jewel among publishing houses.

To Dick Smith for sharing his talent as a creative photographer, for his friendship, and for showing us how to live our lives as caring and compassionate people.

To Nancy Lewis, who gave me a tour of SAR, Clarice Cole and Carol Cashman—three dear friends who read The Santa Fe Secret manuscript and offered astute comments.

To lovely and gracious Pilar Aguilar for her warm hospitality in her home in the San Ildefonso Pueblo on Feast Day, and to her husband Martin who was one of the dancers. To Taylor McConnell (and in memory of June), who showed us around the Pueblo.

To Bishop Roy Sano, longtime friend, whose family was forced into a Japanese internment camp in Arizona when he was a little boy, which entailed losing their freedom, home, possessions and income. Yet, when Roy shared that journey with me, he did so without bitterness or vindictiveness. I continue to admire his capacity for grace.

To other special friends on my journey: Lynn Ewing, Wilson and Robbie Holman, Karen Wells, and Jane Smith. To Kathy Guier, Marilyn Bailey Ogilvie, Glo Weaver, Henry and Sandra Estess, David and Paula Severe, Phyllis Henry and Mary McPherson (and in memory of Bill and Doug). To Beverly Job (and in memory of Rueben), Charles and Karen Crutchfield, Martha Chamberlain, Elaine Hopkins, Jo Stith, and Joe Yeakel. To Mary Larson, Jimmie Schlender, and Cassandra Welton. Thanks for continuing to encourage me.

To Will McDonald, Jim Hays, Erasmo Estrada and Ed Muir, who design and build unique adobe homes and furniture that contribute to the feel of "The City Different."

To my beloved husband Bill, with appreciation for his patience with my writing, like when we drove the roads from Santa Fe to

Los Alamos so I could consider where and how the chase scene and crash could occur. To Danna Lee, Dirk, Valerie and Bryant with deep appreciation for their love and support and for being who they are. To our grandchildren Chelsea, Sarah, Nathan and Graham for the joy they bring and for their future dreams. And to my cousin Colette Pantalone (and in memory of Ralph), who literally brings the sunrise each morning through her beautiful photography.

And with gratitude for my childhood companion Pal, a white collie who happened to show up again in this story.

And to Vini (protagonist in my first novel and great-grandmother of the President in all three) who continues to peer over my shoulder as I write, asking: Is it just? Is it fair? Then asks with a smile, Does it take the reader on a journey? Ah, Vini, I hope so. It certainly took me on one!